SLEEP TIGHT

C.S. Green is a bestselling author of psychological thrillers and an award-winning writer of fiction for young people under the name Caroline Green. Written under the name Cass Green, her first novel for adults, *The Woman Next Door*, was a No.1 ebook bestseller, while the follow-up, *In a Cottage in a Wood*, was a *USA Today* bestseller and a *Sunday Times* top ten bestseller. She is the writer in residence at East Barnet School and teaches courses for City University and *Writers' & Artists' Yearbook*. She lives in London with her family. *Sleep Tight* is the start of a new series featuring the UCIT.

🐦 @carolinesgreen

Also by C.S. Green (writing as Cass Green)

The Woman Next Door
In a Cottage in a Wood
Don't You Cry
The Killer Inside

SLEEP TIGHT

C.S. Green

HarperCollins*Publishers*

HarperCollins*Publishers* Ltd
1 London Bridge Street,
London SE1 9GF

www.harpercollins.co.uk

HarperCollins*Publishers*
1st Floor, Watermarque Building, Ringsend Road
Dublin 4, Ireland

First published by HarperCollins*Publishers* 2021

1

ISBN: 978-0-00-839076-1 (HB)
ISBN: 978-0-00-839077-8 (TPB)

Typeset in Sabon LT Std by
Palimpsest Book Production Ltd, Falkirk, Stirlingshire

Printed and bound in Great Britain by
CPI Group (UK) Ltd, Croydon CR0 4YY

For Roy Lownds (11/03/31 – 24/08/19)
Much missed by all your family.

Sleep, those little slices of death.
Edgar Allan Poe (attributed)

1

Kirsty

He's no regular stalker.

There's no shadow of a figure in her peripheral vision as she goes about her day. No footsteps behind her in an alley as she comes home from work.

Instead, he visits her in the darkest part of the night, padding soft and deadly into her dreams at 3 a.m., when she is at her most defenceless. In her own bed.

The sleep rituals are the only weapons she has.

First, she makes herself turn off the iPad, even though she wants to watch another episode of her reality show. But the blue light scrambles your brain and keeps you awake. This is just basic advice. Next comes the bubble bath – not too warm, not too cool – with the meditation audiobook playing from the phone lying on the sink. She doesn't really like baths; she always ends up getting sweaty or chilled, but all the advice suggests that this is the right thing to do for A Good Night's Sleep.

That's how she thinks of it: in capitals. A destination. The Holy Grail.

She's drunk the mug of hot chocolate – the best part of her routine – and eaten the banana. (They give you serotonin or something like that. She's a bit hazy on the science.)

Now for the lavender oil, which she spritzes on the pillow, but not too much because someone told her that can have the opposite effect to the one desired.

Climbing into bed, she lifts up her thriller from the bedside table and looks at the picture on the cover. It shows a woman half-turning under a streetlamp, eyes wide and startled, like someone being followed.

With a small shudder, she puts it back on the nightstand. It's quite good, but maybe not for bedtime reading.

Instead she twiddles with the dial on the clock radio until she finds Radio 4. It's not her thing at all in the daytime, but droning, posh voices seeping into the room are comforting at night. Someone on there is talking about moving to a Scottish island for a year and doing something involving sheep. It's incredibly boring, but isn't that what you want at bedtime? Excitement is not what she needs right now.

Closing her eyes at last, she pulls the duvet with its freshly changed cover up to her chin and inhales its clean scent, breathing in and out very slowly. The lamp is still turned on and the orange glow bleeds through her eyelids, but she isn't ready to turn it off yet.

She's not ready for the darkness.

Her parents say she resisted the lights going off from when she was a little girl, even before the night terrors began. And it only got worse.

There was that time on holiday in Devon, when she was eight, and she screamed so ear-splittingly that someone in the next chalet called the police. Her parents, clad in dressing gowns and dozy from too much sun and wine, had to explain that the unearthly sound had been made by a sleepy little girl and not someone being brutally murdered.

Over the years there were various rituals she had made her

long-suffering parents carry out before bed, checking everywhere for bogeymen.

But the bogeymen still somehow snuck in, if not physically, then covering her with their slick shadows until she woke up thrashing in panic.

Sleep paralysis they call it.

Lately, it always follows the same pattern.

First, coming to in the pearly light of her bedroom, the familiar furniture appearing as dark, blocky shapes around her. Awake.

Then, the creeping figure. There's a flare of white panic in her mind before the sweet relief of realization comes.

No, wait, it's just that thing again. It's just the sleep paralysis. It's not real. None of this is real. I'll wake up soon.

Except . . . the face doesn't go away. Instead, it becomes more defined, more corporeal, until it is visible in high-definition detail, hovering above her as she lies there, powerless and unable to move a single muscle.

The faces used to vary. Sometimes it would be an old man or woman with leathery, crinkled skin and cruel, glittery eyes. But lately, it's always a man, features hidden, eyes staring down at her through slits in a balaclava.

And that's when she realizes this time is different. She's not dreaming. This isn't sleep paralysis. This is happening.

The surge of horror at this realization is always the tipping point. She breaks free from the sleep-state and finds herself shivering, gasping, out of her bed, carpet under her curled toes, back slick with sweat.

But lately, that moment is taking longer to come.

Friends and family have never understood that it's worse than a 'bad dream'. That's OK. She's used to being a freak. But what makes her feel really lonely – and really scared – is the people who should know, her fellow parasomniacs.

They don't believe her when she tells them there's something different about this.

It's as if he, whoever he is, is somehow . . . breaking through whatever barrier exists between the waking world and the nightmare one.

But she's driving herself mad with thoughts like these. That's not even possible. Is it?

Don't they say we only use 10 per cent of our brain or something, and the rest is a mystery? It's only her silly brain playing tricks.

Tonight, she is going to sleep peacefully all the way through. He won't come this time. She is quite determined.

She lies still and breathes slowly through her nose, eyes closed. The bedside clock ticks. Radio 4 burbles on . . .

The scream of a car alarm outside. Eyes snapping open, insides cold with acid shock, heart punching her ribs. She must have been dozing but she's wide awake again.

Annoyed at having this promising start compromised, she makes herself switch off the lamp. The shipping forecast is a low drone in the background, and she lets the words soothe her, repeating them slowly in her mind.

Viking, North Utsire, South Utsire, Dogger, Fisher, German Bight.

Viking, North Utsire, South Utsire, Dogger, Fisher, German Bight.

Viking, North Utsire, South Utsire, Dogger, Fisher, German Bight.

Bight Utsire, German Dogger, Fisher Price . . .

Jerking awake. Focusing once more.

Viking, North Utsire, South Utsire, Dogger, Fisher, German Bight.

Dogger, Dogger, Alfie and Annie Rose and picnics, picnics and cider and when Tim Watts stuck his tongue in my mouth in the rec and fried chicken on his breath . . . Viking, North Utsire, South German . . . South . . .

Finally she sleeps. But at 3 a.m., her eyes snap open.

He's back.

2

'Yeah, you can sod off, too,' mutters Rose at the driver of the white Range Rover, whose mouth is chomping away in silent reproach on her left.

Technically, she was in the wrong, having not exactly seen him trying to back out from that driveway, but she has an unreasonable dislike of people who drive big SUVs. Sailing high above the hoi polloi below, they have a sense of entitlement that irks her.

'Don't start, Gifford,' says DS Colin Mackie – Mack to everyone – from the passenger seat.

'Don't start what?' she says, although she knows the answer.

'The Eco Warrior stuff,' he says, and she laughs.

'*Eco Warrior* stuff?' she repeats, drawing the words out. 'Would you like to call me a member of the Burn Your Bra Brigade next? And oh, hey, has political correctness gone mad?'

Mack makes a sound that is somewhere between a sigh and a laugh.

'Don't make fun of the elderly, young lady.'

There is silence for a moment before Rose says, 'Anyway, it's not that so much. I just don't like those cars.'

'I'm extremely well aware of that fact,' says Mack, and his tone makes her dart another look.

Maybe she came across grumpier than she meant to. She

slept badly – again – and Mack doesn't exactly look like a man who is well-rested and at one with the world.

He has some sort of situation going on at home with teenage offspring, involving bunking off school, but she can't remember the details. His phone pings with a text and he fumbles it from his pocket, then frowns at the screen.

Before Rose can say anything further, the satnav announces their destination is the next road on the right.

The properties on this street are 1930s, semi-detached, each with a brown, chipped moustache of tiles over its bay windows. White-suited CSIs are coming in and out of the house on the end. A small group of gawpers are standing around, stamping their feet against the chill November wind and talking to each other; thrilled horror lighting their faces.

Rose swiftly parallel parks into a space further down the street. As they exit the car, several heads turn in their direction.

Her stomach is rumbling as she reaches the gate. Should've had a proper breakfast, she thinks. She'd got it into her head that a banana and a yoghurt would be a good idea, especially after the massive plate of fish and chips she'd had for dinner the night before. They weren't even from the posh chippie, which was five minutes further from her house.

Rose and Mack pull on their gear once they leave the car. A CSI she recognizes – Dominic Something – gives her a small nod as they pass him on the way into the house.

The hallway smells of hair products, with an undertone of fried food. The walls are covered in bumpy, yellowing anaglypta. The dusty sideboard squatting in the hallway is far too big for the space. A combination of mirror and cabinet with an ornate acorn-engraved top that almost meets the ceiling, it's covered in fast-food flyers and junk mail, plus a single, dusty-looking stud earring.

There is a room off to the left, presumably a living room, and a uniformed officer she doesn't recognize is standing at the doorway. The sound of quiet weeping can be heard coming from inside the room, punctuated by bubbly nose-blows and indistinct mumbling.

'Who's in there?' says Mack in a low voice.

The uniform speaks so quietly they have to lean in to hear him. 'Flatmate,' he murmurs. 'Name of Sofia Nikolas. She's the one who called it in.'

'Right,' says Rose, 'make sure she has enough tissues and tea, and we'll be back in a bit.'

'Up here?' says Mack, gesturing upwards, and the uniform nods confirmation.

They climb the stairs, which are covered in a swirly seventies carpet of browns and purple. The carpet is worn and gritty, even through the protective bootees.

The house is typical of this area. It's towards the end of a decent tube line into town, which means plenty of privately rented, converted houses or house shares. Landlords charge tenants, mainly the young, a fair whack for the privilege of being able to live 'in' the capital, but the local high street is comprised of chicken and kebab shops, charity shops and betting shops, with a lone Costa Coffee and a Sainsbury's Local for variety.

Turning towards the first bedroom at the top of the stairs, Rose registers the splintered remains of the door, which has clearly had to be broken down for access.

Inside, there is a sweet, flowery smell she can't immediately place. The room is much nicer than she'd anticipated, based on the state of downstairs. The walls are a calming lilac colour. Fairy lights adorn a dressing table and one wall is taken up with a huge photo board covered in laughing, smiling faces and postcards.

She moves in closer to get a better look. The postcards range from pretty prints of landscapes or cute animals, to a single arty, and strikingly ugly one; the kind that comes from gift shops in the V&A or the British Library. Some kind of gothic creature.

There are several people in the room, including DS John Tennant from CID. Her DCI, Stella Rowland, is just inside the door, blocking the view of the bed. She is talking in a low murmur to the chief pathologist, Derek Peterson, a man destined to die on the job rather than retire.

Rowland is about a foot taller than Rose and an entirely different species of human. She has never, to Rose's knowledge, dripped coffee on her blouse, or laughed so hard she's peed her pants, even a minuscule amount. She's never said anything rash, or stupid. Always serious, always focused, she simply functions on a higher plane. Rose feels like a grubby, emotional child in her presence. Rowland has never liked her and, since the thing that happened a few weeks ago, the atmosphere between them is chillier than ever.

Batting this frequent, intrusive worry away, Rose's eyes finally find the bed.

The usual feeling starts the moment she sees the body. Rose forces herself to take a slow sip of air. It'll pass. It always does. The dimming around the edges of her vision; a shadowing of her consciousness. Bone-deep cold and a crawling sensation, like tiny fingers scrabbling at her skin.

It has always been her reaction to stress, ever since she was a little girl. That's how she frames it in her mind, anyway. In fact, it is more complicated than that. It started when she first began sensing voices in the house that shouldn't be there. Rubbing her nails hard against the skin of her arm helped to distract her from it. Over time, that patch of skin has developed a tendency to flare up whenever her senses are on high alert.

The victim looks to be maybe late twenties, early thirties. The flowery white duvet is pulled up to her chest, almost as though she has been tucked in by her mother at bedtime.

Her eyes are closed. Her skin is pale; like Rose, she looks the type who would burn after five minutes in the sun. There is no obvious sign of injury, but the very fact that CID have called in the Major Investigation Team means something is amiss about this young woman's death.

She swallows and breathes in. That sickly sweet smell again . . .

'What's the story, ma'am?' says Mack. DCI Rowland says something she doesn't hear to the photographer who's taking pictures of the rest of the room and looks down at the body, frowning.

'Hannah Scott, 32-years-old,' she says crisply. 'Nursery worker. Couldn't be roused from her locked room by the flatmate this morning, so she called it in. No sign of forced entry to the house. So when the paramedics arrived, they thought at first this was natural causes. Maybe adult SIDS. But when they took a closer look at her eyes, they found signs of burst blood vessels consistent with suffocation. That's when they called us in.' She pauses. 'It appears the victim was screaming in the middle of the night too.'

Rose looks up sharply.

'Screaming?' she says.

Rowland fixes her with one of those weary gazes that encompasses her entire feelings on the subject of the human race.

'Flatmate downstairs heard it,' she says. 'At three a.m. Went back to sleep, would you believe.'

They all consider this for a moment.

'That's odd,' says Rose, and Rowland looks down at her own notepad.

'Apparently she suffered from nightmares. In fact,' she pauses, 'when the flatmate called 999, she said "the bad dreams . . . she has these bad dreams and she won't wake up".'

'So the door was locked?' asks Mack, and Rowland nods.

'Key was still in the lock,' she says, 'when the paramedics broke in.'

'That's weird,' says Rose. 'Doesn't that mean you can't open a door from the other side?'

'Weird indeed,' says Rowland. 'But someone got in, because she didn't suffocate herself.'

Rose comes closer and stares down at the body. The victim has long, fair hair with a russet streak at the front. It lies prettily on the pillow in a way that seems horribly out of place in this room of death.

'What's with the smell?' says Mack, looking around the room. 'It's very strong in here.'

'I think it's lavender,' says Rowland. 'People use it to help them sleep. The pillow reeks of it.' She wrinkles her nose.

Rose can't stop looking at the soft hair, curled on the pillow. She pictures Hannah Scott washing it carefully and blow-drying it for the last time. There is a pair of GHDs on the dressing table, fine blond hairs sprouting from the tongs.

'I'd like you two to focus on getting a statement from this housemate, Sofia,' says Rowland. 'Did she have a key to this room? Who else had access?'

'Right, let's go,' says Mack, and they head back downstairs. Before going into the sitting room, they stop to peel off their protective clothes and bundle them into a pile near the front door.

Sofia Nikolas has cried so much that her features have almost become indistinct. Her eyes are red and puffy. Rose notices she has those fake eyelashes that last for ages. But quite a few of them have fallen off, giving her a disconcerting *Clockwork Orange*, spidery effect on one side. She has round, chipmunk cheeks, a snub nose and thick, dark brown hair that has been scraped back into a fat ponytail. She is wearing a fluffy onesie and currently cuddles a red, tasselled cushion, her feet in woolly pink socks pulled up next to her on the scuffed blue sofa.

'Sofia?' says Mack gently. He and Rose sit down across the coffee table, so they are facing her.

She gazes at them, blurrily.

Rose gets out her A4 investigator's notebook, new for this job, and flips to a fresh page for this first interview. Everything relating to the case will be kept here, from briefing notes to interview notes, witness interviews, and CCTV notes. At the end of the case it will be handed over to the Disclosure Officer. Rose still gets a slight schoolgirl pleasure about cracking open a fresh notebook.

'I'm Detective Sergeant Colin Mackie, and this is my colleague Detective Constable Rose Gifford,' says Mack. Sofia stares back at him and says nothing. 'Have you been offered a tea or coffee?' he adds.

Sofia leans to pick up a toilet roll that's sitting on the table. She yanks off a length before blowing her nose, then nods.

'Yes, but I feel sick,' she says in a small, snotty voice. 'He put sugar in, and I don't take it.'

Stroppiness over the poor tea revives her a little and she finally meets eyes with Rose, who offers a small smile of sympathy.

'We know how difficult this is,' she says, 'but it's very important, if we're to find out what happened, that we get as much information as we can straight away.'

Sofia sits up and gives her shoulders a wiggle, as though physically shaking some courage into her limbs. But almost immediately a beseeching expression washes over her face and she visibly shrinks.

'Can I ask something first?' she says.

'Of course,' says Rose.

Sofia swallows and plucks at the cushion. 'Did she have a heart attack or something?' she says. 'I mean, I don't think you would all be here if it was that, but maybe it *is*, is what I'm thinking.'

The two police officers regard her in silence for a couple of seconds.

'We don't know for certain,' says Rose gently, 'but it looks likely that someone did this to her.'

Sofia squeezes her eyes tightly shut and cries soundlessly, nodding, as though her suspicions have been confirmed. Her fingers pluck, pluck, pluck at the tassels on the cushion.

'Are you OK to continue, Sofia?' says Rose.

After a moment the other woman nods and opens her eyes again, swiping fresh tears away with the heel of her hand.

'Let's get it over,' she says nasally.

'Perhaps we can start off with a few basic facts,' says Mack in a soothing, gentle tone. 'Who lives in this house, as a general rule?'

Sofia takes a deep breath then begins counting off on her fingers, which have elaborate nail art – tiny black cats, by the look of it, against a white background.

'Well, there's Mohammed,' she says in a rush, 'who's been away working in Dubai for three months. He's in the downstairs bedroom and he's the one who's been here the longest. We hardly ever see him.' She draws breath in again before continuing. 'Then upstairs it's me and, and . . .' Sofia's shoulders begin to shake, and she clutches the crumpled, disintegrating toilet paper against her nose. Her words come out in a wail as she completes her sentence: '. . . and Hannah . . .'

Sofia sobs into her fisted hands. Mack and Rose quietly wait. Rose catches the eye of the uniformed officer standing sentry by the entrance and says, sotto voce, 'Do you think you could find more tissues or kitchen roll for her?'

He nods and leaves the room, emerging a few moments later with a wodge of kitchen roll, which he hands to Rose with a 'best I could do' shrug.

Rose goes to Sofia and holds the rosette of paper towards her.

'Here you go,' she says. 'It's still going to sandpaper your eyelids off, but at least it won't turn to mush.'

Sofia looks up with a grateful smile before taking the offering and blowing her nose loudly.

'OK to keep going, Sofia?' says Mack after another beat. 'We do realize how difficult this is.'

A car alarm goes off outside. Sofia flinches and closes her eyes.

'Yes, I can go on,' she says, her voice weak but resigned-sounding. 'I know this has to be done.'

'That's great,' says Mack. 'You're doing really well. Now, you were telling us who lives in the house. How long have you all been here?'

Sofia sighs. 'Let me think,' she says. 'Mohammed was here when Hannah . . . when Hannah and me moved in. That was a year ago.'

'You say you and Hannah moved in at the same time,' says Mack. 'Did you know each other before?'

Sofia looks as though she may dissolve again. Her chin wobbles and her eyes fill with fresh tears, but she swipes them away and clears her throat before giving a savage nod.

'We work . . . worked together at Little Angels,' she says thickly. 'I've been there two years and she was my line manager. She was ever so kind to me.'

'OK,' says Mack. 'What can you tell me about yesterday evening? Were you at home?'

Rose feels a rush of admiration for her boss in taking it so steady. She can't stop thinking about that scream.

Sofia's shoulders stiffen and her hands begin to work at the soggy kitchen towel; twiddling it through her fingers into a twisty point.

'I was out with, with my . . . boyfriend until about ten,' she says. 'Then I came home and went straight to bed.' Her eyes are cast down as she speaks. 'I'd had a late night the night before and was shattered.'

'Did you see Hannah when you got back?' says Rose, making a note on her pad: *Boyfriend?* Interesting pause before it.

'No. But I could hear her in her room,' says Sofia. 'I think she'd had a bath, because the bathroom was all steamy.'

'What exactly could you hear?' says Mack.

Sofia shrugs. 'Hannah moving about in there, you know.'

'Did you call out to her or anything?' says Rose. 'Exchange any words?'

'No.' Eyes pinned to her hands, which are twisting the kitchen roll so hard that it's beginning to shed dandruffy flakes onto the carpet.

Rose and Mack trade glances.

'Can you be sure that she was alone in there?' says Mack in a gentle tone.

A flare of anger, bright and hot. 'Like I said, it sounded like it was only her. I can't be sure because I didn't go in, did I?'

'That's fine,' says Mack. 'Did your boyfriend come back too? What's his name?'

Sofia reaches quickly for the cold cup of tea on the coffee table and then puts it down again. A blush is staining her throat and chest, where the onesie is open, and Rose watches it creep up to her cheeks. Interesting.

'What do you want to know that for?' The hand is now pulling the onesie together at the neck, as though to contain the heat rising from her skin.

A sympathetic smile from Mack. 'Routine, that's all,' he says. 'Did he come home with you?'

'No,' says Sofia firmly. Mack and Rose exchange glances again.

'The thing is,' says Mack, 'that from what we can tell, there is no sign that anyone broke into the house. So, we need to make sure we speak to everyone who may have been in the house in the last twenty-four hours. Do you understand what I'm saying?'

Sofia stares down at the floor, silent. Footsteps outside thud down the stairs and the front door opens and closes.

'His name,' says Rose. 'Can we get that, please?'

Sofia's eyes are brimming and a tic jumps in her right cheek. She murmurs something, too quietly to hear.

'What was that, Sofia? I didn't quite catch it,' says Mack.

Eyes up. Chin raised. Defiant.

'Leon,' she says, 'Leon Gavril. But he has nothing to do with anything.'

Rose looks her in the eye. 'Tell me,' she says, 'does Mr Gavril have a key to this property?'

Sofia shakes her head so hard her ponytail does a little dance at the back of her head.

'Who does have a key?' says Rose.

Sofia scrunches up her brow in thought. 'Well, only the people living here. Us.'

'What about a key to Hannah's bedroom?'

'No one!' This is in danger of becoming a wail and Sofia scrubs at her raw nostrils again. 'So I don't see how anyone could get in there! Are you sure this isn't some sort of accident?'

She casts a desperate look at their faces, which give her the answer she needs. The wild panic in her eyes causes Rose to hurriedly speak. This interview has a limited shelf life before Sofia breaks down again.

'What about your landlord?' she says. 'Does he or she have a key to that room?'

Sofia shrugs. 'I dunno. Probably.'

'What about previous tenants?' Rose says, half to Mack, but Sofia is shaking her head.

'New landlord changed all the locks when we moved in,' she says. 'He bought the property off someone else and he said he always does that, for security.'

'Right, OK,' says Mack. 'Are you absolutely certain that no one else has a key to the front door at least?'

'Yeah, I—' But Sofia doesn't finish her sentence. She draws in a breath and her eyes go wide. The plucking resumes on the poor cushion again.

'What is it?' says Mack, sharply.

Sofia is breathing heavily and her eyes flick from Mack to Rose.

'It's just, I remembered something,' she says, and when there is no response she continues. '. . . I put a spare key under that statue thing in the garden a while ago because I kept locking myself out.' Then, in a rush, 'But no one knew about that key!'

Mack sits back in his chair and lets out a sigh. 'Right, we'll certainly be checking that out. Now, Sofia,' he says gravely, 'I believe you told our colleagues that you heard Hannah screaming last night?'

There's a long pause. Sofia's breaths are coming faster. Little puffs in and out, like she is having to contain something rising inside.

'Yeah,' she says in a strangled voice. Then, in a rush, 'Thing is, though, Hannah had these terrible nightmares. I said so, I think, didn't I? When I called? She often woke up making noises like that. I used to go in at first, then I . . . stopped.'

Rose and Mack wait, Rose's pen hovering over the pad.

'So, was this "noise" the same as usual, or different in any way?' Mack's voice growing sharper by the minute.

Sofia's eyes are stricken. 'I don't know!' she says. 'But I hear all sorts from her room, so I don't pay no attention.' Stress is creeping into her diction and her cheeks flush under her tan. 'She was always waking up saying someone was in her room,' she goes on. 'A . . . a man. But there was never no one there!'

There's a brief pause, during which Rose and her sergeant's eyes meet.

'There weren't no one there,' repeats Sofia, her voice pitifully quiet. 'So when she did it last night, I didn't think nothing of it.'

She starts to sob quietly, her shoulders hunched.

'OK,' says Mack, gentle again. 'Are you sure it was three a.m. when you heard this?'

The young woman rubs at her nose and eyes with the scraggly piece of kitchen towel and nods miserably.

'I didn't check the time or anything,' she says. 'But that was always when she did it. Bang on three every night.'

3

By the time they pull into the staff parking bay at the back of the station, a smattering of icy rain has begun to fall from a low-slung sky. There's a headache-inducing quality to the light and Rose squints as she heads into the Tesco Metro across the road. She pulls air in, filthy as it is. Anything to get rid of that sickly lavender which clings to the insides of her nostrils. The pavement has patches of leaves that haven't been swept yet and a single yellow leaf shines unnaturally bright at Rose's feet.

Rose scans the shelves. It's probably going to be a late night and she needs to stock up on sandwiches, drinks, crisps, and chocolate for her and Mack. She'll hide the stash under the desk, dipping in as and when needed. By a certain point in the evening, it would be safer to leave the bag with a pack of Labradors than her colleagues in the Major Investigation Team.

It's quiet in reception as she passes through. There's no one being signed in or out and the six-foot-five Desk Sergeant, Omar, is filing paperwork and singing something in his rich baritone. It's probably from *Hamilton*, which he's seen four times.

'You're wasted here, you know that,' she says with a grin, and he does a flourishy bow.

'I aim to please,' he says, then, peering at what she's carrying, 'What you got for me in there then, young Gifford?'

'Well,' says Rose, pretending to rummage inside the Tesco

bag. 'I've got lots of nice carrot sticks and a big tub of delicious humous. Want some?'

'Bloody liar,' says Omar with a sigh. 'I can see the Walkers logo through the bag.'

Rose hears him muttering, 'Humous, honestly!' as if she had suggested larks' tongues or stuffed monkey heads.

There's a crackle of energy in the air and Rose realizes everyone is heading into the briefing room.

The room has never been big enough to accommodate the whole team; already all the seats in the rectangle of laid-out tables are taken. Rose stands by the door, breathing in the smell of dusty, ancient radiators working overtime and the particular chemical tang of institutional carpeting. Once again she remembers that sickly lavender.

She keeps her eyes fixed on the whiteboard, which so far has two or three photographs of the crime scene along the top but is otherwise blank. She senses a dark head to her left swivelling in her direction, but she doesn't react.

Don't look at him, she thinks.

'Right,' says Rowland loudly as the last few stragglers enter the room. She turns to the whiteboard and writes the words OPERATION SANDPIPER in her blocky writing.

'That's what we're calling this one.' She pauses and turns back to the room. The burble of conversation peters out and dies as everyone faces the same way.

'We have a thirty-two-year-old victim,' says Rowland, 'name of Hannah Scott. Nursery worker. Time of death between three a.m. and seven thirty. No sign of forced entry into the house. Locked bedroom, with a key in situ when the door was broken down. Cause of death, suffocation, likely with the spare pillow on the bed, judging by the pattern of saliva found on it.'

People exchange grimaces and there is a low murmur around the room.

'Any signs of sexual assault, ma'am?' asks Tom Skinner, a DC with the eye bags and crumpled shirt of the brand-new parent.

Rowland shakes her head. 'It didn't look that way, but until we get the pathology report, we can't be sure. So, we have no signs of robbery and no obvious sign of sexual assault – yet.'

'How did they get into the property?' says Tom.

'There was a spare key, under a birdbath in the back garden,' says Mack. He and Rose had checked this out before leaving the property. 'But it was covered in cobwebs,' he continues, 'and didn't look as though it had been touched for ages. We're getting it looked at.'

'Hmm,' says Rowland, 'it's a weird one, this. You'd almost think it was someone who just died in their sleep if it weren't for the signs of suffocation.' She pauses. 'And the locked bedroom is very odd. There are some locks that can be opened from the other side even when the key is in place, if you have another key. It seems likely that's what happened here. But we need to find out exactly who has a key to that room.'

Tom speaks up again. 'I've spoken to the landlord . . .' he glances down at his pad, 'a Mr Amir – but he's currently in Pakistan. Flew out two months ago, after his mother died. He says the door can be opened from the other side, but the only spare is in a safe in his house, which is all locked up. We went to Muswell Hill to check out his property, and it has CCTV everywhere and a top-of-the-range alarm system. Highly unlikely anyone stole it from there.'

Rowland grimaces. 'Well, whoever killed her got in somehow,' she says. 'They didn't float through the wall like a ghost.'

Everyone mulls over that thought.

Rose clears her throat.

'Ma'am?' she says. 'I noticed something that seemed odd.'

All eyes in the room fix on her.

'Go on,' says Rowland.

'Well,' says Rose, 'it was her hair. It looked almost artfully tidy. I mean,' she pauses, getting into her stride, 'if someone was suffocating you, you're going to thrash about like crazy, I'd think.' Rose turns her head from side to side to illustrate the point. 'The crown of her hair at least should have been bunched up. Even if she *had* died in her sleep, which she clearly didn't, it would be messier than that. She was so . . .' she hunts for the word, '. . . *neat*. She looked like Sleeping Beauty, lying there, didn't she? Weirdly perfect.'

Everyone stares at her and she tries to combat the flush creeping up her throat by sheer will power. Rowland, apparently deep in thought, turns back to the board.

'Yes, there was something stagey about it, now you mention it,' she says. 'I'll get the CSIs to look for a hairbrush and get it checked out for prints. And,' she adds, 'if that's the case, it might lead to certain assumptions about the killer, perhaps?' She frowns at one of the pictures of the victim on the white-board. Then, something occurs to her, and she turns.

'Obviously I don't want anyone using that . . . rather *striking* description of our victim . . . outside of this room.' She is addressing everyone, but she is looking at Rose with a scalpel glare. Rose looks down, hiding her irritation at being chastised.

'Maybe it was someone who cared about her,' says Mack, 'and they wanted her to be left in a dignified way, despite what they'd done?'

'Maybe,' says DC Kev Wallis, bald and round with a full-on eighties moustache, 'he's a sick little bastard.'

There's a ripple of grim laughter at this.

'So . . .' Rowland raises her voice to get the room's attention again. 'I want to know everything about this young woman's movements last night. And about her nearest and dearest.' She pauses. 'Tell me about the flatmate,' she says, looking at Mack and then Rose, who hands Mack her notes.

'Sofia Nikolas,' says Mack, reading from Rose's notebook. 'Twenty-three years old, works with the victim. Couldn't rouse her this morning and got scared, so she called 999.' He pauses. 'Says the victim had bad nightmares and was always crying out in the night.'

A murmur goes around the room at this.

'Go on,' says Rowland, tapping the whiteboard pen against her other palm.

'Well,' says Rose, picking up the narrative, 'it's a bit odd because it seems Sofia got used to it. And she did it at the exact same time every night.'

The room falls silent and Rose knows everyone is having the same thought. It's the one that has been going around and around in her mind since Sofia Nikolas said those words. Imagine if she had written something off as one more bad dream when in reality she had been listening to her friend being murdered in her bed?

'OK,' says Rowland wearily. 'What do we know about her love life? Any boyfriends?'

'Sofia claimed not,' says Mack, 'but that didn't ring true. She was very uncomfortable when we asked her about her own boyfriend, a fella by the name of . . .' he looks down at the notebook and flips the pages back, '. . . Leon Gavril.'

'Could be that he's playing away from home,' says Wallis, and Rowland nods.

'Yes, might be that she doesn't want him interviewed for that reason,' says Rose, glancing at Mack for encouragement. 'But when we questioned her about Hannah's love life, she was very . . . guarded. We were speculating that maybe this Leon Gavril had been at it with both of them? Or there was some sort of issue there.'

'OK,' says Rowland. 'Run him through the PNC, see there's anything to be found. And continue with the house-to-house on the street, in case anyone saw or heard anything unusual. Is there any CCTV on the corner where that betting shop is? It's a cul-de-sac, so we're looking for any vehicles or pedestrians entering or leaving Michenden Crescent within that time frame. Kev, what do we have on the victim's phone? Anything?'

Kev clears his throat before speaking to the room. 'Nothing beyond some chatty messages between her and her parents in Leeds, who' – he looks up – 'should be here soon, I believe. But the techs are getting everything off it and looking at whether she blocked anyone. They have her iPad too. We also have Sofia Nikolas's phone.'

'Right,' says Rowland with an approving nod. 'Let me know what comes up there. Mack and Rose, you look up this Leon Gavril and see what we've got. Then I'd like you to track him down. Did you get his contact details?'

'Only a phone number,' says Rose. 'Sofia says she's never been to his place, which goes to support the theory that he's shagging about.'

Leon Gavril, it transpires, has a conviction for Common Assault after a domestic violence incident six years ago. His record has been clean since then.

Mack and Rose share a family-sized bag of Maltesers as they crawl through the rush hour traffic towards the address found on the system. Gavril may have since moved on, but it's a start.

As they wait at traffic lights, Mack glances over at Rose in the driving seat.

So,' he says, 'what's going on with you and Sam then?'

Rose buys time by muttering an obscenity at the driver in front, who's taking his time noticing the changing lights.

'Hmm? What do you mean?' she says, with unconvincing nonchalance.

Mack laughs.

'Come on,' he says, before attempting to throw a Malteser into his mouth, and missing. It pings against his chest and then rolls down under the seat, where it no doubt joins a graveyard of mouldering litter. The shabbiness of the vehicles is one of the ways the cuts are being felt. It used to be that officers would take an afternoon off every once in a while to get them cleaned, but with budgets and staffing the way they are, no one has time any longer. The result is dusty paintwork and a mild crunch under the feet from gritty car mats.

'Damn,' he says, then, 'anyway, don't try and kid a kidder. My fine detection skills are not only honed by my years on the job, but by having two scheming children.' He pauses. 'You seem to be ignoring each other. I thought you were mates?'

'We are!' says Rose hotly, realizing she is nearing 48 mph in a 40 zone. She forces herself to ease up the pressure on the accelerator. 'There is absolutely nothing going on!'

Mack doesn't reply. He simply passes the bag of Maltesers in Rose's direction and holds it under her nose. There's something about the silent kindness and understanding of this small gesture that gives Rose a tender feeling in her chest.

She wishes she *could* begin to describe what is going on between her and Sam Malik. They met at Hendon in the earliest days of their police training. Sam, naturally friendly and open, had been kind to the weird, quiet girl skulking at the back on the first big night out. After a few pints – and a few more shots – they were bellowing 'Mr Brightside' in a karaoke duet outside the kebab shop.

Skinny, with a longish nose and glasses, he was geeky and cute. This is what she saw when she looked at him then, anyway. A mate. A chum.

They went their separate ways for several years until Rose began working here at Silverton Street Station for MIT14 and they met up again. They started to hang out once more, neither of them being in a relationship at the time. He was in uniform and was determined to stay that way, enjoying the excitement and variety of being a response officer, travelling around the area and acting on 999 calls. Rose loved seeing his family again: his noisy, warm mum and his quiet, gentle dad, plus sister Zainab, a hilarious force of nature.

Then there had been that night when everything changed. The 'almost night'. Almost coming together. Almost being a couple.

But however much Rose might like the idea, it has to stay that way.

Because how can she ever explain what is going on in her life to someone as normal as Sam?

They pass the squat 1930s Wood Green tube station and then the glass curves of the cinema as they head south along Green Lanes, one of the main traffic arteries of North London.

The grand old building of the crown court is near here. Rose remembers giving evidence for the first time there in a rape case. The defendant had watched her with a knowing smile the whole time she was in the dock and she had hated herself for blushing when she wasn't embarrassed but merely furious and determined. These days, she slaps on extra foundation whenever she appears in court. She's found one with a greenish tinge that counteracts redness, though she has to be careful she doesn't go too far and end up looking like the Hulk.

The address is a seventies block of flats off Green Lanes. Leon Gavril lives on the ground floor. The windows, screened by wooden blinds despite the hour, give the flat a blank, unwelcoming look.

Mack raps hard on the door, which is covered in slightly peeling blue paint.

Nothing happens for a moment or two, then the blinds ripple and bend in the middle before snapping back into parallels again.

Rose opens the letter box and calls out:

'Mr Gavril? We're from Silverton Street police station. Can we have a quick word?'

Still nothing.

Rose raps harder on the door. 'We won't take up too much of your time, Mr Gavril, if you could open the door for us?'

Finally, they hear scuffling sounds from the other side and after a great deal of fumbling with chains and locks, the door opens. A tired-looking, round-faced woman in her mid-thirties with long fair hair hanging lankly on her shoulders stares out at them. She is dressed in a greyish tracksuit top that has a crusty stain on the shoulder.

'Yes, can I help you?' she says with surprisingly crisp diction. She has half her body still hidden behind the door and her expression is suspicious.

Rose smiles and brandishes her ID card.

'Sorry to bother you, but I'm DC Rose Gifford and this is my sergeant, DS Mackie. We're from Major Investigation

Team 14, based at Silverton Street, and we're looking for a Mr Leon Gavril. Does he live at this address?'

Some flicker of emotion passes over the woman's face and she fiddles with a lock of hair. Her nails are bitten to the quick, her grey eyes puffy.

'Sort of,' she says quietly. 'But he's not here.'

'Right,' says Mack in an easy tone. 'Can I ask what do you mean by "sort of"? Is this his address, or not?'

The woman licks her lips, which look dry and cracked. Her eyes dart from left to right, minnow fast.

'Um, I mean he does live here, yes, but he's not home.'

'Can we get your name please?' says Mack.

'Kate,' she says, 'Kate Morley.' Her eyes grow panicked. 'I haven't seen him for a few days.'

'OK,' says Mack. 'Could we ask you to—'

The sound of something falling elsewhere in the house causes the woman's eyes to widen further.

'Is someone else in the house, Ms Morley?' says Rose.

'Only me and Carli, my baby,' she says quickly.

'And how old is the baby?' says Mack.

'She's . . . she's five months old.'

There is a short pause, but it's long enough to make the woman blush furiously. Rose almost feels sorry for her. It's like watching someone who can't swim being sucked underwater.

'Ms Morley,' says Mack, voice raised for the first time, 'we are here in relation to the murder of a young woman and we think Mr Gavril can help with our inquiries. If there is someone in the house with you, we need you to cooperate. If you'd rather come down to the station for a chat, that's absolutely fine.'

Face hardening now, the other woman glares at them.

'I already told you,' she says. 'I don't know where he—'

The clear sound of a squeaking step behind the door. Kate Morley is grasping the door so rigidly the tips of her fingers are bleaching white. Her mouth opens and closes. The two police officers exchange silent glances and Rose hurries away from the front door and down the side alley.

She gets to the end in time to see a huge man dressed in a vest top and tracksuit bottoms climbing effortlessly over the back fence.

'Stop! Police!' she yells as he begins to run. Rose sets off in pursuit, yelling into her radio. 'Suspect on the run down the Fredericks Close alleyway, heading south from the property!'

Lungs burning, she follows, silently cursing how long it's been since she went to the gym.

'Stop!' she yells, but the man, Gavril no doubt, continues to run. He is so muscular he isn't running all that fast, but he's still getting away from Rose, whose chest is on fire.

He reaches the end of the alley slightly ahead of Rose, who painfully bangs a hip against some communal bins, then disappears from sight. She careers around the corner to see him catch his foot on the edge of the pavement and sprawl forward with an anguished grunt. He almost rights himself, but it gives Rose long enough to hurl herself at his broad back. He's slammed down onto the pavement and she twists his vast arms – muscles like tennis balls inside stockings – to be handcuffed together.

He is no longer resisting. She can smell the sweat rising from his back, his shoulders as wide as one of her armchairs at home.

'Fuck sake!' he yells. 'All right!'

'Leon Gavril,' she gasps out, 'I am arresting you on suspicion of the murder of Hannah Scott. You do not have to say anything . . . Shit . . .' she draws some much-needed air into her tight lungs, '. . . but it may harm your defence if you do not mention something when questioned that you later rely on in court. Anything you do say may be given in evidence against you. Do you understand?'

'I didn't murder no one,' he says through bared teeth as she slips on the cuffs, which only just fit his thick wrists.

'Right,' says Rose breathlessly, 'well, you'll get plenty of opportunity to have your say down at the station, Mr Gavril.'

Mack arrives, and when he catches Rose's eye, he gives her a grin and a nod of approval.

'You OK?' he says as they lead the suspect to the car. 'You look like you're about to have a stroke.'

'All right, Mo Farah,' she pants, 'like you're any fitter.'

Mack laughs as they reach the car. He opens a door and helps ease Gavril into the back. 'In you go, young man,' he says. 'No more nonsense from you, please.'

'I want to see my brief,' says Gavril sulkily.

'All in good time, my friend,' says Mack, still grinning. 'All in good time.'

They check him in with Omar, who runs through the usual drill. Gavril does a lot of sulky eye-rolling but is otherwise compliant. He answers all the questions about alcohol, drug dependencies, and self-harm attempts with a series of grunts.

Rose can't stop looking at his arms as he stands next to her and marvels at their sheer breadth. She has never been able to understand the appeal of pumped-up men.

A vivid mental picture of Sam's slim brown fingers cupping her face causes a simultaneous tingle of lust and a bone-deep feeling of regret. The image is then replaced by Gavril pressing his meaty hands over a woman's face and watching her fight for breath as she lies in her cosy, lavender-scented bed. Rose's fingers instinctively reach for the spot on her arm; she scratches so hard she later finds a pinprick of blood on her jumper.

Gavril wants a specific solicitor, rather than the duty one, and he is led away to a cell to wait for their arrival.

Rose goes to the kitchen area to make some tea. She hopes the fact she's made an arrest on an hours-old case will give her immunity from having to do one for the entire office. She decides she'll gulp it down right here on the spot if she has to, even if it means taking off the roof of her mouth.

She's stirring in some milk when someone comes into the kitchen behind her. Turning guiltily, she flushes when she sees Sam, who crisply nods then goes to the kettle.

'What was that meant to be?' she says, trying, and failing,

not to sound sarcastic. It's her Achilles' heel; the source of much aggro with teachers when she was at school, and partly why she and Rowland don't get on.

'What was what?' says Sam, his back to her now as he opens the fridge and pulls out a Tupperware container. He is a big maker of healthy stuff; a chopper and a slicer who never eats fish and chips two nights running.

'The weird nod,' says Rose, feeling small and mean, even as the words leave her mouth.

Sam closes the fridge with his hip and then turns to face her. His expression is completely impassive. Her insides cool and shrivel.

'I don't know what you want from me, Rose,' he says quietly, then, 'But hey, well done on the arrest. Great stuff.'

'Your mum would be proud of your excellent manners,' she mumbles, too quiet for him to hear, but beyond a sharp frown, he doesn't acknowledge it. Sam leaves the room.

Miserably, she sips the tea, staring at the cardboard sign above the kettle that says, *There is no Washing Up Fairy. Clean up your own shit*, which has been here as long as she has.

It's not fair. It's not fair on Sam and it certainly isn't fair on her.

Back in the office, Rowland calls the team over for an update.

Everyone is tired. There is a palpable sense of burned-out energy and stale mouths.

'Right, people,' she says, 'the clock is ticking on Gavril, so we need enough evidence to charge or he's on his way home tomorrow. Luckily, we have some interesting findings from his flat. Tom?'

DC Tom Skinner grins.

'We found ten wraps of coke laid out nicely on the kitchen table.'

'God,' says Mack, 'no wonder he was skittish when you showed up.'

'Bet he nearly shat himself!' This interjection from Kev,

complete with a waving motion as though to clear a bad smell, earns a gust of laughter that is dowsed in a moment by the distasteful expression on Rowland's face.

'Has he been arrested for that, as well?' says Rowland, and Tom nods with satisfaction.

'Good.'

'But,' says Rose, 'the reason he ran away *might* have nothing to do with Hannah Scott.' She had a feeling that picking up Mr Gavril had been a little too easy.

'Yes,' says Rowland with a frown, 'that's very true. But it gives us some leverage that could make him more willing to talk to us. We could suggest talking to the CPS about whether he's on this side of the line with regards to it being possession.'

'There's something else,' says DC Ewa Duggan, a quiet officer with a soft Polish accent. Ewa came to the UK for a gap-year holiday when she was nineteen, ten years ago, and met her Glaswegian husband within days. 'I've had a message from Tech, and it seems that Hannah Scott had blocked a number and deleted a whole series of messages from—'

'—our Mr Gavril, by any chance?' says Rowland, with a rare smile. It's disconcerting, because, thinks Rose, she looks completely different. She bats away that other image. *Puffy eyes. Mascara streaks. Shiny snot snaking from one nostril that hasn't even been noticed in the state of distress.*

'Yep,' says Ewa, returning the grin.

'Right,' says Rowland, the smile switching off. 'He has asked for a solicitor from Crossnans, so we're going to have to wait until the morning. We'll reconvene here at seven a.m. When the solicitor arrives, I'd like you, Colin, to interview him with Rose.'

Then, 'Get some sleep, people. The PACE clock is ticking and we're losing valuable hours, so tomorrow's an important day.'

The room fills with sounds of shuffling and the scraping of chairs.

4

Rose drives home on autopilot. Eyes stinging and knee throbbing from her tussle on the ground earlier, she yawns and forces herself to concentrate as the lights from oncoming cars dazzle and spread across her vision. But despite the tiredness and the aches and pains, she can't help the smile that comes at the thought of bringing in a suspect in this murder so fast. It was her and Mack who went to the house, but she, Rose Gifford, was the one who brought him down. This gives her a pleasing, toasty sensation inside.

She reaches the quiet street in the East Barnet suburb where she lives shortly after 11 p.m. and, finding nowhere to park, drives around the neighbourhood looking for a space. In the end she must park three streets away and as this puts her near the main road again, she sits in the car contemplating whether she needs to go to the Costcutter on the High Street.

All she wants is a glass of wine and then bed, but she knows she won't sleep well on an empty stomach. She doesn't want one of those nights where she spends hours hovering on the verge of sleep, so decides to at least get some toast and Marmite down her first.

The pub on the corner is at chucking-out time and, judging by the lairy, flushed faces and the plethora of Arsenal shirts over middle-aged bellies, there was a match on earlier. Their upbeat mood suggests their team won, which is something to be grateful for.

Rose walks towards the Costcutter with her head down and hears her phone ring from inside her bag. She stops and fishes in the voluminous but crammed leather sack, which is at least partly responsible for the near constant shoulder pain that plagues her. Unable to find her phone, she curses when it stops ringing, silently praying that it isn't Rowland calling with something that can't wait until morning. Rose isn't entirely sure whether the other woman sleeps and if she does, it's possible that she hangs upside down like a bat for a few hours.

Finally finding the phone, Rose looks at the screen and taps recent calls.

Sam.

She stares at the phone for a few moments, contemplating whether to return the call, but instead slips it back into her bag.

Bypassing the bread and Marmite waiting in Costcutter, she goes to the chip shop on the corner for the second night running.

Turning the key in her front door and balancing her hot, wrapped bag of chips with the other, she hesitates inside the door. She can't hear anything and a sense of relief washes over her.

Maybe she has the place to herself tonight, which would be ironic considering the whole Sam situation.

Passing the darkened living room, though, her senses prickle and she tentatively pokes her head around the door and then gives a little yelp when she sees the shape hulking in the nearest armchair.

Her mother is sitting with her hands folded in her lap, staring straight ahead. As usual she wears the purple jumper with the tiny mirrors sewn into the neck, which smells of smoke and the Chanel No.5 knock-off from the market. Her brittle hair is pulled back into a claw grip, brassy red streaked with grey. Small eyes are ringed in black liner and her pink lipstick is greasy and bleeding into the cracks around her mouth. When Rose thinks about that mouth it is either saying something bitter or pulling like a drawstring around a fag. She turns and smiles benignly at Rose, revealing yellowing teeth, but does not say anything. She never does.

Rose tuts loudly in response then heads towards the kitchen, where she opens the chips and stuffs a few into her mouth. Pouring a large glass of red wine from the bottle by the sink, she sits at the table and finishes the chips. But the stodgy, greasy dinner sits like a brick in her stomach.

After a few minutes she forces herself to get up and check the living room again, snapping on the harsh yellow overhead light as she enters.

As she had hoped, the room is empty.

Rose Gifford has been having these visits from her dead mother for years, proving that humans can get used to anything.

She has become accustomed to finding her sitting on one of the kitchen chairs, or, once, appearing to do the washing up, her hands moving silently and rhythmically while not disturbing the smeary, crusted plates in Rose's neglected sink.

At first, she told herself it was some kind of psychotic episode, even though nothing specific seemed to have sparked it. It was when she was early in her training at Hendon that it happened for the first time. She had come back into the silent house to find her mother sitting in the kitchen as though she were simply waiting for her dinner.

When it happened a few days later, Rose had been too scared to go to the doctor about it, in case she was told she was mad and therefore couldn't become a policewoman.

But here's the thing. Rose knows, as well as she knows the sun rises in the East and sets in the West, that this isn't some rogue twist of her synapses, firing wrongly and creating things that aren't there. She knows. Her mother really is haunting her.

And Rose doesn't even believe in ghosts. Isn't that what she has always said, all these years? Despite all evidence to the contrary. The irony of how delighted the old phoney would have been about this is almost amusing. Anyway, Rose somehow grew used to it and managed to treat it as an annoying aberration she hoped to outgrow.

But a week ago, things took a more disturbing turn.

She'd been to the pub with Sam. They were celebrating having charged two senior members of a notorious Haringey gang who had been grooming boys as young as thirteen to carry drugs and intimidate rivals. It was a case the team had been working on for over five months and everyone had got sloshed. Even Rowland came along for one.

Afterwards, Rose and Sam had somehow ended up coming back to the house.

Rose had been trying to ignore the fact that something had changed lately.

He had not long come out of a relationship with a woman called Lucy. Bloody perfect Lucy, with her posh voice and swishy hair. Rose had been greatly surprised by the lurch of hope in her stomach when he told her they had split up. It seemed to come from nowhere, but once thought, it couldn't be unthought. Neither could the moment when she was watching the actor Dev Patel in a movie and realized a) how much she fancied him and b) how much he resembled Sam.

She'd quashed these feelings though. She'd had no time for a relationship. Too complicated.

But on this evening she'd invited him back to her house for another drink and some magnetic force had pulled them together the moment they were inside the front door. Just like that, they were joined at mouths and hips, making their way up the stairs like a clumsy four-legged creature.

Rose hates naff sentimentalism but yes, it had felt like coming home, or being peaceful for once.

They'd cuddled up in the bed after, joking about Rose's icy feet and sharing a laugh about something particularly coruscating that Rowland had said to Kev Wallis earlier that day, then drifted off to sleep in each other's arms.

Rose had snapped into consciousness about an hour later, adrenaline throbbing through her body and her heart punching against her ribcage. There was a heaviness on the bed and when she lifted her head from the pillow to look, there she was, sitting so her knees were trapped and frowning, not at Rose, but at the prone body of Sam, who was turned with one naked shoulder out of the bed and facing the other way.

Rose was screaming, 'Fuck off and leave me alone!' while leaping from the bed before she could help herself, and a very confused Sam woke with an exclamation of shock.

Explaining she'd had a nightmare, she forced herself back into bed but lay awake for hours. Her mother had migrated to the chair by the window, where she kept up her silent vigil all night.

In the morning, Rose had been exhausted and sullen. Sam had repeatedly asked what was wrong until she told him that the night before had been a mistake. They needed to go back to being friends again.

The hurt look on his face had almost undone her. Rose had forced herself to remain stony-faced, saving her hot, desperate tears of frustration for when he had left the house.

She'd said, 'Are you happy now, you annoying bitch?'

But she was speaking to thin air.

Adele Gifford, widow, so-called medium, crook, had been dead for ten years. Technically, she wasn't Rose's real mother, she was her grandmother. But she had brought Rose up from birth. Rose's birth mum, Kelly, had given birth to her at seventeen and then died from a drug overdose when Rose was three. She had no memory of her mother at all and, having always called Adele mum, it was impossible not to. As for her father? Could have been anyone – from the things Adele said, anyway.

Throughout her childhood in this house, Rose had resented the punters who turned up to have their supposed 'readings' done. She would come home from school to find the curtains drawn and the air thick with grief and the sickly neroli oil her mother burned when she saw her clients.

The living room door would be firmly closed, but often when Rose was carrying a snack of bread and peanut butter up the stairs to her room, she would see the 'clients' leaving the room, dabbing at eyes and thanking her mother for whatever it was the old charlatan had claimed to do for them that day.

Most were women of a certain age, longing for their dead husbands and, Rose suspected, lonely enough to be half paying simply for the company. But occasionally there would be someone with the harrowed, stumbling air of those for whom death has come far too early in their lives: the parent of a dead child, or the man in his thirties Rose remembered, whose wife had died on a supposed holiday of a lifetime. These were the ones that made her furious, the poor, sad souls who were looking for something her fraudulent mother could never give.

If Rose sometimes felt a hollow-cold sensation in her stomach and glimpsed something out of the corner of her eye, she knew to ignore it.

Like today, when confronted by Hannah Scott's corpse, when the feeling came again…

But this has nothing to do with her job. She simply won't allow it.

Rose is a police detective, who lives in the real world of gritty, messy, criminal behaviour, of clear right and wrong. Of black and white, not shadowy grey.

If she keeps telling herself this, maybe it will be true.

5

Rose sleeps fitfully. When the alarm goes off at 6 a.m., she feels she's had scant break from her own tumbling thoughts and restless limbs. There were no more visits, no frantic tugging at the bedclothes (another horror she has had to deal with lately). But as always she slept lightly, constantly on guard, and this state of vigilance leaves her feeling depleted.

Only half awake, she stands with her hand over the bath and waits for the mean spitting from the shower to warm up. It may happen suddenly, scalding her hand, or it may not get warmer at all. It's one of the many things about this house that she has got used to over the years.

One day her landlord is going to sell this place and she won't be able to live on her own in London any more. Not on her salary. When her mother died, she took over the rent; but the landlord – a shady friend of her mother's – is ancient, so it's inevitable that one day this old-fashioned agreement will be replaced by the harsh realities of capitalism. This is a two-bed-roomed house within the M25 and even if the kitchen dates back to the 1970s and the hot water has a mind of its own, at least it is hers.

Under the warm dribble of water at last, she lets it run over her face to wake her up.

Out of the shower she blasts her bushy, conker-brown hair

with her aged hairdryer then pulls it back in a ponytail, before slicking some mascara onto her lashes. She wants to look crisp and professional for the interview this morning but can never seem to quite pull that look off. Still, this is the best she can do, in her black skirt and patterned top under a grey jacket that's too tight across the shoulders.

Breakfast is a can of Diet Coke and a couple of handfuls of dry Cheerios. She can't be late.

Gavril's solicitor is a young woman from a firm known to and respected by the team. Her hair is short and glossy, her complexion as fresh as you'd expect from someone who gets plenty of quality food, sleep, and exercise.

It turns out that, despite appearances, Gavril's wife Kate Morley comes from a middle-class family. Although she and her family had fallen out in recent times, the legal representation has come via the father's recommendation. A decision has been made not to arrest Morley, who was suffering from post-natal depression and had been believably distraught over lying about Gavril's whereabouts.

'Hi, I'm Rabea Anand,' says the solicitor, 'from Crossnans.'

'DS Colin Mackie, and this is my colleague DC Rose Gifford.' They shake hands.

'Have you had some time with the client?' says Mack. Rabea Anand nods.

'If we can have a quick word before we go in?' she says.

They go into the room reserved for the softer interviews, which has a couple of slightly greasy sofas and a Georgia O'Keeffe rip-off from IKEA on one wall. No one sits.

'Look . . .' says Anand, spreading her hands in an open gesture. 'The truth is, the reason my client panicked and ran was because of the drugs. They were only for personal use, but he had a complete meltdown, in his words, when he heard you at the door. All reason flew out of the window.'

'Go on,' says Mack with a small smile.

'Well,' says Anand, frowning, 'he denies any knowledge of this young woman's death, but he is willing to fully cooperate on that if you might consider recommending to the CPS that he is charged only with possession.'

Mack sucks in his breath in a stagey way and turns to look at Rose.

'Hmm, I'm not sure,' he says. 'My DC had to give chase, and your client weighs about ten times as much as her. She put herself in danger to get him.'

'Look,' says Anand in a low voice. 'You know you have absolutely no evidence linking my client to this murder. If you'd rather he gives a No Comment before the clock runs out and you let him go, that's up to you. But that would be a great waste of everyone's time.'

Mack looks at Rose again. He's smiling; he enjoys this horse trading – they all do, to some extent. Keeps all parties on their toes.

'What do you think, DC Gifford?' he says.

Rose pretends to spend a moment thinking it through.

'I think we'd like Mr Gavril to tell us everything he knows about Hannah Scott,' says Rose. 'And we'll see what we can do.'

Inside Interview Room One, there's a musky smell, not unpleasant, like someone has brought in a fairly clean animal and snuck it under the table. It seems to be coming from Gavril, adding to the aroma absorbed into the walls via the many despairing and desperate characters who have sweated, cried, and farted in here.

Gavril is dressed in a grey tracksuit top and bottoms and the top strains across his chest. He sits back with his arms crossed and his legs spread wide, so tiny Anand must sit almost sideways in the seat. Rose wishes she could flick him hard on the leg with something, simply to see his expression, but instead gives him a professional, cool smile. She has a vivid muscle memory of how it felt, pushing that powerful body against the car. Then the image flips and she pictures those meaty hands pressing down on Hannah Scott's terrified face, arms slightly bent, but effortless, as her body flails and fights for air. Rose narrows her eyes at him.

The recording begins with its usual long awkward hum. They have been promised an upgrade to the new digital system any day, which will get rid of this once and for all. Rose wonders whether she will miss it, in a funny way.

Mack begins with the customary spiel, detailing exactly who is in the room.

'So, Mr Gavril,' he says, sitting back comfortably in the chair. 'Or can I call you Leon?'

Gavril shrugs and Anand gives him a look.

'Leon it is, then,' says Mack. 'So, Leon, you have been arrested for the murder of Hannah Scott and also for possession with intent to supply Class A drugs.'

Gavril's nostrils actually flare, which Rose finds oddly fascinating to watch.

'I didn't touch Hannah, not like that,' he says. 'And that coke was just for me, no one else.'

Rose looks up from the notes she is taking, and exchanges a glance with her sergeant, both clocking the wording of that denial about Hannah Scott.

Not like that. Interesting.

'OK, Leon,' says Mack. 'We may have a little wiggle room on the items we found in the upstairs bedroom of the property at Manning Court, but I would like to hear from you why you ran from us yesterday.'

Gavril's eyes flick briefly to Rose, and she meets his gaze coolly. There is a gratifying flush to his cheeks and he mumbles something indistinct.

'Could you speak so that the tape picks it up, please, Leon?' says Mack.

Gavril swallows and glances at Anand, who gives him another nod.

'I was scared,' he says, his voice low and deep. He doesn't look like a man who uses these words often. His right knee is jumping up and down, his fingers tapping out a rhythm.

'Scared of what?'

'I was . . . worried about the fact that I had that gear on the kitchen table. I wasn't about to take it. I wouldn't do that with my daughter in the house.'

Rose glances at her sergeant. Mack indicates she can pick this up.

'Wait,' says Rose. 'You'll have to excuse me, but I'm a bit confused.' She pauses. 'You were scared because you had coke out on the kitchen table. You wouldn't take it with your daughter in the house. But you left it on the table when you ran away from me and my colleague, with your daughter in the house. I think you might need to explain that part, because I'm struggling to keep up.'

Gavril sinks his huge head into his hands and sighs bitterly. 'Look, I can't explain it. I just lost my shit for a minute.'

'How well do you know Sofia Nikolas, Leon?' says Mack, and Leon's head jerks up again.

'I know her a bit,' he says, sitting back in his seat. His body language couldn't be more defensive if he pressed himself against the wall behind him.

'She says she's your girlfriend,' says Rose.

Leon looks at his solicitor, but she merely continues writing neat notes in her notebook. Rose knows she would have been the sort of girl with a pristine pencil case at school.

'Look,' says Gavril in a smaller voice as though all the bravado has drained away like air from a puncture. 'I've been having a thing with Sofia, just casual-like, but Kate don't know about any of that. She's been really down since having Carli and things ain't been . . . well we haven't been . . .' he flails for a moment longer until Mack puts him out of his misery.

'Right,' he says, 'we're not here to judge anything like that, Leon. All we care about is getting to the bottom of a very serious crime.' A pause. 'How well did you know Hannah Scott?'

Gavril's Adam's apple bobs like a ping-pong ball in his throat and he looks wildly at his brief. She leans into him and whispers in his ear. Rose catches '. . . cooperation' and nothing else. Whatever she said doesn't seem to have reassured him that much because his eyes are roving around the room like those of a cornered horse.

'A little,' he says. 'She was around and whatnot.'

'Did you have a key to her bedroom door?' says Rose.

Gavril leans forward, slapping one meaty hand on the table. 'No way,' he says. 'Why would I?'

There's a sharp knock at the door then and Ewa Duggan puts her head round to peer in at them.

'Sorry, sir,' she says, 'a quick word?' Her eyes are bright.

Mack stops the recording and he and Rose go out to the corridor.

They come back in a few minutes later.

Gavril and Anand sense the change in energy immediately and both sit up a little straighter as the two police officers take their seats and Mack resumes the recording.

'So, you say you knew Hannah Scott "a little",' he says, glancing down at Rose's notes as though he needs the reminder from only a few minutes earlier.

'Yeah,' says Gavril, and his nostrils do the flarey thing again. His right leg is tapping out a rhythm under the table at double-quick time. 'That's right. She shares the house with Sofia, so I saw her around and about.'

'Around and about,' repeats Mack. 'So you weren't close?'

Gavril pauses and then gives the smallest shake of his head.

'Sorry, Leon,' says Rose, 'for the benefit of the tape, would you mind being clearer? Was that a denial?'

Gavril swallows again and flexes and unflexes his fists on the table. 'Yeah, that's right,' he says.

'Thank you,' says Rose, wrong-footing him with a smile.

Mack frowns. 'Well,' he says, 'in that case, Leon, can you

41

explain why traces of your semen have been found on the sheets in Hannah Scott's laundry basket?'

The effect of this on Gavril is like someone has punched him in the stomach. He folds over the table, head in hands and starts to cry. Then he turns helplessly to his solicitor and mumbles something.

'I think,' says Anand, 'my client needs a break.'

'No problem,' says Mack, and Rose begins to gather up her papers.

Rose and Mack walk down the corridor to the kitchen in silence.

Once there, he turns and sighs, before leaning against the sink and facing her. She sits down at the table, avoiding something that looks like a globule of mayonnaise, rapidly hardening, with her elbow.

'Why am I not punching the air?' says Mack. Rose sits back in the chair with a heavy sigh.

'Probably the same reason I'm not,' she says. 'We don't have any hard evidence that he murdered her. Shagged her, sure. He behaved like a total twat all over the place. But he does have an alibi, unless Sofia Nikolas is going to say something different when she discovers she wasn't the only bit-on-the-side her married lover had.'

Mack takes a cup from the drainer and fills it with water, which he drinks in one go.

'I think we're going to speak to her again,' he says. 'Just in case that alibi magically disappears, as you say. I only wish I was convinced Gavril was the man who did this.' He pauses. 'Something about this doesn't feel right.'

'No,' says Rose, rising from the table and wriggling her sore shoulders. 'I agree. But he knows more about it than he's letting on.'

6

Kirsty

She struggles to focus all day at work. When her supervisor says something about how she looks, suggesting she could, 'do with a night in' as she almost dozes over her tub of salad in the staffroom, she doesn't know whether to laugh or to cry.

Nights in are all she has these days. She starts thinking about bedtime as soon as she gets inside her front door, with a mixture of dread and longing all mixed together. The trouble is, having had a small glimpse of how things could be, she almost feels worse.

Not too long ago there was a period when she managed to sleep right the way through for three days in a row. It was incredible. When she woke, she felt so disorientated by the unfamiliar experience of seven straight hours that she'd been slightly tearful in the shower.

She'd even stopped checking in with the group, daring to believe that her need for them was coming to an end. Much as she loved the support she got there, she sometimes wondered what it would be like not to stumble out of bed and frantically start reading whether anyone else'd had as bad a night as she had.

But then, the cruellest thing happened. On the fourth night, she'd woken at three, screaming and thrashing in the bed.

The man in the balaclava was back, leaning over her, as though trying to steal the breath from her lungs.

And this time, something was different.

She'd experienced the crushing weight on her chest many times before. It was a standard part of the package when it came to sleep paralysis. Someone in the group said this was an element of sleep paralysis that had made its way into a ton of folk tales around the world. They said it as if it was meant to be a comfort. Something being a problem for hundreds of years did not make it less scary. But the feeling of a weight pressing down on her, of being unable to move, was par for the course.

The last few nights, though, the man in the balaclava had lingered longer each time before she thrashed her way back to consciousness. And (she was aware this was a strange word to use about something that was only in her own mind) it was as if he was getting . . . bolder. Last night she had distinctly felt his fingers at her throat before she had been able to vault that last step to full wakefulness.

She shudders, realizing her hands are touching her neck, as though recreating the sensation of those cold fingertips.

This is ridiculous. She'll make an appointment to see her GP, a kind but harried woman in her early forties, to get some sleeping tablets. That's what anyone sensible would do.

The only thing that has put her off is the feeling of helplessness that will come with chemically aided sleep. She'll be ensconced in a blackness she can't control.

And it suddenly feels, oddly, as though she needs to be alert.

7

'So, Leon, why don't you tell us why we found your semen on Hannah's clothing, and while you're at it, you can fill us in on why she blocked a number that belongs to your phone?'

Gavril is tipped back in the chair, as though trying to place himself as far away as he can from the two police officers opposite. Rose blinks eyes that feel gritty from time spent under the sickly strip light above and takes a sip from her water bottle.

When he sits forward, the chair legs hit the ground with a noise that makes everyone flinch, him included.

'You're going to try and twist everything I say, I know how this works,' he says in the voice of a sulky kid. Rose feels a sudden urge to slap that arrogant face and fire rises in her own cheeks.

'Mr Gavril,' she says, and he looks at her with a frown. 'There's a man and a woman in this police station,' she goes on, 'who have had to go and look at the dead, murdered body of their youngest daughter. All we are interested in is getting answers for them. Nobody in this station is in the business of stitching anyone up. We want the truth, that's all.'

She is breathing a little heavily and can sense Mack looking at her.

Maybe she sounded too emotional in her outburst, but seeing Hannah Scott's family arriving in the office earlier had been so upsetting. Mrs Scott was a small, round woman whose eyes were swollen into slits and whose hands were shaking so much that she thrust them into her pockets to hide them. The father was a tall, stooped man with a bald head whose Geordie accent was strong when he said, 'We just want to know what happened to our Hannah, you see. Who did this.'

Gavril deliberates for a moment, then rests his meaty arms on the table, folding them one on top of the other.

'Does Kate have to hear about any of this?' he says. Mack shrugs.

'It depends on what you tell us, Mr Gavril,' he says easily. 'But we are not in the business of maliciously wrecking people's relationships. They tend to be pretty good at that on their own.' Gavril frowns deeper, unsure if he is being got at or not. 'I can assure you,' Mack continues, 'we are only interested in solving this case and, as my colleague says, finding some peace for those poor people out there.'

There is a brief silence and Gavril's body relaxes a little. Anand locks eyes with Rose and she senses the lawyer thinking, 'Here you go. But remember what we agreed.'

'She was a really sweet girl,' he says. 'You're going to see when your people do whatever they do with the phone that there weren't nothing there beyond a few . . . sexy messages between us. I wasn't hassling her or nothing.'

'Why'd she block you, then?' says Rose.

Gavril gives her a dirty look.

'Because she was pissed off that I dumped her, that's why,' he says. 'I started seeing Sofia and she was angry about it. She maybe wanted to get me off her phone.'

'How did Sofia and Hannah get on?' asks Mack.

'All right, I suppose.' Shrug. 'Not as good as once . . . you know.'

'Did they fight about you?' says Rose. She glances at Mack, confident they are thinking the same thing, i.e., could Sofia have been the one who killed Hannah? She didn't look physically stronger than the victim, but maybe, when you are so vulnerable in your bed like that, less force would be needed.

Gavril gives a loud, false laugh, clearly guessing their line of thought.

'Nah,' he says. 'Not her style. Sofia is more likely to sulk than properly kick off about something like that. She's gentle as a kitten.'

'How long ago did you break up?' says Mack.

Gavril shifts in his seat.

''Bout three weeks,' he says.

There is a silence. An idea comes to Rose and before she can talk herself out of it, she speaks.

'In that case, Leon,' she says. 'Can you explain why our forensic team believe your semen sample is only a few days old?'

She's not sure who tenses up more: Leon Gavril, or Mack. Sensing her boss looking at her, she keeps her eyes fixed firmly on the man opposite.

The solicitor looks up from her pad sharply and her brow twitches with a frown before she looks at the pad again and writes something down.

Rose's heart is beating hard. Can they all hear it?

Gavril sighs loudly and sits back in the chair, body language defensive once again.

'Look,' he says, 'that was a one-off.'

'OK,' says Rose, because Mack is still too quiet. 'We're listening.'

'Thing is,' says Gavril, shifting in his seat, 'she was a terrible sleeper. Always having nightmares.' He makes an exasperated face. 'They were both nuts about this stuff, her and Sofia. But she was nothing like Hannah. Sofia did a bit of sleepwalking sometimes. But Hannah, I mean, she would wake me up all the time if I slept there. It was fucking wearing, man, I tell you.' He pauses, then continues, 'One time, she smacked me right in the face in the middle of the night because she thought I was an intruder. All I was doing was lying next to her.' He gives an incredulous smile and then, just like that, Rose sees it: the full realization – perhaps for the first time – that the woman he slept next to, even for a short time, is dead. Murdered. A spasm of real sadness washes over his face and he stares down at the table, swallowing visibly. His leg has started up its percussive movement again.

Neither of the detectives speaks, as if by mutual consent. It's one of the things Rose loves about working with Mack. They seem to know when to wait and when someone needs to fill the silence.

Anand is looking at Gavril too, pausing in her neat note-taking. He returns her look and then faces the detectives again, his eyes a little reddened.

'So,' he says, 'there was a night last week when I was staying over with Sofia. I got up to get some water from the kitchen and almost jumped out of my skin when I saw Hannah in there, sitting at the table in the dark.' He pauses.

'Go on,' says Rose quietly.

Air hisses from between Gavril's teeth, like he is deflating. 'She was shaking all over and crying because she'd had such a bad nightmare,' he says. 'Kept saying someone was coming for her in her dreams and she had to stop it.'

'Coming for her?' says Mack, brow creased. 'In what way?'

'It was just her being upset, like I said,' says Gavril. 'She'd said it when I was right next to her, talking about these bad dreams. She was a bit . . . sorry to speak ill of the dead, but she was a bit mental.'

'But that didn't stop you having sex with her, did it?' says Mack softly. 'Is that what happened, Leon? You climbed out of one woman's bed in the middle of the night, then had sex with her mate?'

Gavril buries his huge head in his hands and when he speaks, his voice is muffled.

'I gave her a cuddle, to comfort her,' he says. 'But one thing led to another . . . You know.'

Looking up, his face seems momentarily both older and younger than it did before. There is the pleading look of a small boy who has been naughty, combined with the baggy eyes of a man in his mid-thirties who has been accused of murder.

'We do indeed,' says Mack tightly.

Gavril puts both hands flat on the table in front of him and searches Rose's face with his eyes.

'I would never have hurt her,' he says. 'She was such a sweet girl. I did not do this, you have to believe me.'

'So,' says Mack, ignoring this. 'Back to the night she was killed. Did you spend the whole night with Sofia?'

Gavril sighs heavily. 'I was there until about midnight,' he says. 'Then I went . . .' he falters over the word, '. . . home.'

'We shall be checking that, Leon,' says Mack, 'with all relevant parties.'

'OK' says Gavril, whey-faced. 'But please don't tell Kate I wasn't out with a mate. She'll fucking skin me if she hears about Sofia.'

Mack stops the interview.

Gavril appears to be a lot more worried about his wife finding out about his shagging habits, thinks Rose, than being charged with murder.

Which, she can't help thinking, means either he didn't do it, or he knows full well they have nothing on him.

The minute the door closes behind them in the corridor, Rose says, 'Mack . . .' but her sergeant is marching away from her.

So much worse when he is disappointed in her. She'd prefer a bollocking.

But then Rowland emerges from the observation suite, her mouth a grim line, and Rose changes her mind.

'DC Gifford, a word in my office, please.'

Rose walks behind her, feeling much as she did when she thumped someone at school. This is not a helpful memory.

As they pass Mack's desk, some subtle communication occurs between him and Rowland, whose back is still to Rose. He rises from his seat, giving Rose the briefest of glances as he does so. There's nothing there. Not a scrap.

Rose knows full well what she has done.

Mack follows her into the boss's office and closes the door behind him. No one sits down.

Rose clenches and unclenches her sweaty fists. She forces her face out of the defensively sulky lines she knows it is taking from sheer terror.

'Can you tell me,' says Rowland, in a dangerously controlled voice, 'why you told Leon Gavril that forensics were able to precisely date that semen?'

Mack joins in. 'You know that's not true, Rose!' he says. 'Why did you say it?'

Rose swallows.

'I'm sorry,' she says. 'It just came to me. I felt sure he was lying about the last time he had sex with Hannah.'

'Oh, you *felt sure*, did you?' says Rowland, her voice is raised enough for the heads nearest her office's internal windows to bob and check out what's going on. 'That's OK then. Let's not worry about telling *lies* in interviews and making the whole bloody thing inadmissible, shall we?'

Rowland is breathing heavily, for once displaying extreme emotion.

'I had to look into the faces of a couple of devastated people earlier,' she says, voice tight, 'and tell them that we were doing everything we can to find out who held a pillow over the face of their daughter until she was dead.'

This echo of what Rose herself said deepens her shame even further.

'Ma'am . . .'

'And now you may have compromised the whole case with your reckless behaviour.'

'Look,' says Rose, her face burning, 'I really am sorry. I messed up. It won't happen again.'

'No, it won't,' says Rowland crisply, 'because you're off interviewing. You can get cracking on the phone evidence from Hannah and Gavril's phones. Assuming you can be trusted to do that.'

'Yes, of course, ma'am, but . . .' Rose begins, fading off when Rowland holds up a silencing hand.

'I'm not interested.'

Then she turns her narrowed gaze to Mack.

'As for you, Colin,' she says, 'you should know better than to let that happen. You should have stopped the interview right there and then.'

'Ma'am,' says Mack quietly. Nothing more to be said.

That's almost the worst part; that she has got her boss and friend into trouble too.

Outside the office, Rose grabs Mack's arm to stop him from walking away.

'Mack,' she says in a low voice, 'I'm so sorry. I never meant to jeopardize this case. I feel terrible.'

Mack looks into her eyes, as though studying her, before replying.

'You could be an excellent police officer, Rose,' he says wearily. 'But you still have a lot to learn. More perhaps than I realized – and that's my own failing.'

With these crushing words, he walks off towards the kitchen. Rose tries to swallow the hot, hard ball of tears she can feel clogging her throat and watches him go.

8

In the briefing, Rose keeps her head low.

The effort of holding in the swell of misery inside has given her nostrils a pinched, reddened look and her eyes sting. An attempt to improve things with the small amount of make-up she carries in her handbag hasn't done much. Why did she do such a stupid thing? She knew as soon as the words were out of her mouth that it was a terrible mistake. She got carried away, so certain that Gavril was lying, she almost risked the case.

It's clear that several of her colleagues are onto something by the way everyone is darting glances at her. When she catches Sam's eyes, she sees a look that is both quizzical and sympathetic, like he honestly believes she has been unfairly treated. This makes her feel even worse and she slides her gaze away, focusing instead on the notebook in front of her.

'Right,' says Rowland, and the voices fall quiet. She smooths a hand down her neat, black skirt, as if it would ever be mussed up like normal people's, thinks Rose. 'We have had to let Gavril go.' There's a disappointed murmur around the room at this and Rose doesn't know if she imagines the frown the DI flashes her way. This brings a corresponding burst of anger inside. It isn't as though they had any real evidence. Sure, she messed up badly, but she isn't the reason they haven't been able to make an arrest.

The hot injustice is a welcome kind of energy after the churning shame she had been feeling, and so she forces herself to sit upright, raising her eyes to the room at large.

'There simply isn't enough evidence to convince the CPS that he was responsible for this crime,' continues Rowland over the hubbub. 'And now . . .' the noise retreats again, 'we are out of the crucial Golden Hour since this crime was committed. We need to redouble all efforts here.

'The pathology report shows no sign of recent sexual contact on the victim,' she goes on. 'No drink or drugs. If anything, she was a bit of a health nut. She had various herbal remedies in her system,' she looks down at her notebook, 'Acai berries, echinacea . . . ones I don't know but all of it available over the counter. Her medicine cabinet looked like Holland and Barrett. But nothing was toxic, even in combination.'

She turns to DC Bello. 'George, what have we got from house-to-house?'

Bello looks down at his pad, then up at the boss. 'There was a party two doors down that night. Several people mentioned that it was especially noisy and busy in the close.'

'Party on a bloody Tuesday night?' says Kev Wallis. 'I'm guessing they're students?'

'You guess right,' says Bello to a small ripple of laughter. 'We've almost managed to track down everyone that was there and will continue to interview them over the coming days. It means there is a fair amount of footfall registered on the nearest CCTV, located on the corner. We're in the process of matching up who claims to have come in or out that night with the images. But,' he says, with a frown, 'it's not the only way into the close, because there is an alleyway coming from Belford Park Road to the south of the address. And there is no CCTV for that end of Belford Park Road.'

Rowland pinches the bridge of her nose and lets out a sigh. 'Thoughts, people, about the significance of the party?'

There is a pause. Rose wants to speak but feels as though something is stoppering up her throat.

'Well,' says Tom, 'it could be that someone from the party committed the crime . . .'

'Opportunistically? But why?' says Rowland sharply, and Tom makes a helpless gesture.

'Maybe the party was a good cover.' All heads turn towards Rose.

'Go on,' says Rowland, her eyes as expressionless as a shark's.

Rose swallows, then forces herself to lift her chin and her voice. 'If this was pre-meditated, which would fit with the neatness of the killer . . .' 'I mean,' she clears her throat, gaining confidence because no one has shot her down yet, '. . . the whole freaky thing about her hair and the bed being so tidy. And if that was the case, then it's suspiciously good timing to have it happen when the close was more chaotic than usual.'

There's a brief silence and she almost holds her breath until Rowland makes a grudging face of agreement.

'Yes, you might have a point,' she says. Then, 'How well did the victim know the residents of that property? George?'

'She didn't,' he says. 'Not according to them or to Sofia Nikolas, anyway. You know what this city is like. Neighbourliness isn't top of most people's priorities, is it?'

'OK. Well, it's something to think about,' says Rowland. 'What about phone evidence?'

Ewa Duggan takes up the narrative, reporting that the data from Gavril, Sofia, and Hannah's phones has been uploaded and she's working her way through it. Rose doesn't know whether she imagines Ewa giving her a sympathetic look.

Being told she is rubbish at something can have one of two effects on Rose.

When she was at school, and the shame of her nasty clothes and weird mother followed her like a smelly cloud, she retreated into herself and agreed with everyone concerned that she wasn't worth much. But then when she messed up her GCSEs and her mother told her that it didn't matter anyway because she could 'follow her into the family business', it had provided Rose with a kind of helium that made her rise up, up, up, until she could float away from it all on a cloud of successful re-takes.

Tonight, she's opted for the second approach. The office is largely deserted as she hunches over the telephone evidence from Leon Gavril and then Hannah Scott, the remains of two cups of coffee, a can of Red Bull, and an empty family pack of Walkers Sweet Chilli crisps on the desk. Rowland is in her own office and Rose can see the blond head bent over the desk, the warm yellow glow of the lamp casting a buttery pool on the desk.

It is much less atmospheric out here in the general office, and Rose has only the nasty overhead strip lighting to help keep her awake. Helpfully, it has started to buzz. It's not even a constant buzzing, which would be tolerable, but more a sound that comes and goes just as she is getting used to one or other states.

Her back aches and her eyes are sandy and sore, but she is grimly determined that she will not go home before her DCI does tonight, even if that means being here until the bloody morning cleaning staff arrive.

Extraction reports are PDF documents of many, many pages that detail all the activity that has occurred on a person's telephone. In Rose's experience, they're about as exciting as they sound.

She has had the task of cross-referencing the records of four men in a recent drugs case over the last few months, which resulted in her going to bed and literally watching columns of numbers scrolling across her mind for hours until she could sleep. It's painstaking work, but she is determined to give it her all.

Rose feels another stab of self-disgust every time she thinks about the telling-off earlier. A diet of television cop shows growing up had somehow fed her the idea that the ends always justified the means, although what goes down on telly is a far cry from what is acceptable in real life. Telling lies to suspects in the interview is a huge no-no and Rose knows this. But she had been so sure that Gavril was lying about when he last had sex with Hannah Scott that, for a wild moment, common sense had taken a back seat. There was scant comfort in the fact that she had been right.

She takes a swig of the Red Bull, which is warm and sticky in her mouth, then pops in some peppermint chewing gum, in an attempt to refocus.

Ewa Duggan had already been through many of the texts and WhatsApps on Gavril's phone. Scanning them, Rose finds herself fast becoming tired of reading messages that were variations on a single theme:

I will fuck U L8r

He'd sent that one to a variety of women, excluding his wife. The messages between him and Kate Morley tended to be along the lines of: *Don't 4get bread* or *Need newborn nappies*, interspersed with a frequent '*Where RU????* thrown in plaintively.

What a tosser. She grimaces and carries on reading.

The recovered messages between Gavril and Hannah Scott brought no revelations and seemed to back up his story that she blocked him after he dumped her. The exchange right before this happened began with a dick pic from Gavril, which makes Rose shudder, and ends tragically with, *Can't wait to CU* followed by a row of kisses, a heart, a face with hearts for eyes, and more kisses. Then *U too babe.*

After another hour spent going through all this, Rose turns to Hannah's phone.

There is a series of WhatsApps between the victim and her sister, Stephie.

The sleep issue seemed to crop up quite often.

Hannah: *Had a better night last night. No bogeymen!*

Stephie: *So glad 2 hear. Remember when Mum and Dad had to lock ur bedroom door and climb out window to convince u no bad guys could get in LOL.*

Hannah: *I'm not alone in doing mad shit like this! U shd see some of the stories in that FB group. Ppl do insane stuff when they are asleep.* 😂

Stephie: *Glad u got something that is helping. Love you, u mad bitch* ♥ 😂

Rose makes a note to mention this group to the team searching the victim's computer in the morning, as nothing like this has appeared on the phone so far.

At last, Rose sees Rowland's office go dark and the door opens. Her boss is shrugging on an elegant pale blue mackintosh and yawning, uncharacteristically without covering her mouth. Rose catches sight of a dark filling and feels a stab of satisfaction that the woman doesn't have perfect teeth.

'Oh, I didn't realize you were still here,' says her boss as she reaches her desk. 'I think that's probably enough for one day, don't you?'

'I won't be much longer,' says Rose, attempting a smile.

Rowland doesn't say anything else as she heads towards the door.

'Ma'am?' says Rose, and the other woman stops and turns to face her.

'Yes?'

Rose hesitates. 'I really am sorry about earlier. I will never do that again.'

Rowland regards her for a moment before replying. 'No,' she says, 'you won't.'

And with that she disappears through the door.

Rose can't help thinking Rowland is glad to have something real to hold against her.

Because this frostiness isn't only about her error in that interview. It goes a lot deeper than that.

It happened about a month ago, a weekend when Rose wasn't working. She had met up with an old friend from Hendon, who had ended up moving to Southampton to work for CID there. Aisling had always been a good laugh and after a few drinks in a slightly touristy pub in Soho, Rose was feeling mellow as she headed up the stairs to the Ladies.

As she had reached the landing, a familiar voice made her stop in her tracks. Peering inside the small upstairs bar, she saw Rowland, sitting inside the door at a small table, her hands stretched across and enfolded by a man whose identity Rose took a moment to place, because of the baseball cap he was wearing. When she did, she muttered, 'Oh fuck' under her breath.

It was Deputy Assistant Commissioner Martin Thomlinson. A very big cheese, who happened to be married. Rose had been transfixed as her boss, normally so together as to be almost robotic, began to cry. Then Rose managed to gather herself and she scurried off to the Ladies, heart pounding at what she had witnessed.

She thought, as she dried her hands, that she had got away with it, but then the door to the Ladies had swung open as she was about to leave and she was presented with the blotchy, tear-stained face of her boss. Rose had attempted to hide how stricken she had felt but it was clear from the look on the other woman's face that she'd failed.

The woman had glared at her and said nothing as Rose muttered 'Ma'am' under her breath. She'd had to squeeze past to escape. Nothing had been said, but Rowland had been even frostier than usual with her ever since. And this latest slip-up certainly wasn't helping.

Rose wonders whether a transfer might be on the cards and lets out a heartfelt sigh.

'Fuck this,' she says quietly and logs off her computer. Time to go home, such as it is.

There was never one moment when Rose understood what Adele Gifford really was. The knowledge had seeped into her gradually. Had she ever believed Adele Gifford was genuinely helping customers reach the spirits of their loved ones? Maybe. Once.

But the true nature of her mother's business wasn't something she could understand when she was eight, nine, ten. All she knew was that Adele would get excited about once a month when a man she referred to as Mr B would call on her. Her mother would take ages getting ready and be in high spirits on these occasions. Rose remembers being very small and delighting in helping her mother try on different outfits and necklaces. She always liked fifties-style fitted dresses in rough silk or cheap alternatives, and favoured stilettos on those evenings. It seemed thrilling to Rose, who would creep into her mother's bedroom afterwards and smear Adele's lipstick over her own mouth, puzzling over its greasy feel but liking the clown look it gave her as she made faces at her reflection.

She still doesn't know whether the male visitor had a surname that started with B, or whether her mother had named him after the Mr Big character in *Sex and the City*, which she adored. Adele claimed he looked like him and Rose supposed his bulk and heavy eyebrows were vaguely similar to that character.

He radiated something that seemed to send her mother into a dizzy, embarrassing mood, but its impact on Rose was like a dark cloud that made her feel cold and hollow in her stomach. She would pretend to be ill when he came, which suited Adele Gifford well enough as she waved her off to bed and adjusted her tight neckline to show off her cleavage.

Rose thinks it was when she was about twelve that she understood about the money laundering. She saw it on a television programme. Adele never regulated any of her viewing and there was a second old television in the dining room that

Rose would watch for hours while her mother drank and entertained in the room where, in the daytime, she carried out her 'business'.

Maybe it was that woman who turned up one night. The memory of it makes her queasy even now.

They had been watching television together when the doorbell had rung. She thinks it was some soap or other, although she doesn't remember which one. Adele had looked anxious and then cautiously gone to the bay window to peek through the nets. What she saw presumably angered her, because she swore and told Rose to go upstairs.

Rose had argued that she wanted to watch the rest of the episode and then Adele had shouted at her so viciously she found herself scurrying from the room. She pretended to close her bedroom door with a bang and then lurked on the landing, listening.

She heard her mother speaking angrily in a low voice and then the response: a woman's voice, much younger, saying something about being ripped off and it not 'being fair any more'.

The two women had gone into the front room and Rose had hovered then gone to her bedroom and tried to curl up with a book. Half an hour later the doorbell went again. She crept out to see him, Mr B, arriving in a dark coat studded across the shoulders with raindrops. His face was consumed by a look of anger that made Rose's stomach curdle.

After this there had been shouting and then banging noises. Rose had been too scared to come down but had continued to lurk on the landing. Peeking round the bannister, she saw the door open and her mother emerge, ashen-faced and holding a hand to her mouth as though trying to stuff in a scream.

'Mum?' she'd said, and her mother had met her eyes and made a desperate motion for her to go back.

Rose was too frightened to do anything but comply.

The next morning, her mother was uncommunicative.

From that point on, her drinking got steadily worse until

finally, seven years later, she was killed in a hit-and-run accident on her way home from the pub. Her blood was four times over the legal limit.

Rose had been old enough to look after herself by that time. Going to Hendon to train as a police officer felt like a new start, washing away the shabby, criminal element of her upbringing.

Which is why it's absolutely crucial that she doesn't mess this up. She won't let herself be dragged back into the world she came from.

9

A few miles away on the fringes of the city, a woman yawns widely as she taps at the screen in front of her.

Sitting in the pool of icy light from the lamp on her desk, she is alone in this vast room. It's an old building and prone, as old buildings are, to night-time exhalations and creaks that can sound disconcerting to those who are unfamiliar with them.

Despite what she does for a living – or maybe because of it – she doesn't mind being here late at night. She has no truck with some of the things people say about this old place, even her own colleagues. The noises. The occasional smells. The sudden dips in temperature. Most things can be explained, she has found in the years she has been doing this job. And the ones that can't? Well, that's the reason she gets up in the morning. Why this department exists.

Popping a sweet into her mouth, she sighs. She's spent the last half hour looking through the CADs – Computer Aided Dispatch transcripts of calls from the public to the emergency services. Since civilians took on the job of uploading the data, every tiny detail tends to get logged, even the seemingly irrelevant ones. This might be an annoyance to some, but in this building it's considered a boon. It makes her job so much easier to be able to carry out searches using certain unusual search terms that may otherwise never have been recorded.

Her eyes begin to prickle and she's close to giving up for the night, but then she sees something that makes her sit up straighter in her seat. It's not much, but that little fizz at the back of her skull means she takes notice. Some might call it intuition. She prefers to think of it as experience.

She mulls over the information, looking up at the ceiling and idly popping in another sweet.

Then she busies herself by looking up the directions to Silverton Street nick for the morning, before turning off all the lights and leaving the office.

Once the building is in darkness, all that can be heard is the gentle squeak of a trolley as it is pushed through empty, echoing corridors.

10

The next day the rest of the team is busy interviewing people who attended the party at the house two doors away from Hannah Scott's place.

A series of young people troop through the station, many of them looking simultaneously terrified and thrilled. There is a noticeable smell of weed that drifts after one young man with a shaved head and large holes in his ear lobes, and when Kev Wallis does a daft stoned wobble and grins at Rose, she is grateful for his lame joke.

Mack has been busy all morning. When she sees him going into the kitchen at 2 p.m., she hurries in after him.

Ewa Duggan is in there, reading a Polish newspaper and eating from a Tupperware box. She glances up and nods before looking back at her paper. Rose decides it's now or never; Ewa is one of the most discreet people in the station, so hopefully she will at least pretend not to listen in.

Mack is spooning instant coffee into a cup and he holds up the jar when he sees Rose, an act that makes something that is tight inside her loosen a little.

'No, you're all right,' she says. 'Just wanted to catch up.'

'Oh, OK.'

There's an awkward silence while Mack waits for the kettle to boil.

Rose wishes, not for the first time, that she was good at small talk. At building bridges. But Mack speaks first.

'I had a call from Hannah Scott's mother,' he says, meeting her eyes.

'Oh God,' says Rose. 'Was she . . . checking in?'

'Yep,' says Mack. 'Wanted a progress report, I think, but she couldn't get the words out because she broke down almost immediately.'

'Oh no,' says Rose.

'She didn't hang up,' says Mack, 'just cried and cried down the line. I had no option but to wait it out.'

'That's rough.'

'Not as rough as it is for them,' he says heavily. 'I hate it when we have nothing to give the families. It's like hurting them again and again.'

There's an awkward pause.

'So is there anything coming from our party-goers?' she says as he pours water into the cup and stirs.

'Nothing yet,' he says, and runs a hand down his face. He looks tired. 'We've had the lock on the door looked at, and it hasn't been tampered with.' He sighs. 'It's a complete shit show, frankly. We've got nothing.'

'You look bloody knackered,' Rose finds herself saying.

Mack looks at her then laughs. It's a deep laugh, from his belly.

'Well, thanks for that,' he says. 'I can always rely on you to give it to me straight, can't I?'

Rose is uncertain for a moment, but there is warmth in his grin that gives her courage.

'Look,' she says, 'I couldn't feel worse about yesterday.'

Mack eyes her wearily. 'I know, kiddo,' he says. 'I know.'

'How long do you think she's going to keep me in the doghouse? I want to be interviewing with everyone else.'

Mack picks up his mug and takes a sip before replying.

'I have no idea,' he says. 'But stick with what you're doing, and I'll have a word once we're through the worst of this. OK?' His eyes are soft when they meet hers.

She squeezes his arm. 'Thank you,' she says quietly.

Mack leaves the room and Rose looks at Ewa, still studiously reading her paper.

As she too goes to leave, Ewa looks up and gives her a wink. From anyone else it would be annoying, but as she goes back to her desk, she feels grateful for the small warmths she has experienced from other members of the team. She may have cocked up and Rowland may hate her, but at least she still has mates. Back at her desk, she resolves not to think about Sam, who hasn't been in all morning.

At midday, Rowland calls another briefing. The energy in the room has shifted. In the earliest hours of the investigation there was a sense of excitement, a positive buzz that everyone shared.

Now, with the clock ticking and no arrests imminent, faces are tight and there is no banter as people file in and take their places.

That's when she notices someone she has never seen before at the back of the room: a short, squat woman in her fifties with reddish dyed hair and an eager expression. Her hawk-like gaze is currently fixed on Rose so keenly it's as though she is vibrating with fervent energy. How rude. Rose looks away.

Rowland has her poker face on as she takes her place at the front of the room. She surveys the team as if she is deliberately scolding each and every one of them with her eyes.

'So, it's two days since Hannah Scott was murdered,' she says, 'and we have absolutely nothing. This morning Mack spent half an hour on the phone to her distraught parents, trying to explain why their daughter's murderer is still out there.' She pauses to draw breath, trying to compose her irritation. 'I want a renewed push on this. I want information on every violent offender within a five-mile radius of that house. I want every aspect of that woman's life analysed and pulled apart. I want to know all her movements on the day she died, from the moment she got up to the latest actual sighting of her. I want her workplace visited, her gym, anywhere she used to frequent regularly. I want her relationship history. I want her health history. Because right now, the information we have isn't good enough, people.'

There is a general shuffling of feet and a few cleared throats.

'Boss, can I say something?' All eyes turn to Rose. 'She mentioned to her sister that she was in a Facebook support group for her sleep problems. It's probably not all that relevant, but I wondered if it's worth a look?'

Rowland frowns. 'Add that to the list of things to check out please, Rose.'

'Yes, maybe,' she says. With that, she turns back to the rest of the team and sets about allocating jobs.

'Mack . . . you and Rose go to the nursery,' she says, once everyone else has been given their assignments. 'Speak to her boss, her friends, the people she worked with every day. I don't believe Sofia Nikolas was what you'd call a friend,' she says archly. 'Let's go much wider.'

She hesitates, and then, as though with great reluctance, gestures towards the mystery woman at the back.

'By the way, this is DS Sheila Moony,' she says. 'She's sitting in today from a division called UCIT.'

All heads turn towards the newcomer, who does a little wave that doesn't fit her general demeanour. Her squat little hands are covered in rings and her nails are varnished red, but her face is free of make-up and pulled into a tight frown.

'I'm only doing the rounds, so you can ignore me,' she says in a husky voice.

'What's UCIT?' says Mack, and the woman fixes her gaze on him.

'If you want the full title, it's Unit for Compliance: Information and Training,' she says brightly. 'There will be some online work for you all at some point.'

The word 'compliance' immediately sucks all attention away from the woman and back to Rowland. Rose doesn't know what it means, but it sounds like something dull she has no time to do.

The briefing is ending but as they are about to leave the room Rowland says, 'Needless to say, none of this can get out to the press. I've prepared a statement to camera that the Press Office has sent off, but we don't want any of the specifics getting out, is that clear?'

There are murmurs of agreement as everyone files out of the room.

Rose scurries to pick up her bag before the boss can change her mind.

She drives. Mack rubs his face and yawns as they merge into the traffic. He lets out a small sigh.

'Nice to be allowed out again,' says Rose.

He looks across and gives her a small grin. He doesn't say anything further and Rose waits a moment or two before speaking.

'Mack,' she says, hesitantly, 'are we . . . I mean, are we OK?'

Mack turns to face her and she glances at him before looking back at the traffic.

'Of course we are,' he says. 'We've discussed all that. You got the bollocking and you won't be doing any nonsense like that again, will you?'

'God, no!' says Rose hotly. 'I have *so* learned a lesson there. I promise.'

'Well,' says Mack, 'we're all good then.'

They drive in silence for a few minutes. When their progress is slowed by traffic lights, Rose tries again:

'. . . only,' she says, 'I feel like there's a weird vibe. Between us. You and me.'

Her cheeks are roasting. She hates this type of conversation and would usually go to great lengths to avoid it, but she needs to be sure that all is good with Mack so the world can return to its correct axis. And something still feels off.

Mack lets out another sigh. He's been doing this a lot lately, it's as if he has a slow leak.

'Ah, Rose,' he says, 'it's nothing to do with you, mate. It's . . .' he pauses. 'Kid stuff.'

'Well,' says Rose, 'I have a great deal of expertise with kids, having been one for thirty years.'

Mack laughs and the sound is so welcome she feels instantly warmer.

'I'm not sure anyone is expert enough to understand my daughter,' he says. 'Her least of all.'

'What's going on with her?' says Rose. She has met Mack's daughter Caitlin a couple of times. A clever, quiet child, with a shy smile and perfect manners, Rose had found her endearing, even though she could never think what to say to her.

Mack pauses and looks out of the window to his left.

'She's got quite bad anxiety,' he says, 'and has started having panic attacks at school. She's frightened of her own shadow.'

His voice is heavy, and Rose senses the pain and helplessness behind his words.

'Oh bless her,' she says. 'I'm sorry to hear that. So much pressure on modern kids, isn't there?' She read that somewhere. Her own teenage years were far from being a bed of roses and she finds it hard to believe this generation could possibly have it worse, but this feels like the correct response.

'Sometimes I think it's because of my job,' says Mack. 'She's obsessed with knife crime and rape, and all the bad things she reads about. I can't understand it, because Connor is so straight-forward. As long as he's fed regularly and transported to various sporting events, he's happy. But Caitlin . . .' He lets out a sigh that is heavy with worry. 'I'd have hoped,' he continues bleakly, 'that having a copper for a dad would make her feel safer instead of more afraid.'

Rose glances his way, and he manages a weak smile.

'I'm sure you do make her feel safe,' she says. 'I mean, who wouldn't feel safer with you around? I've seen some of your moves in the face of the criminal fraternity.'

This earns another genuine laugh. 'Well,' says Mack, 'I'm grateful for the vote of confidence.'

Rose can tell Mack has something further to say so she lets the silence expand until he's ready to speak.

'The thing is,' he says, 'I think she hears me talking to her mother sometimes. You know, about cases. Not,' he quickly adds, 'that I breach confidentiality, but you can't help talking about your day, can you?'

Rose pictures the two weary people, curled in their respective armchairs in front of the telly, exchanging easy confidences over late-night cups of tea, and thinks about how lucky Caitlin is, really.

'No,' she says, 'of course not.'

They drive along in silence.

'Oh, hey,' says Rose, 'who was that Moony woman?'

Mack makes a face. 'No idea, but if they think we're going to be finding time for non-essential training, they're having a laugh.'

Rose has to park a good way down the road from the nursery, but they hear the hubbub of children's voices from the Little Angels nursery a couple of minutes before they come to its security gate.

A small boy with a mini Spurs shirt and fat red cheeks is looking through the gate as they press the buzzer, staring at them with wide, fascinated eyes.

Rose grins at his serious expression. She quite likes children – admires their anarchy and wild joy – but has no desire for her own, suspecting she would have no skill for motherhood.

She pictures herself at nine or ten, silently eating cold beans for the third night running, while peals of drunken laughter rang out from the living room. When she started her periods at thirteen and went to Adele, tearful with cramps, she'd been told: 'It's all part of being a fucking woman, so get used to it.'

No, she hadn't been taught the rules she'd need to know to look after a child herself. Not that there was much prospect anyway, the way her life was going.

A clear, bright voice comes through the intercom, asking who is there. Mack replies, and a moment later there's a loud buzz. They push open the metal gate and enter the play area.

The building is a purpose-built modern structure with lots of shiny glass. A huge sign says, *Little Angels Nursery, Ages 3mths–3 Years. Where you're little ones can shine.* Mack and Rose exchange wincing looks.

'I wouldn't be able to stand looking at that grammar every day,' murmurs Rose. 'I think I'd have to get a tin of black paint and go at it in the night.'

'I think some graffiti is probably justified,' says Mack equally quietly.

The noise level is making Rose's ears hurt. They walk across the concourse, which is coated with a slightly spongy blue covering, with large colourful splotches all over. There is a play area built around a bright blue pirate ship and toddlers are crawling all over it and emerging through tunnels with focused expressions.

A round-faced little boy with an oversized fireman's hat hanging over one eye stares up at Rose with unabashed curiosity. She finds herself making a funny face at him and is rewarded with a shy smile.

A tiny girl of about two is busily trying to pull her dress over her head, revealing a small pot belly, a saggy nappy, and chubby knees. An adult voice calls, 'Olivia! Remember we keep our clothes *on* during the day!' Olivia drops her dress and gives a mutinous look that wins Rose's immediate respect.

A large woman in her late thirties in a bright yellow polo shirt with a Little Angels logo approaches as they reach the main entrance. She has white-blond hair tied into a tight pony-tail, giving her a startled look, and thick false eyelashes that fascinate Rose. They look as though they must be a great weight for that delicate skin to carry. She is frowning deeply as she gets closer, then manages a weak smile.

'You here about Hannah?' she says in a wary voice. 'I'm Sandra, the manager here.'

'I'm Detective Sergeant Colin Mackie and this is Detective Constable Rose Gifford,' says Mack. 'Is there somewhere we can talk?'

'Come this way,' she says, and they bypass the main reception and follow her across the front of the building past what is presumably a sand and wet play area. Several children of barely walking age are elbow deep in sand that has largely been turned to sludgy brown mud. One red-haired boy is patting his hands into it with some violence and making a noise that sounds like, 'gah, gah, gah!' with a look of outright fury in his eyes. Sandra opens a gate at the end and they go through a fire door into the main building.

'Quicker to come in this way,' says Sandra over her shoulder as she leads them down a corridor painted bright yellow until she reaches a door marked *Sandra Langley, Manager*.

'Come in and take a seat,' she says.

It's a small office with a desk, two chairs this side of it, and shelves crammed with box files. The desktop is clear apart from a computer and a pink mug that says, *Keep Calm and Watch Strictly*.

The two police officers sit down, and Sandra Langley sits at her desk and clasps her hands together in front of her, settling in with a small wiggle of the shoulders.

'We're all absolutely devastated about Hannah,' she says. She has a hard set to her face that makes the words sound vaguely defiant rather than genuine.

'Yes,' says Mack, 'I can imagine you are. I'm very sorry for your loss.'

As the woman dips her head in acknowledgement, Rose gets a strong feeling that she is resentful of their presence. Odd.

'The reason we're here, Sandra . . .' says Rose, then, 'Can we call you Sandra?'

'You can.'

'. . . the reason we're here is that we want to build up as full a picture of Hannah's life as possible, and that includes her workplace. So, to start off, can you tell us what she was like as an employee? She'd been here, what, three years?'

Rose flips open her notebook and pen in readiness.

'That's right,' says Sandra. 'Well, she was one of the best on my team. She had lots of patience with the little ones and was always smiling and happy. Usually, anyway.' She falters and both Rose and Mack look up at her expectantly.

'Did something change about the quality of her work lately?' says Mack. Sandra looks away, chewing her lip.

'Well,' she says, meeting their eyes once more and looking flushed around the throat '. . . it wasn't that she wasn't on top of things. Only, she had a few days of coming in looking a bit . . .' she searches for the word and then, seeming to give up on finding a better one, '*rough*, I'm sorry to say. Told me she wasn't sleeping.'

'When did this start?' says Rose, pen poised over her pad.

Sandra twists her lips and looks to the sky, thinking.

'I only became aware of it about two weeks ago,' she says. 'She always looked nice. Hannah made the best of herself, you know. I encourage all my staff to maintain a professional front.' She gives a self-conscious pat of her own hair at this. 'But Hannah was letting things go.'

'In what way?'

Sandra squirms in her seat. 'Just . . .' she swallows, '. . . looking like she'd been up all night, you know.' She pauses. 'Bit scruffy,' she says, then, with heat, 'And it's not like that's the most important thing, not at all. But there was an . . . incident with one of the babies that I couldn't let go without . . . without me saying something.' Noting their expressions, she adds hurriedly: 'A one-off thing.'

'What happened?' says Mack gently.

Sandra begins to fiddle with a thin gold cross around her neck.

'She had one of the babies on a changing table and she . . . lost focus for a minute. She was staring out the window, like she was miles away, and it was only the quick actions of one of my other staff that stopped the little mite from rolling right off and falling to the floor.' She sniffs. 'Doesn't bear thinking about.'

'Who was the other member of staff?' says Rose.

'It was Esin,' says Sandra. 'She was good friends with Hannah and wouldn't have said anything to me in a million years, but I happened to see it as I was walking by, and . . .' she lets out another sniff. 'Well, as I say, I had to give her a talking-to.'

'How did Hannah respond?' says Rose. Finally we're getting to the reason for this strange attitude, she thinks.

Sandra takes a deep breath and lets it out in a shudder. Her eyes have begun to shine ominously and she swallows to get control of herself.

'Not well,' she says in a tremulous voice. 'She burst into tears and worked herself into a right state. I had to send her home for the rest of the day. But you'll understand that I had to give her a verbal warning?' There is such a beseeching tone in her voice that Rose and Mack both find themselves nodding reassuringly.

'Of course,' says Mack. 'The children's welfare must come first, mustn't it?'

'That's exactly what I told her at the time,' she says with satisfaction. 'I said to her, I said, "Hannah . . . it's the safety of these children that must come first. You not getting a good night's sleep cannot be allowed to interfere with your work."'

'And what did she say?'

Sandra deflates at the memory. 'She said she would go to the doctor. Get some pills or something. I don't know if she did, but we didn't have any more problems.'

There is a brief silence while Rose finishes writing her notes.

'Can we speak to Esin?' says Mack. 'Is she in today?'

Sandra's face hardens. 'Yes, she is . . . But I'm not sure if she is free at the moment.' Then, clocking the expressions on their faces, she adds hastily, 'I'm sure someone else can take over whatever she's doing. I'll go and find her.'

She leaves the room and Mack and Rose exchange looks. Mack raises one eyebrow.

'Never ceases to amaze me how people want to cover their backs in these sorts of circumstances,' he says. 'I mean, as if the way she bollocks her staff is our concern.'

'I know,' says Rose quietly. 'But I reckon she feels like shit because Hannah died.'

74

'Yeah, probably,' says Mack wearily.

Less than a minute later the door opens and Sandra comes in, followed by a large woman in her late twenties, with dark, worried eyes and a heart-shaped face framed by her hijab. Her hands are clasped together in front of her and her shoulders are rigid.

Rose and Mack stand up.

'Hello,' says Mack. 'I take it you're Esin?'

The other woman nods, her expression terrified.

'Nothing to be worried about,' says Mack kindly. 'We want to talk to you about Hannah, that's all.'

Esin's eyes immediately fill and she blinks hard several times, nodding her agreement. Sandra begins to come into the room too and Mack holds up a hand to stop her.

'Actually,' he says, 'it would be better if we could have the room for a while. Would that be OK?'

Sandra visibly stiffens and Rose pictures a chicken with its feathers ruffled.

'Of course,' she says huffily, and leaves the room.

Esin sits down and begins to fiddle with the hem of her flowery tunic, eyes skittering around the room. Her breathing is audible, as though she has come from doing some exercise. She is very overweight, but Rose is sure that the puffing is a result of distress rather than exertion.

'So,' says Mack, more briskly, 'we're told that you and Hannah Scott were friends – is that right, Esin?'

'Yes, that is right,' says Esin in a tiny voice. She has a slight accent, which Rose can't identify. Then, as if there is a need to prove something to them, she adds, 'Hannah was lovely person. Look, this is us, together last year.'

She reaches into a pocket for her phone then spends an age running her finger down the screen until she finds what she is looking for.

'Look . . .' she holds the phone out, and both Mack and Rose lean forward.

The photo shows the two women leaning into the camera

and laughing, while pointing to a poster for the *Harry Potter* play in central London.

'We're both mad about Harry Potter,' she says. 'We did the whole thing in one day.' She pauses and her voice is trembling when she speaks again. 'I sometimes call— called her Hermione when she was being bossy about something.'

Her eyes fill with tears as she stares down at the phone.

'We're very sorry indeed about what has happened to Hannah, Esin,' says Mack gently. 'And we're doing everything we can to find who is responsible. Part of that is building up as full a picture as we can about her in order to catch who did this terrible thing.' He pauses. 'So, can you tell us whether Hannah ever said anything to you that suggested she felt threatened or intimidated by anyone?'

'Yes,' says Esin firmly, nodding at the same time. 'Yes, she did.'

Mack and Rose exchange surprised glances. Rose feels her heart give a kick of excitement.

'Oh yes?' says Rose. 'What exactly did she say?'

'The man,' says Esin, eyes widening, 'she was scared of the balaclava man.'

'Which balaclava man, Esin?' says Mack.

Esin looks around the room, as though checking no one else has snuck in during the course of this short conversation. Then she leans forward, conspiratorially. Rose and Mack do the same, almost unconsciously.

'The man who came to her in the night,' says Esin, eyes wide.

'Well, that was bloody pointless,' says Mack as they trudge back to the car. 'And I honestly thought we were onto something there.'

Rose murmurs her agreement. When Esin had paused before delivering the bombshell, Rose had been convinced some significant piece of evidence was about to present itself. Instead it turned out to be more talk about the victim's famous nightmares.

The sun has come out since they went inside the nursery and, almost unconsciously, the two police officers turn their faces to the warmth. The hubbub of children playing recedes as they walk down the side road to their car.

Rose drives and as they set off, she glances at Mack and opens her mouth, then hesitates.

'What?' he says, sensing her desire to say something. 'Spit it out, Rose.'

'Well,' she says carefully, 'everyone keeps going on about this sleep thing, like it's all Hannah Scott ever talked about . . .'

'Go on.'

'It's just . . .' Rose pauses, concentrating on turning right at a busy junction, then continues, 'What if it *is* relevant to what happened to her?'

Mack is silent. She takes this as encouragement to go on.

'I mean,' she says, 'I don't know in what way, but – and I'm thinking out loud here – what if the killer relied on the fact that she was wandering around in a haze of constant exhaustion? Maybe it helped him in some way?'

Mack is frowning, tapping his fingers against his knee, which is a thing he does when he's mulling something over.

'You mean,' he says, 'someone could have followed her home without her noticing, because she was sleep-deprived? Is that what you're saying?'

Rose can feel her confidence ebbing. 'I don't exactly know what I'm saying,' she says. 'But . . . I guess that is possible?'

'Hannah wasn't the only person who lived in that house,' says Mack. 'If someone weird was hanging around, staking the place out to break in, wouldn't Sofia Nikolas have noticed?'

They have stopped at traffic lights. The car is silent as they both ponder.

Rose lets out a heavy sigh and is beeped by the car behind for failing to spot the lights have changed from red to green.

'Oh all right, dickhead,' she murmurs, then, louder, 'I guess that is unlikely. It must be someone who's been to that house at least once.' She goes on, 'Which would make sense. I can't imagine crimes like this are opportunistic. This feels too careful to me.'

Mack sighs. 'We still have sod all with regards to motive.'

His phone rings and he answers.

It's clearly Rowland and Mack begins to fill her in on everything that was said at the nursery.

As he comes off the phone, he mutters something Rose doesn't catch.

'What was that?' she says.

Mack looks at her with a puzzled frown. 'I don't know. She said something odd at the end, after I told her about Esin's mad notions.'

'Oh yeah?' Rose is looking the other way, waiting to turn right across a busy junction.

'Yeah,' says Mack. 'She said, "Oh, she's going to love that. That is all we need."'

Rose turns to look at him.

'Who does that mean?'

'No idea,' says Mack, but his face is scrunched, eyes lost in thought. Then, 'You have to admit, this is turning into a weird one, isn't it? The case?'

'Yeah,' says Rose, 'you can say that again. Everything about this feels off.'

Mack is still looking thoughtful and when he speaks, his words cause Rose's foot to jump off the clutch as she is braking at a junction. The car stalls.

'Sorry,' she says, restarting the engine. Her hands are trembling on the wheel and she has to work hard at keeping the tremor from her voice.

'I didn't quite catch that,' she lies. 'What did you say?'

'Oh,' he says, distracted. Then: 'I asked if you believe in ghosts.'

11

Rose licks dry lips and keeps her ashen face turned away. She manages to affect a laugh, which sounds shrill to her own ears.

'Why on earth would you ask me that?' she says brightly. In her mind she is screaming her emphasis on the word 'me'.

Why on earth would you ask *me* that?

'I don't know,' says Mack with a yawn that makes his jaw audibly crack. He rubs his face briskly. Maybe he hasn't noticed her oddness. 'Just wondering.'

'Of course I don't!' *Must not screech. Must speak like a normal human.*

Mack's silence next to her is as disconcerting as the initial question.

'Don't tell me you do, Mack?!'

He is silent for a moment and then gives a short laugh. 'Well, not really,' he says. 'Not in the traditional *woo-woo in a white sheet* kind of way. But . . .' he pauses. 'I've had the odd experience that has made me wonder.'

Rose is desperate to know what these experiences were but daren't ask. Her heart is beating uncomfortably hard in her chest and she feels sick.

'Right,' says Rose flatly. 'So maybe Rowland was right, and a ghost did it.'

Mack laughs. 'No one is saying that. But we haven't exactly got a lot right now, have we?'

Rose is too churned up inside to continue this line of discussion. So instead she diverts it.

'These weird dreams she had,' she says. 'Worth having a word with her GP, in case she reported anything that sheds light on her state of mind about all that?'

Mack reaches for his phone and dials the station. 'Good idea. I'll get the name and address.'

They're told the GP, a James Oakley, will be free at lunchtime, which is – conveniently – in ten minutes. Soon they're pulling into a car park that is full apart from a bay currently being vacated by a people carrier. Rose enjoys the stars aligning twice in such a short period of time as she parks.

There is a library next to the surgery that looks as though it was built in the 1930s. Sharing a design with some of the tube stations around the area, it's reddish brown brick, curved at the front with narrow, rectangular windows made up of smaller panes of glass.

In the moody lighting of an impending downpour it appears to be glowering at them as they exit the car.

The surgery is a tatty building that perhaps came twenty years later than the library, an ugly box with graffiti on one side of the wall and four parking spaces marked for the GPs.

Inside they find a waiting room with a mixture of elderly people and mothers juggling small people, many of whom are coughing ripely.

'Hand gel at the ready,' says Mack quietly, making Rose smirk. It's one of his endearing quirks; that this tough policeman has a near phobia of germs, especially anything to do with sickness. He once told Rose he would take a dead body over a vomiting drunk any day.

'That little boy over there looks ready to blow, so watch your shoes,' Rose murmurs and Mack shoots her a warning glance.

They approach the reception desk where one of the two receptionists is coming off the phone. In her fifties, with brutally short hair and large hoop earrings, she flicks her gaze between the two police officers with barely concealed hostility.

'We're closing for lunch,' she says. 'You'll have to come back at two.'

Mack explains in a low voice why they are there, and she flushes as though caught out, then looks even grumpier than she did before. Rose breaks into a friendly smile, for sport, momentarily confusing the receptionist.

'His last patient has just gone in,' she says. Then, 'So you'll have to wait over there until he's finished.'

'Fine,' says Mack, eyeing the waiting room with suspicion. A small boy coughs exuberantly for several seconds, visible spit spraying over the toys he is playing with, then starts to cry as his mother rubs at his face with a tissue.

'Come on,' Rose tells Mack. 'I can get you a suit and bootees from the car, if you like?'

'You might have to,' he replies as they sit down on the nearest seats.

Rose pretends to look at messages on her phone but all she can think about is that conversation in the car. Darting a look at Mack, who is frowning at his own phone, she wants to ask him more while simultaneously wishing the conversation could simply be wiped from her memory.

She joined the Force in an attempt to escape from a certain type of thinking. It was something she had wanted to do since she was eight years old.

It all started with that policewoman, standing in Rose's potpourri-stinking hall in her smart uniform and hat. She looked like something clean and bright in a house filled with darkness and grime.

Rose has never really known what had been going on that day. Some drama had occurred, with shouting and banging around downstairs. Then her mother had blood on her face and was crying. Then the police were there. In the years after, her mother had claimed to have no memory of the incident. Rose had been hiding on the stairs, breathless with panic that her mother was going to be taken away, and trying to ignore some of the spiteful whispers around her from unseen mouths.

There were wonderful new sounds to focus on instead: radios crackling and calm, authoritative voices that didn't belong here. Rose wanted to fill her ears with those sounds and not let them seep away again.

There were two of them, a man and a woman, Rose recalls. The man did most of the talking and the woman stood behind him. Suddenly, whatever it had been was over, and they were leaving. The policewoman glanced up at Rose peeking through the stairs and stopped.

She'd smiled at her, eyes warm and twinkly, and seemed about to say something, but Adele had sharply told Rose to go back to bed. For a second, though, Rose had felt something pass between her and this policewoman, something she wasn't able to unpick or understand.

When she got back into her bed that night, trembling from the combination of cold and the unexpected drama that had woken her, she couldn't stop thinking about the policewoman. For a tiny pocket of time, she'd felt less alone in the world.

A man is approaching them, he wears a tentative half-smile.

'Hi,' he says in a low, pleasant voice, 'I'm James Oakley. I believe you wanted to see me?'

'Yes, thank you for making time,' says Mack, and they both rise and shake his hand.

'Follow me to the consulting room,' says Oakley, 'We can talk privately in there.'

He leads the way down a corridor to a room at the end. All three enter, then he closes the door and gestures for them to sit. It's quite a large room, as befits one of the partners in the practice. Along with the desk and two chairs, bed and screen, there is a bookshelf with some pot plants and files of the *British Medical Journal*.

Oakley is in his early forties. He's not tall, five foot nine at most, and is dressed in suit trousers and a blue shirt, with a navy tank top over it. Tired but friendly blue eyes are framed by dark-rimmed glasses, and he has a neat beard that's slightly more reddish than his light brown hair. He's quite hot, in a tired-dad way, Rose thinks, although there aren't any personal pictures on the desk for clues about his life outside the surgery.

'So, I understand you're here about Hannah Scott,' he says, with a sigh. 'I still can't believe this has happened.'

'Did you know her well, Doctor Oakley?' says Rose.

'Oh, please,' he says, waving aside the formality. 'Call me James. As to how well I knew her, I have been looking at my notes and she had been to see me' – he glances at his screen – 'six times in total, over a period of two years. I'm not supposed to tell you what about though,' he says, looking visibly uncomfortable, 'unless you can convince me otherwise.'

Mack nods. 'Of course,' he says. 'I know how much this goes against the grain, but we think understanding Hannah's state of mind could help us to get a broader picture of what happened and ultimately help us find out who killed her.' He looks Oakley in the eye. 'Obviously we can come back with a warrant.'

Oakley visibly relaxes. 'No,' he says, rubbing his jaw. 'I felt I should say it for the record. I do want to help.'

'Great,' says Mack. 'So did Hannah speak to you about any mental health issues she may have been having . . . Any delusions? Anything like that?'

'No.' Oakley shakes his head firmly. 'I don't think there was any reason to suspect Hannah had any mental issues. She was plagued by these awful night terrors, that's all.'

'Can you tell us any more about that?' says Rose.

'Certainly.' Oakley looks at his screen again. 'The first mention of it was at the start of this year. In fact, until then, she had only been for contraceptive advice and for a chest infection. The sleep issue seems to have become a problem this year.'

'Did something trigger it?' says Rose.

Oakley looks into the distance, frowning as he remembers. 'As I understand it, she'd had this problem from childhood,' he says. 'But she had been able to manage it until recent times. I tried to ask about stresses in her life, sleep hygiene—'

'Sleep hygiene?' says Mack.

'Yes,' says Oakley. 'It means your habits around bedtime. Warm baths. Not staring at screens or working out before bed. That kind of thing.'

'Ah, right.'

'She seemed obsessed with all that,' says Oakley. 'I tried to tell her that becoming anxious about bedtime rituals was counterproductive in itself. But I could see she wasn't taking it in. I put her in for a referral to a sleep clinic – there's only one for the entire capital and the waiting list is horrendous – but it hasn't come through.' He looks visibly upset and pauses. 'She's not going to need it now, is she?' He coughs and sits up straighter. 'I'm sorry,' he says, blinking hard. 'I've obviously lost patients before, mainly elderly ones. But I've never had a patient . . . be killed by another person.'

'Yes,' says Rose. 'This must feel quite different. So, can you tell us how she described these night terrors, as you called them?'

'Yes,' says Oakley, relieved to be able to impart facts again. 'I think the correct term for what she had is sleep paralysis,' he says, 'although there may have been an element of night terrors as well. What happens when we sleep normally is that our muscles become so relaxed we can't move. Essentially, that's what stops people wandering around when they're dreaming – though of course people still do that. But sometimes those signals become scrambled, leaving us half-awake and half-dreaming, with a sensation that we can't move. People who've experienced it say it feels as if someone is pressing on their chest, and sometimes they see horrible faces that are very lifelike.'

Mack grimaces. 'Sounds awful,' he says.

Rose pictures waking and seeing her dead mother on the bed and shifts in her seat.

'Yes,' says Oakley, 'I believe the effects are extremely realistic. Hannah told me that it was getting worse . . . the sensation of immobility was lasting longer each time.'

'What did you say to her about it?'

Oakley blows air out through his cheeks. 'To be honest, beyond giving out sleeping tablets – which she tried and didn't like, incidentally – there wasn't much I *could* advise. Sleep is a complex thing and even the specialist clinics have mixed success. Oh, one thing I suggested was that she try to find a support group. I believe she reached out online, but I never got the chance to ask her again.'

Rose nods and continues to write notes on the pad. It feels as though they have what they came for, such as it is. The energy in the room shifts.

'Well,' Mack begins, 'thanks for your time, James. We'll leave you to get on with your lunch.'

They all stand but before they can leave, Oakley says, 'Can I ask you a question?'

'Of course,' says Mack, 'fire away.'

'Does this sleep thing have something to do with her murder? I don't understand the connection.'

Mack sighs audibly. 'It probably has nothing to do with it,' he says. 'But we have to explore all avenues at this stage of the inquiry, and understanding the victim's state of mind might be useful.'

'I see,' says Oakley. 'Well, please don't hesitate to come back if I can help in any way.' He looks burdened, his shoulders rounding. 'It's such a waste. She seemed like a very nice young woman.'

They drive back to the station in a flurry of stormy rain, wind buffeting the car. Both are deep in thought. Rose guiltily thinks about her mother's visits and attempts, through various mental gymnastics, to ascribe the nocturnal ones to some form of sleep paralysis, as described by the doctor. But even if that was happening, how does it explain the times she is sitting there in the full light of day?

When Mack's phone rings, Rose can tell from his silent alertness and the way he sits up straight that something's up.

'Right, on our way,' he says, hanging up and turning to Rose with a gleam of excitement in his eyes.

'We're off to arrest Sofia Nikolas,' he says.

'*What?*' says Rose. 'Why?'

'It appears our Ms Nikolas ordered a copy of Hannah Scott's bedroom key from an online locksmith three weeks ago.' Mack taps the dashboard with both hands. 'Let's go!'

12

Sofia Nikolas looks like she is trying to make herself into a small knot, scrunched with her arms around her knees, on the bed in cell 4.

Her face is pale and her lips have a bloodless look, despite the fact that she keeps chewing them. When she isn't biting her lips, she is gnawing at her nails. It's as though she may consume herself entirely soon. Every now and then she gives in to a small flurry of tears.

Rowland, Mack, and Rose are all looking at her on the CCTV camera that is behind the front desk.

'What was she like when you arrested her?' says Rowland.

'Well,' says Mack, biting into a Snickers bar and then answering with his mouth full. 'She was weirdly compliant. Barely said a thing, other than asking if she could go and change out of her work clothes.'

Sofia had been at the nursery and, while they had tried to make the arrest with as few onlookers as possible, it hadn't been possible to do it without Sandra the boss being there.

'So it didn't seem like a total shock then?' says Rowland. 'You'd think it might.'

'Hard to say,' says Mack. 'People react in all sorts of ways, don't they?'

'Hmm,' says Rowland thoughtfully. 'Well, in the meantime we have another search going on at Nikolas's place.' She glances at her watch. 'Duty solicitor on his way for her, as she requested. You two can do the interview in due course.'

'Great,' says Rose, and attempts tossing a smile in Rowland's direction.

'Don't mess it up this time, Rose,' says the other woman, swatting it away. 'I'm taking a chance even letting you back in that interview room after what you did the last time, but Mack here has persuaded me it was very much a one-off.'

'It was,' says Rose quietly, instantly deflated. 'Thank you for the opportunity.'

Rowland mutters 'Hmm' again and walks off. Rose mouths a 'thank you' at Mack. He nods and compresses his lips into a quick, warm smile in return.

Rose grabs a late lunch of a claggy cheese and onion pasty from Tesco and a can of Diet Coke. She eats on the go as she makes her way back, thinking that, along with sorting out where she lives, it's high time she did something about her diet.

She would have been looking forward to this interview if the boss hadn't felt the need for that last sign-off. Maybe she ought to think about a transfer somewhere else when this case is over. It feels as though the bad blood between her and her superior will always count against her, and any mistake is going to be magnified by ten. A stab of resentment passes through her.

When she gets back to her desk, the pasty a greasy slab in her stomach, a briefing is called.

'Right,' says Rowland when quiet falls in the packed room. 'We have arrested Sofia Nikolas and I would like to know why she felt the need to order a copy of Hannah's bedroom door key online, and then have it sent to a PO box under her own name.'

'That does look decidedly off,' says Mack. 'But why go to

all that bother? Why not simply pinch the key when Hannah was out and get a copy that way?'

'This way she didn't have to remove the key,' says Rowland. 'All you need is a photo.' She pauses, then continues. 'But do we think she would have been physically capable of suffocating Hannah, even if she had a reason to?'

'What if it was a joint enterprise with Gavril,' says Tom thoughtfully. 'Some revenge thing after Sofia found out he'd slept with Hannah. Maybe she coerced him into it? Threatened to tell the wife?'

Rowland seesaws her head. 'Possible, I guess. It would help if we knew where this key is now. Let's start by searching the drains and the bins at both properties.'

Rose thinks about the day she arrested Gavril. That chase down the alleyway.

'Ma'am,' she says, 'have the communal bins at the end of the alleyway behind Gavril's property been searched? They were quite far down, so wouldn't have been the ones for his flat, I don't think, nor is that the likely main route he would take back to the main road. But worth having a look, just in case?'

Rowland nods at Tom. 'Get onto the search team,' she says, 'and mention that.'

Good thinking, Rose, thinks Rose, then, *Don't mention it, boss.*

Rose makes a coffee and then goes to her desk to work on the interview plan for Sofia Nicolas. In her earlier days she would write out everything she planned to say, but now she will simply list bullet points, then send Mack a copy for any changes to be made.

Mack is reading it when there is a shout from Tom across the office.

Everyone looks up as he stands and does a triumphant pump of his fist.

'Just heard from the search team,' he says, grinning. 'They found a black balaclava in the refuse bin at the end of the alleyway by Leon Gavril's house.'

An excited murmur goes around the room.

'And that's not all,' says Tom. 'The bedroom key has been found in the pocket of one of Sofia Nicolas's coats.'

Rowland is at her office door. Not quite smiling, but clearly pleased.

'OK, people,' she shouts over the rising noise. 'Let's not get too excited here. This is still not going to be enough for the CPS as things stand, but it's a start.'

She turns to Ewa. 'Anything on Nikolas's phone?'

'I'm waiting to hear about deleted messages,' she says.

Mack cranes his neck to catch Rose's eye.

'All set?' he says, and she stands up, enjoying the thrum of excited energy in her body.

'Yep, let's do it.'

Sofia Nikolas is sitting in the interview room radiating a mutinous expression when Mack and Rose enter.

The solicitor, a man called Kevin Jefferies they know reasonably well, nods and greetings are exchanged. Mack starts the recording and goes through the drill.

Rose is expecting a series of 'no comments' to emerge like spat pips from Sofia's mouth as soon as questioning begins, but before either of them can come out with the first question, Sofia speaks.

'Look, can I say something?' she says.

'Of course,' says Mack. 'This is your opportunity to do exactly that.'

It's clear from his body language that Sofia's solicitor has counselled against this course of action before they came in the room. But he says nothing, merely gestures with an open palm that she should continue.

'The thing is,' she says, placing her fingertips together in a steeple by her chest, as though saying a prayer. 'I know why you think we done something to Hannah.'

'OK,' says Mack, settling back in his chair. 'And why would that be, Sofia?'

'It's because of that stupid thing me and Leon did, isn't it?' she says. 'Someone told you? But it was only a joke, you see. A stupid thing. It didn't mean nothing.'

'What stupid thing is that?' says Rose, and Sofia looks quickly between her and Mack and then back again, as though trying to work out whether she is being caught out.

'It was a joke, you see,' she says in a smaller voice. 'We never meant anything by it. Not really.'

'What did you do, Sofia?' says Rose gently, and the other woman bursts into sudden tears, covering her face while her shoulders heave.

They don't speak. Rose pushes the box of tissues across the table, reminded of a similar role the other day at the crime scene.

After a few moments, Sofia blows her nose noisily and then places the hand with the scrunched-up tissue in front of her on the table, staring down at it.

'The thing is,' she pauses and sniffles before continuing. 'She kept going on about this bloke in the night, this *balaclava man*,' she says after a moment. 'I got sick of hearing about it all the time.'

'OK,' says Mack, 'carry on.'

Sofia looks up at him, eyes brimming with tears. Her nostrils are pink and her eye make-up has gathered in the corners of her eyes.

'You're going to think badly of me,' she says, voice tiny.

'Sofia,' says Rose, 'you have been arrested for the most serious crime there is: murder. This isn't a game. We're giving you this opportunity to get everything off your chest and unburden yourself. I suggest you do that.'

The other woman nods miserably and then begins to speak, her hands twisting together in her lap.

'So it was Leon's idea, really,' she says. 'A Halloween prank. We'd been at a party, drinking a lot. A bit of weed as well. You know.'

'Go on,' says Mack.

'Well,' continues Sofia, dabbing at her raw-looking nostrils with the tissue, 'Leon had a balaclava that he sometimes wore under his helmet on his motorbike. He had it in his pocket and he said we could play a joke on Hannah. Creep into her room and give her a fright.' She pauses. 'You know . . .' she says again, her eyes desperately seeking reassurance that isn't forthcoming.

'So this was Halloween night?' says Mack. 'End of October?'

'Thereabouts,' says Sofia.

'And was this the only time you played this "joke"?' says Mack, his emphasis on the last word, revealing how he feels about it.

'So why did Mr Gavril throw the balaclava in the bin near the back of his house?'

Sofia's eyes flare with bright panic, then she looks down again.

'I think he was worried what it would look like, after, after, you know . . . what happened to Hannah.'

'Indeed,' says Mack. There are a few seconds of quiet, then, 'Moving on, Sofia, can you tell us why you ordered a copy of Hannah's bedroom door key from an online locksmith?'

Sofia's mouth opens and closes. She turns wide eyes from Mack to Rose to her solicitor and then back to Mack again.

'What the fuck are you talking about?' she says. Then, 'Sorry, sorry, but what do you mean?' her words skidding. 'I don't know what that means?' She turns to the solicitor. 'What are they on about?' she says, and begins stroking her throat in an odd way.

'We found the order on your phone, Sofia,' says Rose, evenly. 'And the key was sent to a PO box in your name.'

'What PO box?' says Sofia wildly. 'What key? I didn't buy a key!'

Her fingers are practically clawing at her throat and she begins to cry loudly. 'I can't breathe!' she says. 'I can't fucking breathe!'

'I think my client needs a break,' says Jefferies in the manner of one who has been in this position many times. 'And maybe some tea, please?'

Sofia's whole body is shaking, hands over her face, almost hyperventilating.

'Try and breathe slowly, Sofia,' says Rose, placing a hand on the other woman's shoulder. 'You're all right. You're having a panic attack. Come on, breathe slowly in for four and then out for four.'

Sofia obeys, drawing a shaky breath and flapping her hands. Rose can't tell if it's theatrical or genuine.

'Right,' says Mack. 'Stopping the tape at 18.43 for a fifteen-minute break.'

In the observation suite a few moments later, they find Rowland watching the Leon Gavril interview, which is being conducted by Tom and Kev.

'How's that going?' says Mack, and Rowland makes a face, then stifles a yawn.

'Want to guess his favourite two words in the English language?' she says.

'*No comment*, by any chance?' says Rose, and Rowland rolls her eyes and throws a piece of paper rather expertly into the bin.

'Yep,' she says. 'What about our Ms Nikolas then?'

Mack fills her in on what has happened so far.

'Did you feel she was putting it on?' she asks. It's obvious it is only Mack's opinion she is seeking.

'Hard to say,' he replies. 'She looked like we'd punched her in the stomach when we mentioned the key. It felt as though it did come as a surprise. But, as we all know, people who have done bad things can be very good at pretending otherwise.'

It's a long, exhausting evening.

They interview Sofia twice more and even when a series of deleted messages is unearthed between her and Gavril that reference the dumping of the balaclava, she refuses to admit that she ordered that key or had any idea of its existence, even when confronted with evidence to the contrary. For his part, Gavril keeps up his mantra of 'no comment', despite the best efforts of Rose's colleagues.

Rowland calls a briefing at ten thirty, her face even grimmer than it was earlier.

There has been a development. The service providers have released all the data for the other two phones found at Gavril's property.

As a result they have been able to place him in several locations around Manor Park and Turnpike Lane from midnight until 6 a.m.

'Fairly obvious what he was up to,' says Rowland drily, 'hence the radio silence. Probably thinks this will affect the deal he was offered.' She pauses. 'And it bloody might too – I haven't decided yet.' Rubbing her eyes, she looks around at the team.

'We only have Sofia Nikolas's word that she heard that scream at three a.m.', she says. 'Are we giving it too much credence?'

Mack shakes his head. 'I don't think so,' he says. 'She isn't that good an actress. Looked like she wanted to crawl out of her own skin when she told us that.'

'OK,' says Rowland. 'We have nothing on these two, not really. Absolutely no chance of the CPS letting us charge them. We're going to have to let them go and start from scratch.'

A sound somewhere between a groan and a sigh goes around the room.

'Yep, I know,' says Rowland. 'Go home and get some rest, everyone. We have a lot of work to do tomorrow.'

13

Crime-scene tape is still across the bedroom door and a dusting of black fingerprint powder is visible on the wooden surfaces in the room: the dressing table, the chest of drawers. The bed.

He gazes down at it. And remembers how it all looked that night. How it felt.

Such a privilege, watching the dancing movement behind those delicate eyelids. A whole world on widescreen under that thin skin, with its tiny, violet veins. The essence of a person suspended between the two states of sleep and wakefulness. Then between life and death.

What did she see right before her eyes snapped open? He likes to think she was dreaming about him, visiting her like before. What a surprise it must have been when this time it was real.

No time to scream, no time to do anything but cling to his arms and pound her heels against the mattress. She was stronger than he would have expected, but she was weak from her rude awakening and unable to do very much. All too soon, the frantic movements grew jerky, spasmodic, then finally her limbs fell still. When he removed the pillow, her eyes had faded like a subtle change on a colour chart.

The bed looks different now, of course, the linen having been taken away to a laboratory where white-coated experts will crowd over it like flies, looking for the tiniest fibre or skin flake that might lead them to their quarry.

But they won't find anything, beyond the one thing he has deliberately left behind. He is far too careful, too meticulous, for that. It's the purpose of all those visits in advance of the big event.

He knows about the hidden key, because he watched the other one in the house use it months and months ago. It had been easy to get it copied, then replace it again. He knows which stairs creak, and that he needed to step over that patch of oil near the back door that may otherwise have yielded a footprint.

At least, it's one important reason for the visits. The other is simply the pleasure that comes in pre-preparation.

It's about becoming familiar with the way they look sleeping and understanding all their habits: the hands that creep together, squirrel-like, under the chin, or the peculiar way someone's lips move as though they are having a conversation in their sleep.

Knowing all about their private nightmares.

It's time to leave. In a day or so the forensic work will be finished, and the house will return to something approaching normality. All the belongings will be stripped away, and the room will be made ready for a new tenant, should someone have the stomach for it.

But this is London. There will always be someone new, willing to step into the space left by the dead.

And as this household will have to move on, so too will he. But it won't be long until he can do this again. He is already preparing for it.

It all started so long ago, when he was a child.

He'd never needed a lot of sleep, but he didn't make much of a fuss about it, unlike his sister, later. He liked to pad around the house on soft feet and watch his sleeping parents. The comforting smell of their bedroom and their funny little noises. They were a happy unit of three. But when his baby brother was born, all that changed. His mother would cry a lot and everyone snapped at him. He couldn't see how this small, grumpy creature could be so powerful in their household, or why he should be *allowed.*

He hadn't gone in there intending to hurt him that night. But as he'd bent over the crib and watched the small face, for once not scrunched up and wailing, he'd been fascinated by the stillness of the baby. It was like he was dead, lying there all doll-like. He'd found himself going to pick up the pillow with the tiny elephants all over it from the nursing chair without even thinking about it.

The next day his mother had made terrible noises, like a cow giving birth he'd once seen at a farm. His father, hair wild and eyes red and piggy, had gently explained that his brother had died in the night from something called cot death.

He'd felt sad for a time but enjoyed the three of them being alone again.

But he knew it wouldn't last forever and a year later his sister Helena was born.

Helena was a terrible sleeper.

At first, he would sleep through her nocturnal wanderings, but after being shocked awake on one occasion to find her attempting to climb onto his bed to reach a shelf above – it was never clear why – he felt that he needed to stay alert.

He came to know the signs. He'd hear the tell-tale snuffly noises that preceded one of her episodes and snap to wakefulness, heart racing with the thrill of not knowing quite what she would do next. Once, she began to climb out of their bedroom window; if it hadn't been for their mother happening to pass at that moment, and coming into the room, she could have ended up anywhere. They lived on the ground floor, then.

There was a thrill in understanding that he might have been

the only one who could stop her from falling and hurting herself.

His interest in the whole business of sleep continued to evolve as he grew older and forged his place in the world. It is still a constant source of amazement, how much money is invested in something that animals do without thinking. People spend a fortune on oils and apps and masks; getting the perfect night's sleep is becoming the modern religion.

What's more, it's so blinkered to think that lying down and switching off is all there is to sleep. To him, it's like living in a two-storey house and remaining completely unaware there is a whole other level above you.

14

'Fancy making last orders?' says Rose to Mack as she harvests coat and scarf from under her desk, but the suggestion is met with little enthusiasm.

'Nah, best get home,' he says. 'I feel like I've barely seen my family for days.'

'Fair enough,' says Rose, with a bright smile that masks how grim the thought of seeing her own home is right now.

She leaves the office and stands in the biting cold air, momentarily lost. Mack gave her a lift in this morning, so she will be getting the tube home. She could have just the one drink, to take the edge off going home to that miserable house. And it might help her stop picturing dead women seeing monsters in their sleep.

Rose is ensconced at a corner table with her pint of cider and two bags of dry-roasted peanuts.

There are two pubs that the staff at Silverton Street tend to use and this is the less popular one. The main one, the Dame Alice, has gone all craft ale and quinoa salad, but The Coachman is as yet untouched by gentrification beyond its hopeful sign advertising *Teas and coffees served all day including expresso and cuppochino.*

A bunch of men in dusty work gear appraise her as she sits

in the opposite corner and she hears a low comment and a snigger from that table. With a sigh, she pointedly ignores them and rummages in her bag.

She has a book on her – a thriller that someone had been raving about – plus a free newspaper picked up as she passed the station – but she can't concentrate on reading. Instead, she gets out her notebook and begins to flip through.

As she finishes off the peanuts, she writes 'Sleeping Beauty' at the top of a fresh page and circles it. Sometimes it helps to summarize everything that she knows so far in the hope that something might come to her in a new way. Rose starts to list the meagre evidence they have against Sofia Nikolas and Leon Gavril under a heading: 'sex game gone wrong?'

She's engrossed in this when she senses someone standing near her table.

'Oh,' she says. 'Hi.'

It's that Moony woman, holding a large glass of red wine and gazing down at her with a curiously hungry expression.

'It's Rose, isn't it?' she says and, before Rose can reply, she has plonked herself down in the seat opposite.

'That's right,' says Rose hesitantly. How did she know that? She puts her notebook on the bench seat next to her.

'Yes,' says Moony, smiling a little, as though she's in possession of secret information that Rose isn't party to.

She reminds her of a robin, all stout, puffed-out body, thin legs and bright, curious eyes. But a robin that doesn't take no for an answer.

'Um, can I help you with something?' says Rose. She still has quite a lot of her drink left so she can't exactly make an excuse to leave, much as she doesn't want to have to make small talk with a stranger.

'Well, it's more about whether I can help you, DC Gifford,' says the other woman with a grin that shows a snaggle tooth at the front of her mouth.

'OK,' says Rose. 'I'm not sure what—'

'—have you got anyone for this Hannah Scott murder yet? I hear not.'

Rose takes a long sip of her drink before answering.

'We've got two suspects, but we haven't got enough on them to charge as yet,' says Rose.

'And do you think they did it?' says Moony, studying her face intently.

Rose hesitates, then takes another pull of her drink. The alcohol is hitting her empty stomach a little too fast.

'Not yet,' she says. It's a relief to say it out loud.

'I hear,' says Moony, eyes narrowing, 'that the victim talked about strange nightmares in the period before the murder?'

'Look, I don't know if I should be—' Rose starts to say but is interrupted by the other woman sliding her phone closer towards her.

'You can call Rowland and check it's all right to talk to me,' she says. 'Go on, do it,' she says. 'I work for another division, but we all have exactly the same goals here: to catch the bad guys.'

Rose briefly considers calling her bluff and making the call. What does compliance have to do with the case? But the thought of interrupting whatever Rowland does to relax and slipping even further down her Christmas list is off-putting, to say the least.

'Yes,' says Rose wearily. 'The victim had problems with her sleep.'

'And do you think this is significant?' says the other woman, her gaze pinned to Rose in a disconcertingly hungry way. 'The nightmares?'

Rose hesitates. She does. But she doesn't understand how.

It feels oddly exposing to admit this, so instead she says, 'I can't see what they have to do with someone suffocating a woman to death, no.'

'Hmm,' says Moony thoughtfully and stares into the middle distance.

'How much do you know about parasomnias?' she says.

'I don't know what that means.'

'Night terrors,' says Moony. 'Sleep paralysis. Nightmares that feel as though they are really happening.'

Why is she staring like that?

Rose's dead mother sitting on her bed. The very real heft of her on the mattress, pinning Rose down . . .

'I don't know anything about them,' says Rose crisply.

'No, me neither,' says Moony. 'I tend to sleep the minute my head hits the pillow.' She gives Rose a surprising, rather roguish grin, revealing that snaggle tooth again. 'Must be our clear consciences, eh?'

Rose manages a tight, polite smile in return. She doesn't understand what is going on here. Whatever it is, she wishes she had swerved the pub and gone straight to the tube.

'Do you know what we do, DC Gifford? At my division?'

Rose takes another large sip of her cider before replying.

'Isn't it something to do with . . . compliance?'

Moony smiles. 'That's what we always say. But we don't advertise our real remit, which is more about looking beyond the obvious explanations for things.'

Rose can only gawp at her. What is she on about? Something about this woman, this conversation, is making her feel intensely uncomfortable. She scratches her arm and goes to speak when one of the barmen, a thickset man with a beard in his fifties, appears at the table. He pointedly picks up Rose's empty peanut packets from the table.

'Need to ask you to drink up, ladies,' he says.

'Right,' says Rose, pushing her not quite empty glass towards him. 'You can take that. I'm finished.' Then, to Moony, who is looking at her through narrowed eyes. 'Not sure I can help you with anything. It's been a long day and I'd better—'

She reaches behind to get her coat and Moony stops her with a hand on Rose's arm. Rose gets a whiff of cigarette smoke from her.

'Hang on a moment,' her tone is hard now and something about it makes Rose pause.

'I think you need to look harder at the sleep disorder. I have a gut feeling that this is significant in some way and none of you are paying proper attention to it. And if you feel like discussing anything . . . unusual, or hard to explain to the likes of our DCI Rowland – anything at all – give me a call.' Rowland's name was said this time in a way that revealed there was no love lost between these two women.

Which should give Rose yet another reason to disengage.

Moony slides a card across the desk. Rose doesn't look at it but politely takes it and stuffs it into the top of her handbag.

Her heart is beating too fast.

'Why are you asking me about this?' she manages to say, even though the words seem to resist leaving her mouth. 'Why not someone more senior?'

Moony looks at her for a long time then, her expression inscrutable.

'I think you know why, Rose Gifford, even if you don't want to admit it,' she says very quietly. 'You know all about looking into the corners that might otherwise be ignored.'

A hysterical feeling rises inside Rose.

Have to get out of here.

'I've got to go. Sorry. Nice to meet you,' she blurts out, and then grabs her bag and coat and rushes out into the street.

It's only when she gets to the tube that she realizes she has left her investigators notebook on the table, wide open for anyone to see. She pelts back down the road, her whole body pounding with stress. It feels so much further than she would have thought. She must bang on the door to be let in when she gets there. A grumpy barmaid obliges, and to her relief Rose sees it is lying on the table where she left it. Thank God something has gone right for her.

The bitter air hurts her lungs, but she forces herself to draw it in slowly as she walks quickly on a pavement sparkling with frost towards the tube. There's someone curled up in a shop doorway, huddled in blankets so only the bobble of a grubby hat is showing at the top.

She sometimes buys a hot drink or a sandwich for the homeless people who seem to have almost doubled in number over the last couple of years. She almost walks by, too preoccupied tonight, then feels guilty and fishes a pound coin from her purse, before slipping it into the battered McFlurry cup that sits at the person's feet.

Rose barely registers the journey home, the encounter with Moony going round and round in her mind.

'I think you know why, Rose Gifford. You know all about looking into the corners that might otherwise be ignored.'

What did she mean? That she knows Rose's past is less than squeaky clean?

And if she knows, who else does? Rowland? Is that why she doesn't rate Rose, thinks she is basically a bit shit?

Does everyone in MIT14 know her dirty little secret?

15

When Rose opens the front door, weary and hollow with hunger and worry, she immediately notices that there is little difference between the frigid air outside and that of her hallway.

Swearing quietly, she moves down the hall to the kitchen, because the bulb has gone in the hallway and she hasn't yet got round to fixing it. She flicks on the light switch inside the kitchen then goes to the ancient boiler in the downstairs cupboard. The pilot light flickers with a healthy blue light, almost mocking her. Nothing wrong there. So why is it so cold?

She leaves her coat on and comes into the kitchen, bracing herself for the hulking shape of Adele Gifford to be sitting in one of the chairs. But the room is empty. There is an underlying smell of damp that has been there for as long as she can remember, only partly masked by the intermittent blasts of artificial pine smell from the air freshener plugged into the wall.

This is such a shithole. Rose sometimes fantasizes about living in a brand-new flat, with clean white walls and new carpets that smell of a factory, rather than the fag smoke that has seeped into them over many years.

It would be such a relief to leave this place behind.

But much as she tells herself that the cheap rent and the easy access to work are the reasons for hanging on to her rented childhood home, she holds the real reason like a tumour in her chest. Sometimes she thinks she can almost feel it growing.

It's the fear of what would happen if she finally made the break and moved – and her mother came too.

What then? It would mean whatever this is will be a life sentence.

As she moves to the fridge and pulls out milk for cereal, she ponders the strange temperature in the room.

Closing the fridge door, she glances back out into the hallway. With a scream, she drops the carton onto the tiled floor and milk begins to spread and pool.

There's someone lying in the hallway.

Rose's ears fill with her heartbeat as she makes a tentative move towards the door.

Then she sees that it is just an old fur coat.

But it's one she has never seen before. How did it get here?

In the murky light of the hall, only lit from the spill of warmth from the kitchen and the glow of a streetlamp outside, the coat does look oddly capable of moving on its own.

With shaking hands, Rose picks it up, shuddering at the soft, slippery pelt as though it might bite her. A floral scent rises from it, snagging something in the deepest part of her memory as she carries it to the bin in the kitchen. It's an effort to stuff it in there, but she manages to do so, snapping the lid closed with some satisfaction.

It looks like something Adele would have owned, which would explain the feeling she has seen it before. But all her mother's clothes are in the attic, stuffed into bags and shoved to the very back until she can face dealing with them.

This is a new low. This . . . leaving things around.

Why? Why is this happening to her?

She is too mentally and physically tired to unpick it right now.

Her head aches and she takes paracetamol from the cupboard

and downs two, before clearing up the spilled milk and making another bowl of cereal.

At least the heating is working normally again, she consoles herself as she robotically eats the cereal and drinks the sugary milk from the bottom, not even bothering to catch the drip that runs down her chin until she has finished the bowl.

Upstairs she brushes her teeth and takes off her make-up, but as she is about to get into bed, she pauses.

'For God's sake,' she says out loud and goes to get her iPad from where she left it charging in the kitchen. The things Moony said to her in the pub simply won't stop tugging at her brain. There is no way she is going to sleep straight away, even though it is twelve thirty and she is utterly exhausted. She has to be at work by eight o'clock the next morning and she needs to sleep.

But maybe a little research about that very subject is needed first.

Wikipedia tells her that:

> **Parasomnias** are a category of sleep disorders that involve abnormal movements, behaviors, emotions, perceptions, and dreams that occur while falling asleep, sleeping, between sleep stages, or during arousal from sleep. Parasomnias are dissociated sleep states which are partial arousals during the transitions between wakefulness, NREM sleep, and REM sleep, and their combinations.

Rose reads about the different stages of sleep until she starts to feel her own eyes growing heavy.

Before she puts down the iPad for the night, she searches Sleep Paralysis on Google. The first entry under Wikipedia is from an American medical site about sleep. Rose reads about the process Hannah's GP had described earlier; how the body and mind have somehow become suspended in a state somewhere between sleep and wakefulness. The muscles are paralysed, but the brain is creating horribly realistic dream pictures. Combined with the sensation of something pressing on the chest, the experience must be terrible, Rose thinks.

She reads that many cultures have tales of an Old Hag, who supposedly squats on the chest of her victim while they sleep. Turns out that it's also believed to be an explanation for some alien abduction stories.

A loud yawn erupts from her mouth and Rose taps back to the search page, thinking she may finally try to get her head down.

The main post at the top about sleep paralysis features a small, old-fashioned painting.

It's a creepy picture, apparently called *The Nightmare*, by Henry Fuseli. Rose makes a face as she clicks on a link to a dedicated page.

The painting was presented to the Royal Academy in 1782 and depicts a woman in a white nightgown draped on a bed with her head and arms thrown back. Her body appears luminous in the painting against the darkness that surrounds her. But it is the thing sitting on her chest that is so hideous. An apelike demon squats on the woman's body, hunched and otherworldly, looking as though it is contemplating something deeply unpleasant it is about to do next.

She's seen it before somewhere, but she isn't sure where. Anyway, she has been looking at it for quite long enough.

Rose closes the cover on the iPad and places it on her nightstand. Time for sleep. Tomorrow could be another long day.

She goes to sleep almost immediately and doesn't even turn over in the bed for several hours.

It's impossible to tell what time it is when Rose next stirs.

The room is bathed in the glow from the street outside. She can see the detail of her dressing table over by the window and the zigzag pattern bleeding through the curtains. Is it time to get up?

She wants to look at the phone near her bed, but as she attempts to move her hand, she finds she is unable to. A flare of panic rushes through her. What's happening?

That's when she registers a shape by the window. She can't make out what it is, or even whether it is a person, but is seized by the most intense feeling of terror she has ever experienced. Attempting to cry out, she can only feel her mouth stretch and gape soundlessly.

I'm sleeping, she thinks. If only I can wake myself up.

Rose focuses every muscle on straining to move her hand a fraction, but it is as though she is deep underwater and the weight of it is resisting her movement. The shape is suddenly very close, having moved with a sickening, unnatural speed so that it is by her bed. Her hand is free of the duvet now. She can see it stretching out, trembling with the impossible task of reaching the light.

The form looms over her and Rose hears the strangled sound of her own cry. It's a horrible sound, like a dying animal, unlike any sound she thought herself capable of making. The sensation of dread is drenching her and she MUST WAKE UP.

And then her hand is moving so fast that the lamp goes crashing to the ground and she hears the sickening crunch as it lands on top of her iPad. Fully awake, Rose fumbles to pick it up. She is shivering and yet bathed in sweat as she lifts the lamp with its bashed shade and manages to turn it on.

The iPad screen is marked with a spiderweb of delicate cracks. With a groan, Rose carefully picks it up so none of the glass falls out and lays it so she won't tread on it in the morning.

It is 4 a.m. and she hunkers miserably back into bed. It's hard to shake off the horrible feeling she'd had during that dream.

Rose attempts to close her eyes and block out the remnants of that dread.

So that was sleep paralysis. No one can say she doesn't put herself out for this job, whatever Rowland might think of her.

It was a terrible feeling, worse even than the nightmares that

Rose has so regularly. If this was happening to Hannah Scott every single night, she must have been living in a near state of mental collapse.

Is that what drew the killer? Is he tapping into this? If so, how?

16

An hour into processing the interviews from the day before, someone across the room is heard to say, 'Oh, shit,' very loudly.

All heads turn towards Kev Wallis, who has just come back into the office. He is holding one of those thin, blue-striped corner shop bags, through which can be seen the outline of a Ginsters pasty and a bottle of Lucozade, but he is staring down at a copy of the *Standard* free newspaper.

'What is it, Kev?' says Ewa.

Kev holds up the paper, so the front page is visible. A gasp goes up from those nearest to him, but Rose is too far away to read it.

'What does it say?' she says, crossing the room to join the handful of others who have clustered around to look at the paper.

But as she gets close, the words seem to leap out at her.

SLEEPING BEAUTY SEX GAME MURDER reads the headline.

Rose's already tender stomach goes into freefall and heat races up her cheeks. She grabs the paper from Kev's hands and ignores his, 'Hey!' as she reads the story:

Police have had to let go the only two suspects in the murder of nursery worker Hannah Scott, dubbed the

111

'Sleeping Beauty' for the way the body was arranged after her brutal suffocation. Police arrested a man and a woman believed to be close to the victim and are working on the theory that this was a twisted sex game gone wrong.

When Rose manages to drag her eyes up and away to the colleagues surrounding her, she wonders if anyone will say it, or simply think it loud enough to deafen her.

But no, Kev can always be relied upon for this kind of thing.

'That's what you called her in the briefing, isn't it? Sleeping Beauty?'

Swallowing, Rose forces herself to meet his eyes. Something passes between them and she looks away.

'Yes,' she says quietly, 'but we were all in that briefing.'

Kev mutters something and throws the paper into the recycling bin and everyone begins to move away. Rose remains where she is, staring down at the bin and picturing her investigator's notebook sitting unattended in a crowded pub.

She thinks about the group of lads who had given her a little attention as she had come in. She had ignored them, but were they still there when she left? Could they have thought it a laugh to look at what she left behind? She'd been too flustered to notice if they were still there when she went back into the pub to retrieve the book.

She thinks about the page with 'sleeping beauty' written in the centre. Circled and underlined. And 'sex game'.

Her mouth goes dry and she is aware that her hands are shaking as Rowland comes out of her office and says, in a normal voice, 'Briefing, everyone, now.' But she looks as though she is using every atom of her self-control to keep that mask-like countenance and it is somehow more terrifying than if she was yelling and puce-faced.

The phones have already started to ring.

*

The briefing is true to its name in literal time, lasting only a few minutes. But it feels like much longer. Rowland begins by icily telling the team that if she finds out anyone has been talking to the press, they can expect to be hauled in front of a Misconduct Hearing before their feet touch the ground.

'Every one of you knows what this means,' she says. 'In general, we have a good working relationship with the press that operates to our mutual advantage. But when this kind of information gets out about an investigation, it can be enormously prejudicial. It can tarnish the resources we have in solving the case . . .' She seems to run out of steam then. 'As I say, you all know this. I cannot begin to tell you how disappointed I am.' A pause, eyes lowered, as she gathers herself. 'Now get back to work.'

Rose can feel a cold vice clamping her stomach. She pictures herself saying the words out loud. 'It was me.'

She can't do it.

Anyway, there is no time to think it through because Rose's desk phone is ringing off the hook, like everyone else's.

By midday she has dealt with a man who claims he can kill people with his thoughts, another who said he was the real Yorkshire Ripper and that this was his new method of killing, and a woman who said she was going to be the next victim because she was having trouble sleeping.

Judging by the furrowed brows around her and the increasingly terse edge to colleagues' voices, it's clear that several other people on the team are dealing with very similar calls.

But while there are people Rose can quickly dismiss, there are a handful of callers who might be credible. Each and every one must be properly investigated.

It is almost five when Rose is able to leave the station to get something to eat from Tesco's. She has been avoiding having any kind of one-to-one conversation with colleagues in the short breaks to make coffee in the kitchen. This is partly because she has been given a few odd looks simply because she was the person who came up with the killer's moniker. But it's also because she isn't sure she can keep from blurting out the truth to stop it from burning an ulcer into her stomach.

It feels like there is a ping pong ball bouncing in her brain between two competing thoughts:

I can't tell Rowland. I'll be in so much shit and she is already looking for an opportunity to get rid of me. I can't do it.

And:

I have to come clean. If she finds out some other way, the consequences are going to be even worse. I'll lose the only job I've ever wanted. The only thing I've got in my life.

As she stands in the queue at Tesco's, a tub of watery-looking tuna pasta salad and a bottle of diet Coke in her hands, she makes the decision.

It's the only one she can make.

17

Kirsty

She can't stop looking at that story in the Standard, *which is in the staffroom at breaktime. About the woman murdered in her sleep.*

Kirsty keeps lifting the paper up and then putting it back down on the small, round table that is dusted with pastry flakes from where Antonne from Electricals was eating a flaky crois-sant earlier.

She has read the story three times and wishes she could un-read it.

It has nothing to do with me, Kirsty tells herself repeatedly. How can it? This person who was killed happened to be in bed and to look like they were asleep, that's all. And there was that weird sex game thing about the story too. It has no bearing on what has been happening to her. She is simply having night-mares.

She is trying to do something about it. She's been to the doctor. But the GP, a slightly patronizing woman, although she is younger than her, has only been able to suggest short-term sleeping tablets, or a referral to one of the very few sleep clinics that exist (which have endless waiting lists). That appears to be it in terms of medical help.

The trouble is, she thinks, as she runs her mug under the tap, it feels like she has been terrorized in her bed, and who can say that the next stage won't end like this? It's like she is being . . . primed for something.

'Kirsty? I think it's clean.'

'What?' The voice next to her surprises her so much that she drops the mug, a black one with a yellow smiley face on it she always favours, into the sink where the handle neatly falls off.

'Shit!' Tears spring to her eyes.

'Mind your fingers!' Joy, to her left, is a Nigerian woman who has worked in the Lingerie department for at least twenty years. Kirsty likes her, despite Joy's habit of noticing her fluctuations in weight loudly commenting as though this is acceptable. Kirsty has laughed with her colleague Naomi that 'this is what staring at saggy tits for twenty years does to you'. Joy has a sharp, loud voice that has been known to make younger staff visibly flinch in fear, but underneath this, she is kind.

The warm, solid proximity of her proves too much and, before she can stop herself, Kirsty finds herself turning and leaning into her colleague's prodigious bosom, hot tears pouring from her eyes and her shoulders heaving uncontrollably.

A few heads pop up, but Joy skilfully directs Kirsty away with one meaty arm towards the back of the staff room, glaring at anyone who dares to look at them in the process.

Once seated, Kirsty takes the man-sized tissue that smells of perfume that Joy hands her from her pocket and blows her nose.

'I'm sorry,' she says, 'I'm just so tired. I should get back.'

'It's OK,' says Joy. 'It's not going to kill anyone if you're a few minutes late.'

The words 'kill anyone' sets Kirsty off again and it takes several minutes of slightly desperate shushing and another tissue before she can calm herself down.

'What is going on?' says Joy, eyes focused sharply on her. 'This is not like you.'

Kirsty takes a loud, shuddery breath and dabs the last bits of moisture away from her nostrils. Her nose is all blocked up and her head hurts, not to mention what this has done to her make-up. But she senses Joy isn't going to be deterred. What does she have to lose?

She tells her. All of it. About the nightmares and how they are getting more realistic. About the Balaclava Man and this story in the paper about a woman murdered in her bed. Cautiously, she finishes and forces herself to meet Joy's eyes. Her brows are furrowed together in a fierce frown and Kirsty toys with the hankie, hoping she won't be roundly mocked.

'This sounds worrying,' says Joy. 'I think you should go to the police.'

'Wait, what?' This is maybe going too far, she thinks, and dread uncoils inside her. 'Why? It's only nightmares. They'll laugh at me!'

Joy chews her bottom lip and stares back at Kirsty, her eyes unreadable.

'I don't like it,' she says. 'I don't like it at all. What if someone is getting in somehow?'

'But I think I'm dreaming!'

'You think?'

Kirsty's heart begins to beat uncomfortably hard in her chest.

'Well, I must be! But it's just . . . well it seems more real than ever, and lately . . .'

'Go on.'

'I've been conscious of him . . . touching . . . my face.'

The other woman slaps her own leg, triumphant. 'Well, there you go,' she says. 'Something very strange is happening to you, my dear, and you should do something about it!' Then inspiration strikes. 'I know!' she says triumphantly. 'You can borrow my Ziggy. He's small, but a great little guard dog. He'll look after you. He even likes cats, so he'll be fine with yours.'

'Joy!' *The exclamation is loud enough to make more heads turn. Joy gives her a startled look. 'This isn't helping! But look, I'll think about your kind offer . . .' She gets up and hurriedly straightens her hair. 'I need to go back to my section. Thank you for the shoulder and the tissue.'*

Kirsty hurries to the Ladies to fix her make-up. But as she dabs concealer around the red puffiness under her eyes, the idea begins to take root.

She can't go on like this.

18

As she comes back into the station, Omar is on the phone with an uncharacteristically thunderous expression. He says, 'You're going to have to go to the press office, as I keep telling you. No, I can't offer any further comment on this.'

She mouths 'press?' at him and he nods and raises his eyes at Rose in a gesture of frustration. It's been going on all morning, the story well and truly alight in people's minds. A locked room with a dead victim inside. A victim who had terrible nightmares. This only piles even more pressure on the team to get answers. And soon.

A young woman dressed in a smart, fitted blue coat and high-heeled boots is sitting on one of the seats. Her hair is artfully swirled into a bun and she wears thick, meticulous make-up, but she is literally wringing her hands, which have neat white-tipped French manicures. When she sees Rose, she leaps to her feet.

'Are you a detective?' she says eagerly. Rose forces her face into an expression of professional politeness and nods.

'Can I talk to you for a moment?'

Rose hesitates. 'If you're press, then I'm afraid—'

'No,' says the woman, before swallowing visibly and wrapping her arms around herself. 'Someone's trying to frighten me.'

'OK,' says Rose with a suppressed sigh. She wishes she could palm this off on someone else and get her meeting with Rowland over and done with, but clearly she has no choice. 'I can spare a few minutes. Come through.'

Popping her head in to see if the casual interview room is free, Rose gestures for the woman to go in first.

They sit down opposite one another and Rose gets out her notebook, turning it to a fresh page.

'So, Ms . . . er . . . ?'

'It's Kirsty,' says the woman, 'Kirsty Perryman.'

'Right,' says Rose, 'and what is the name of the person trying to, er, frighten you?'

Kirsty lowers her eyes and takes a steadying breath.

'That's the thing,' she is visibly trembling. 'It's in the night. When I'm sleeping. He creeps in and stands over me and . . .' she starts to cry, 'I think I'm going to be driven mad, or, or,' she gulps, '. . . he's going to kill me like that woman in the paper.'

Rose loses the battle with herself over letting out a huge, weary sigh.

A few minutes later, she manages to bundle the woman out to reception, having promised that she will arrange for a Community Support Police Officer to come round and check all her windows and doors, and with a suggestion that she see her GP as soon as possible, blah-di-blah-di-blah.

This is going to mean paperwork. She's required to fill out a Public Protection Notice – known as a PPN1 – to be sent to MASH, the public Multi-Agency Safeguarding Hub, which shares information between various agencies, including police and social services, so vulnerable people get the help that they need. It's not going to be the first form she's had to fill in this morning and she has a feeling it won't be the last, thanks to her unbelievable carelessness and stupidity.

There is only one thing she can do.

*

Feeling like she has lead weights attached to both her legs, Rose drags herself towards Rowland's office.

The boss is writing something on a pad, and she looks up sharply when Rose knocks on the open door before gesturing that she should come in.

Rose enters and closes the door. Rowland clocks this with a frown.

'What can I do for you, Rose?' she says.

Rose licks her dry lips.

'The thing is, ma'am,' she says, 'I think I might have been responsible for the leak. Without meaning to,' she adds hurriedly. 'I mean, I didn't mean it.' She's conscious of repeating the same word but can't seem to stop herself.

Rowland's face is stone.

'Go on,' she says in a dangerously even voice.

'Well,' says Rose, 'I accidentally left my notebook somewhere in public, for a few minutes . . .' The other woman remains silent, forcing her to go on.

'It's possible someone read my comment about "sleeping beauty" and the sex stuff that I'd written in there.'

'Where did you leave it?' The tone is so dry, there is no upward inflection with the question.

Wildly considering naming a more wholesome venue, Rose makes herself say the words.

'In the pub down the road.'

She is dimly aware of seeing Mack peering in through the window at her, but she is too scared to move her eyes away from her boss, whose face has turned pink for the first time that Rose has ever seen.

'The pub down the road.' Deadpan. There's a short silence, then:

'For God's sake, Rose!' Rowland is on her feet and shouting. Rowland never shouts. 'Do you realize what this kind of thing costs us? When details are made public like this, it can derail an investigation completely! How could you be so *stupid*!'

'I'm so, so sorry, ma'am. I don't have anything to say beyond this was an honest mistake and I will take total responsibility for it.'

'Damn right, you will,' says Rowland, who has come round to where Rose is sitting and is looking down at her, eyes blazing. Rose notices that she has golden rings around her green irises. It occurs to her that she has never looked at her boss so closely before. Stupid to think about this right now, but all her words have dried up. She has nothing to say and merely opens and then closes her mouth, before nodding, lowering her head in shame.

'When you came into my squad, Rose,' says Rowland, voice under control again. 'I thought you were . . . a little rough round the edges, but perhaps had good instincts underneath. In the light of your behaviour the other day, and now this, I am sorry to say that maybe I was wrong.'

Tears sting the backs of her eyes, but Rose can feel something else – a tiny flicker of indignation beginning to burn.

She goes to speak, but Rowland cuts her off with a raised hand.

'I don't want to hear it,' she says. 'You're suspended, pending a Misconduct Hearing that will be organized in due course. In the meantime, you might want to contact your rep.'

Rose can hear her own heavy breathing and her heartbeat pounding in her ears.

Suspended.

That flicker of flame suddenly catches a blast of oxygen, and before she can stop herself the words spill out:

'With respect, ma'am, is this *only* about the leak?'

Rowland's face is as tight as a mask now. Her lips pressed into a thin, pale line.

'What are you talking about, DC Gifford?' Her voice is low.

'I'm talking,' says Rose, breathing heavily, 'about the fact that you never cut me a break, ever, and we both know why.'

Rose is already regretting letting the exchange swerve in this direction, but it's too late. Maybe it's the lack of sleep, the stress of the case, she's not sure, but she has never spoken to the boss like this.

It's exhilarating.

It's terrifying.

'Do we?'

Her own voice rising in inverse proportion to the quiet control of the other woman, Rose says, 'Yes, we do!'

When nothing else is forthcoming, she stumbles on.

'It's because of that night I saw you in town . . . when you were obviously having some kind of . . .' she fumbles for words, '. . . emotional upset,' *Oh God, is she actually doing this?* 'with, with . . .'

The look on Rowland's face stops her in her tracks.

'Are you threatening me, DS Gifford?'

'No!' Rose can feel the tears coming and she can't stop them. 'That's not at all what I meant! I only wish you'd understand that I have never told anyone, nor would I!'

Her whole body is shaking but her brain has finally managed to transmit the message to her mouth that she has handled this all wrong.

'Ma'am, I—'

'Get out.'

Rose feels the eyes of her colleagues on her as she leaves the boss's office. She registers someone saying, 'You all right, kiddo?' but isn't able to summon up a response.

Grabbing her coat and handbag, she hurries past the front desk where Omar is doing a shift handover with an officer called Serena, and doesn't draw breath until she finds herself gulping in cold wintry air outside the station.

She needs to get as far away as she can, but she somehow can't seem to make her legs work. There is a bench a short way down the street and Rose hurries to it and sinks down, breathing as though she has been running, and clasps her head in her hands.

The tears won't come now she is able to cry, even though

she is desperate for release from the pain of this humiliation and sadness.

Suspended.

Not good enough to be a copper.

Her worst nightmare has come true.

19

Rose is wrapped in a fuzzy numbness as she opens her front door and does the customary wait-and-listen for the spectre of Adele. The appalling thought races through her mind then that she might appreciate the company on this day of all days, which almost makes her laugh in its twisted logic.

As she places her keys on the ugly old hall table, the tears follow hot on the heels of the laughter, as though her emotions have been given permission to explode out of her at last.

Walking into the living room, she sinks into the most comfortable of the battered old easy chairs and buries her face in her hands. Her shoulders heave and she cries hard and long. It goes on so long, in fact, that she almost scares herself. It is that which helps her to come hiccupping to a stop.

Finally, feeling hollowed out inside, she shakily makes her way to the kitchen to blow her nose and wash her face. Robotically, she starts to make tea, then abandons it halfway through and looks in the fridge for the remains of the bottle of wine.

She pours a glass and drinks half of it in one gulp, then tops it up and takes it over to the kitchen table, scanning the room suspiciously in case there are any nasty, mother-related surprises.

Slumping into the chair in front of her laptop, she stares at the square of the kitchen window, which frames a view of grey sky and the house that backs onto this one.

Now that she has lost her job, she doesn't have to stay in London any more. She doesn't even have to stay in this country. She could finally get rid of this shithole and shed the dingy past like a butterfly emerging free and fresh from the chrysalis as if newly hatched.

Taken with this unexpected positive note, Rose pictures herself hiking up a mountain in some picturesque spot, or working at a beachside café, tanned and happy, with the surf crashing in the background, the only ghost a hangover from some party the night before.

It's tantalizing, but then she imagines herself looking along the shoreline, and a squat little form is standing there, watching her, waves lapping around incorporeal legs that are somehow still mapped with varicose veins.

Her life sentence.

She groans and rests her head in her hands, then snaps open the laptop and begins a desultory review of her social media feeds in an effort to take her mind off things.

Rose isn't much of a one for these things, mainly because she has no wish to stay in touch with anyone who isn't directly in her life.

But a thought comes to her. She hasn't heard anything back about the social media check on Hannah's phone. Might be an idea to take a look herself. When she goes to the 'search groups' function and looks up 'sleep disorders', there are a few, but far and away the biggest is one called Sleepyheads Parasomnia Support Group.

It's a closed group, but before she can talk herself out of it, she sends a 'request to join' email to one of the group moderators.

Her mood has lifted a tiny bit as she goes to the sink and pours a glass of water. Pretending to still be a police officer is all she has got left .

Maybe she can still help Hannah Scott, even though she wasn't good enough to do her job.

The thought of Hannah is enough to conjure the sickly sweet scent of lavender that had hung in the air at the murder scene.

Rose's nails instinctively begin scratching her inner arm, but she breaks off, wincing at the sudden pain. When she rolls up her sleeve, she sees that the skin is red raw. She must have been clawing at this spot without even knowing it.

When she returns to the laptop, she sees a message waiting for her: *Your Request to Join Sleepyheads Parasomnia Support Group has been accepted.*

She sits down and studies the screen.

The banner across the top of the page says *Sleepyheads* and there is a cutesy image of a sleeping kitten draped across the top of an armchair. She reads the group description:

A support group for people suffering from any kind of parasomnia. You can ask for advice here, exchange tips, or share your stories. Remember to be kind! Everyone here is probably as tired as you are! Rude or abusive behaviour will not be tolerated by the moderators.

The group has over a thousand members. Rose feels her research high flag. That's a lot of posts to have to read, and it might all be a dead end anyway. When she types Hannah's name into the Member Search box though, Hannah comes up straight away. Rose's stomach twists as she looks at the picture of the smiling young woman, restored to life and health in the picture.

She is only showing half her face, her long hair obscuring one eye and curling down her cheek. She has an impish look in her eye and clearly wanted to look pretty in her profile shot, even if she wasn't comfortable being her public self.

Rose scans through the hits for her name and it is immediately obvious that she was a prolific poster in this group.

Her last post was on the night of the murder:

Doing my usual bedtime 'routine' but have a horrible feeling the noisy student neighbours are having a party tonight! Grrr!

Someone called LilyFaith replied: Oh noooooo! Can you use earplugs?

Hannah Scott No, I'm far too much of a wuss to put earplugs in!

LilyFaith ??????

Hannah Scott LOL I know it's mad, but I'm afraid I won't hear the bogeyman sneaking up on me.

This was accompanied by a GIF of a woman in a nightgown screaming and shaking her head from side to side.

Rose thinks about this semi-jokey response and shudders at how prescient it turned out to be.

Closing the laptop a little too hard, she goes to pour herself another drink.

Once the bottle is finished, Rose goes to the corner shop to get another.

But it only makes her feel sick tonight and brings on a sharp, throbbing headache.

Mack keeps texting and leaving voicemails, asking her to call him, but she can't bear to speak to him, so she finally turns off the phone.

The night seems to stretch ahead of her. All she wants is oblivion.

She remembers there are some very strong painkillers in the bathroom cabinet that Adele used to take for various ailments. Maybe they will knock her out? Got to be worth a try, anyway.

The use-by date is long gone, she soon finds, but she read somewhere that drugs like this don't really expire. Popping two into her mouth, she drinks from the tap and swallows them, wincing a little as she catches a bitter, chalky taste in her throat.

Right now, she would pretty much do anything for respite from the worries crowding her brain.

She ends up sleeping more heavily than for weeks.

In the morning, the first thing she becomes aware of is the bees in the bedroom. So many bees. Where on Earth have *they* come from?

Batting them away and cracking open sticky eyes, she realises it is the persistent buzz of the doorbell that she is hearing.

Ignoring it is impossible because this is clearly one determined person, judging by the way they keep pressing the bell over and over again. She doesn't remember ordering anything online and no one ever visits...

Grumbling to herself, she pulls on a long cardigan and pads down the stairs with bare feet.

As she gets near the living room, she gets a shock that comes like a defibrillator to the chest.

Her mother is lurking inside the door, staring out, as if she too has been disturbed by the doorbell.

It rings again and Adele turns very slowly to look at Rose, her expression perplexed, her skin so grey and waxy Rose shudders at the graveyard horror of it.

'Will you just,' she squeezes out through gritted teeth, 'fuck *off* . . .'

At this, the spectre, or whatever it is, melts back into the room. When Rose tentatively moves to peer in, the horrible old witch is gone.

The letterbox opens and a pair of familiar eyes are framed by it.

'I can literally see you standing there, Rose,' says Mack, 'so pretending you're not in isn't going to cut it.'

Defeated, Rose goes to open the door a little, giving one more nervous glance around to check she is otherwise alone.

She peers out at him through the crack.

Mack looks at her from the step with an expression of infinite, weary sadness that brings the instant prickle of tears. She will not cry in front of him. She will not. But if he is going to be all sympathetic and disappointed, she is going to have to make him go away. She cannot tolerate that right now.

'Oh Rose,' he says. Then, 'I'm so sorry, kiddo.'

The tears burn and she blinks hard; once, twice.

'No need to be sorry,' she says briskly. 'What do you want?'

'You wouldn't answer my texts.'

Rose shrugs. 'Sorry,' she says. 'But as you can see, I'm not really in a state for visitors right now.'

'It's OK,' says Mack with a smile. 'I'll wait while you get dressed.'

Rose huffs a theatrical sigh. He's clearly going nowhere.

'Suppose you'd better come in then, you bossy git.'

As he comes into the hall, Rose can see him looking around in surprise at her weird, old-person house. Oh well, she has far too many other things to be ashamed about to care. Let him judge her. What does it matter in the grand scheme of the mess she's in?

'Do you want tea, coffee . . . ?' she says in a flat, uninviting way. Mack gives her a small smile.

'You go get yourself sorted and I'll make some.'

She hesitates.

'Go on.' He is already walking towards the kitchen.

Rose almost runs back up the stairs, not enjoying the thought of Mack rooting around in her house. Hastily brushing her teeth, she pulls on a jumper and some jeans over her bed t-shirt. It will have to do.

The smell of toast greets her as she comes down, prompting an approving grumble from her stomach in response.

Mack looks comfortable, stirring what she knows will be the right amount of milk into her tea and putting a pot of peanut butter on the table, along with a plate and fork.

'You're such a dad,' she mumbles, taking a seat.

'I know,' he says. 'But not a very good one, as it turns out.'

Rose is slathering peanut butter onto the toast Mack has placed in front of her.

'Bollocks,' she says. 'Why would you even say that?'

Mack is silent as he sits at the table, his expression grave as he picks up his tea. But instead of taking a sip, he puts it back down again.

'I'll come to that,' he says in a heavy voice. 'But first I want to apologise to you from the bottom of my heart.'

Rose stops chewing her toast and stares back at him. 'Wait, what?' she says. 'What are you talking about?'

Mack meets her gaze, his eyes tired and full of regret.

'It wasn't you who caused the leak, Rose' he says. 'It was me. It's all my fault.'

Too stunned to reply, Rose simply stares at him.

Mack?

How can it have been Mack?

'Rose? Don't you have anything to say?' Then, 'Christ, I wish I still smoked.' She does too, but doesn't want to be all chummy with Mack right at this moment, so she doesn't respond.

'Look, Rose,' says Mack, 'I found out something last night and rang the boss, who told me about your suspension and the lost notebook. It, well, it wasn't that that caused the leak, I'm certain of it.'

'So what happened?'

Mack rubs a hand savagely over his face.

'I think I told you about Caitlin? How she suffers from anxiety?'

'Yeah,' says Rose. It feels like an entirely different conversation is being tacked onto this one and she's struggling to keep up with it.

'Well,' says Mack, 'Caitlin heard me talking to her mum the other evening. I'm telling Libby about the words you'd used to describe Hannah Scott, because they were so chilling, and Caitlin comes bursting into the room in floods of tears.' He pauses. 'I honestly thought she was upstairs watching telly and had no idea she was listening. I wasn't even speaking loudly.' He looks angry. 'It's basic stuff: not sharing that kind of sensitive information. But it had been a long day and . . .' He stops speaking and lowers his eyes before taking a sip of water.

'OK,' says Rose carefully, 'but I can't see your teenage daughter getting on the phone to the *Standard*.' She draws one knee up onto the chair and wraps her arms around it. 'No,' she says with a shake of the head. 'It's kind of you to say this, but it's still more likely that someone read my notebook.'

Mack is shaking his head too, vehemently.

'No, no, you don't have the full picture,' he says. 'She said something in one of her group whatsits on Snapchat. And it turns out that her friend Annabella's dad works on the news desk at the *Standard*. Annabella *told* him.' He pauses. 'We *know* this happened, Rose. There's no doubt about it.'

'Fuck!' says Rose. She is filled with competing emotions that are too complex to unpick, all of them jostling for space to grow.

'Yeah, fuck,' says Mack.

They look at each other in silence.

'Is she OK?'

'Who, the boss?' says Mack. 'I'd say not.'

'No!' says Rose. 'Caitlin?'

Mack raises his eyes and spreads his hands. 'Ah, kiddo, it's very kind of you to even think of that in the circumstances.' He gives her a sad smile. 'Since you asked, she is mortified and cried for most of last night.' He pauses. 'I think she'll be OK. It's simply bad judgement on my part – and bad luck.'

'So, what does this mean for me?' says Rose, making a face. 'I still lost my notebook.'

A thin band of winter sunshine bathes the kitchen in lemon light.

'Rowland knew I was coming straight here this morning, and she told me she wants you to come in for a meeting at midday.'

Hope and nerves flutter in Rose's chest.

'And you?' she says. Mack blows air out through his cheeks and makes a funny face.

'Well,' he says, 'she talked about suspension. I was prepared to take it. Obviously, she is very disappointed in me for discussing a case like this at home.'

'Ouch,' says Rose, picturing this.

'Yeah,' says Mack. 'It wasn't fun. I did feel like a knobbly kneed schoolkid for the entire meeting. But I deserved much worse. I should never have let details of a case come out like that. I mean, it's a long way from deliberately leaking case details to a member of the press. But, in theory at least, I could lose my job over this.'

'Oh, Mack,' says Rose, and her eyes prickle again. 'What about the twenty years of brilliant service?'

'Hmm, well . . .' He shrugs, then seems to rally, sitting up straighter. 'Anyway,' he says, 'I haven't been suspended, even if it would assuage my own guilt. I'll have to go in front of a Misconduct Hearing – and you'll still have to do that too – but for the time being at least, I'm still on the job.' He pauses. 'And so are you, kiddo.'

At that moment, Mack's mobile buzzes with a message and about three seconds later, so does Rose's.

Rowland.

They're needed at the station. Right now.

20

When they get back to the MIT office, Rose avoids eye contact as much as she can, but it is clear from the heads turning as one in her direction that word is already out.

Rowland gives her a nod when she comes into the room and says, 'We'll speak later, Rose. Thank you for coming in,' which, in its odd formality, makes her feel even worse.

Once everyone is assembled, Rowland turns to face the room.

'So,' she says, 'we have had another attempted murder by suffocation. A woman called . . .' she looks at her notebook, 'Joy Kogo called in this morning, in a hysterical state. She was convinced something had happened to a colleague who hadn't come into work. Claimed her friend had been stalked by someone. PC Steve Gibbons called at the scene to check it out and wasn't able to raise the occupant, even though there were signs that someone was in.'

The room is pin-drop silent as the DCI pauses before continuing.

'He and colleague PC Jane Barton were persuaded by a distraught Mrs Kogo, who had waited at the door all afternoon for someone to arrive, that they must gain access to the property, which they then did by force. And they found the woman there, unconscious. There is an alarm system and the door was apparently locked, with no sign of forced entry.

'An ambulance was called, and she was taken to Queen Elizabeth General, where it became apparent that she was in a coma following attempted suffocation.'

'Name?' says Mack.

'Perryman,' says Rowland. 'Kirsty Perryman.'

Rose's gasp makes all heads turn her way.

'Ma'am,' she says, attempting to sound bold but failing, she is sure, '. . . that's the name of a woman who came into the station yesterday and who claimed someone was, well, somehow trying to kill her in her sleep.'

Before Rowland gets the chance to deliver what will no doubt be more stinging words, Rose quickly moves on.

'But not physically,' she says. 'She clearly had psych issues, because she claimed this man was . . . in her . . . well, *nightmares*. No one was ever there, in her house, when she woke up. I'm afraid I assumed she was a bit of a nutter and wrote it up as a PPN1.'

A silence falls and then Rowland lets out a sigh.

'Well,' she says, 'I'm sure each one of us would have done the same.'

Rose's gratitude and relief feel like a physical lifting of something heavy from her shoulders. She's going to be given another chance, perhaps.

'Anyway,' says Rowland, 'tell us exactly what she said, please.'

Rose flips her notebook and finds the entry.

'She said that someone was, and I quote, "coming into my dreams" and that she was scared he was going to "get her". It transpired that she has never found any evidence whatsoever that someone has been in the house, although she also said that her cat "knew" and wouldn't come in at night any more.' Rose looks up from her notebook. 'To be honest, that was the extent of it. I talked to her about basic home security stuff and said I'd send a couple of uniforms round at some point to have a look. But she told me she already had an alarm system. I'm not sure what else I could have done.'

'No, no, as I said,' says Rowland impatiently, 'none of us would have handled this differently. For now, we are going to have to wait and see whether this attempted murder turns into actual murder.'

A pause while these sobering words sink in.

'So how did the assailant get in?' asks Mack.

'Forensics are still looking because it's not obvious at the moment,' says Rowland. 'Whoever it was seemed to know this property well. They think it's possible they knew the alarm code, then retrieved the keys through the letter box using some sort of hook.' She pauses. 'It's how half the cars in London get nicked these days, as we all know. Maybe Ms Perryman thought having an alarm was sufficient security on its own.'

The boss looks around the room. 'One of the big questions is,' she says, 'is there a connection between the murder of Hannah Scott and this attack? If so, could it be a copycat thing because of the leak?'

Rose fights a losing battle with the heat that blasts her face. She keeps her gaze fixed on Rowland, who takes a small red magnet from the side of the whiteboard and then points to one that is already up there.

'So,' she says, 'Hannah Scott lived *here*, in Arnos Grove, and Kirsty Perryman lives . . .' she pauses to stick the magnet onto the map, about three miles away, '. . . here, in Alexandra Park.' What do those places have in common, anyone?'

'They're not that far by public transport?' says Mack.

'Yes,' says Rowland, 'but that doesn't exactly tell us anything. Kev has interviewed Mrs Kogo. Can you please tell us about that? Did you ask her directly if she knew Hannah?'

Kev clears his throat and looks down at his notebook before speaking.

'I did,' he says, 'but if Kirsty did know her, Mrs Kogo knew nothing about that. They work together, Mrs Kogo and the victim, and I think she is a kind of mother figure to her . . .

or wants to be. She said she's been worrying about her, because Kirsty was coming into work upset lately.'

'For the reasons she told Rose?' says Mack.

'Yep,' says Kev. 'She said she wasn't sleeping because she had these terrible nightmares. Only Mrs Kogo wasn't so sure they were nightmares. She was under the impression that someone was trying to frighten her. It seems she let the victim borrow her dog, a . . .' he looks at his notes again, 'a poodle, which was at the scene at the time of the attack. It's possible that it interrupted the assailant – the dog appears to have been kicked.'

A rumble of murmured conversations ripple through the room.

'Is the dog going to be OK?' says Rowland, which Rose thinks has probably surprised everyone in the room.

'Yes,' says Kev. 'Last I heard, it's back with its owner after a visit to the vet.'

'Right.' The boss looks sharply around the room.

'Did Mrs Kogo do this simply to calm her down, or because she believed there was a genuine threat to Kirsty's life?' says Rose.

Kev shrugs. 'Hard to say. Mrs Kogo doesn't seem clear on this herself, but she did say that there's no way Kirsty was making things up because, quote, "Kirsty wasn't someone who was silly like that." She actually encouraged Kirsty to get someone to come over and check over the home security there.'

'Hey,' says Mack sharply. 'Does she know who carried out that work? Because if they knew the property . . .'

'. . . they could get in again quite easily when they wanted to,' Rose finishes the sentence.

'Yes,' says Rowland, nodding. 'Good call. See if this Mrs Kogo knows anything about that. If she doesn't, search the property for any cards or receipts. Failing that, we can check her bank and credit card records.'

'Are there any clues about why he – assuming it's a he – didn't carry this through?' says Tom.

'No, not as yet,' says Rowland. 'It could be that the dog

stopped the attack. According to the two PCs who forced entry, it's a small but feisty little thing.'

The words *'man who comes in the night'* spring into Rose's mind and a shudder crawls up her spine.

'Right, people,' says Rowland as if she has heard Rose's thoughts. 'What do we think about the fact that both women reported having these nightmares before they were attacked?'

The room is silent until Mack speaks.

'Could be that someone was gaslighting these two women in some way? Frightening them at night?'

'But how, though?' says Rose. 'Both of them claimed he was in the room prior to the attacks, even though they both had reasonable security in place.'

Rowland is tapping her bottom lip with her biro.

'I'm not happy about the spare key being bought online by Nikolas and delivered to a PO box,' she says. 'It would have been far, far easier to take the original key out of the house and have a copy made at the nearest key-cutting place. It would have taken ten minutes, tops.'

'Perhaps someone did it from her phone without her knowledge,' says Mack.

Rowland nods. 'I think the likely scenario there, and maybe here too, is that someone very familiar with both properties was able to gain access by using that knowledge. And maybe that person somehow managed to spook two women who happened to be bad sleepers.'

'The sleeping thing might be totally irrelevant,' says Kev. 'I mean,' he looks around the room, 'who here *does* sleep well?'

About half the hands go up in the room. Rose keeps hers down.

'Well, there you go,' says Kev. 'Probably a coincidence.'

There's a pause in which a wave of tiredness seems to swell around them, then Rowland speaks again.

'OK,' she says, 'while we're waiting on forensics, let's look into whether there is any connection between Hannah Scott and Kirsty Perryman.'

'Boss – one more thing,' says Rose as people start to fidget. Rowlands nods and the movement in the room stills again.

'I looked at that Facebook group,' says Rose, 'and found Hannah there.' Does she imagine a momentary flicker of approval? 'And the thing is,' she continues, 'her last post was put up the night she was murdered.' The energy in the room shifts, focusing on Rose.

'What did she say in it?' says Rowland.

'Well,' says Rose, 'it may mean nothing, but she was complaining about the neighbours having a loud party and worrying how it was going to affect her sleep.'

Rowland's eyebrows raise and she nods slowly. 'So, you're thinking this might have alerted someone it would be a good night to break in and kill her?'

'Yes, it's possible, isn't it?' says Rose, feeling a pleasurable increase of her heart rate.

'It's a theory,' says Tom. 'Worth looking into any other conversations she was having online.'

'Yes,' says the boss, already moving towards the door. 'I'll get tech to take a look at the devices of this Kirsty Perryman to see if she is in that group too. Keep digging, Rose.' Then, 'Right, people, let's get busy.'

The room fills with a buzz of conversation, the scrape of chairs and rustle of papers being gathered up. There is a sense of everyone being reenergized by this latest event. It's one of the things about being a policewoman that Rose would find very hard to explain to anyone not in the Force. Bad things happening to good people is the reason for getting up in the morning. There is an undeniable thrill at times.

Rose realizes that Sam is watching her and as she goes to leave the room, he follows her into the corridor.

'Hey, what happened yesterday with you and the boss?' he says. 'Are you all right?' The tenderness in his eyes makes Rose look down at her feet and swallow. She wants to lean against his chest and breathe in his clean, fresh smell. Have him wrap his arms around her and gently rest his chin on her head.

'It's all OK,' she says. 'Bit of a misunderstanding.' She looks up, forcing herself to meet his eye.

He's such a steady, kind presence. She needs him. However difficult things may be in her personal life, she needs her friend.

'Look, Sam,' she says, 'maybe when this calms down we can get together again – I mean, for a drink or something.'

'I'd like that,' he says. 'A drink would be lovely.' But there's something in his eyes she doesn't want to see. 'Rose, I . . .' He runs a hand through his thick, black hair and looks away. 'The thing is, me and Lucy have got back together. Thought I should let you know.'

Rose forces the biggest, shiniest smile across her face. It feels like a rictus grin. It feels like her face might crack from it. Lovely Lucy is back. Of course she is.

'That's great,' she says brightly. 'I'm so happy for you guys!'

Sam looks confused, then mumbles his thanks.

'Anyway,' says Rose, with an exaggerated look at her watch. 'Better get on. But let's not forget that drink!'

She walks away, wincing as though she is actually walking on broken glass.

Back at her desk, Rose takes a moment to swallow down the sadness and humiliation. This has been a long, long day.

Work.

It's the only way to get through it.

She logs into the Sleepyheads group on Facebook and begins to scroll back through Hannah's posts.

There were quite a few about her sleep paralysis episodes. Rose reads a post from a couple of days before she died:

I just wish someone could reassure me that I won't go on like for this forever. I've tried everything, from CBT to herbal remedies that you guys have suggested but it's still happening. And I know how KERAZY this makes me sound but it's like these episodes are getting to be more real. Last night I really thought there was a man in my room but when I woke up there was no one there! Maybe I've finally lost it LOL! – 😄😄😂😂

Rose studies the replies:

Chelsea Girl Sounds really horrible hon. These dreams are very realistic sometimes. Keep doing all the things your doing and remember we're hear for you to vent! Xxx ♥

There are quite a few in a similar vein, including some with a vaguely hectoring tone about not giving up. Some are blatant attempts to sell stuff:

Jason Maddison It is essential during these periods of parasomnia that you maintain routines and maintain proper sleep hygiene. My book *Perfect Slumbers* is just £1.99 on Amazon right now and in it I give you a programme of pre-bed behaviour that works!

Followed by:

John Jones *ADMIN* We discourage commercial posts here so please refrain from linking to products or books that you would personally benefit from by recommending. Any more of this behaviour will result in being excluded from the group. Thank you.

It's hard not to get sucked in. Someone has posted about 'exploding head syndrome', which Rose quickly googles, and discovers that it's a type of sleep disorder where you hear loud noises inside your head as you are drifting off to sleep.

With a huge sigh, she sits back in her chair. Wow, she thinks, and I thought I had some weird shit in my life.

As Rose scrolls through, she notices that the same small band of people tend to reply to Hannah's posts, but there is nothing that stands out. There are a thousand people in the group. Any one of them could have targeted her and used the information she is posting. It's hopeless.

Then Rose's eye snags on something and she clicks on a member of the group called Somnus. Weird name. She googles it and discovers Somnus was the Greek God of sleep, father of Morpheus – who she has heard of. Enlarging Somnus's profile picture, she sits forward.

It's that horrible sleep paralysis painting – *The Nightmare*, was it called? But yesterday she'd had the weird feeling of having seen it before, and it certainly wasn't in this group.

So where had she seen it?

Rose gets up, hoping that moving about will shake whatever it is free from her brain. She wanders into the briefing room, where the photographs of Hannah Scott's crime scene adorn the walls. After staring at the pictures for a few moments, she steps forward to look more closely at one in particular. It's the view of Hannah Scott's bedroom, seen from the doorway, with the dressing table and the noticeboard covered in pictures.

She peers at the postcards on the board and there it is! It had struck her at the time as incongruous. It's the same picture, she's sure of it. Her heart is thudding in her chest because somehow, this *feels* significant. However, as she continues to gaze at the photo, doubts begin to creep in.

Maybe it's nothing. Plenty of people like old paintings, even if this is rather a weird one. Rose has never understood what people see in old stuff, especially when it's ugly. But as she stares at the horrible goblin squatting on that woman's chest, its face full of evil intent, she thinks about Moony's words: 'Night terrors. Sleep paralysis. Nightmares that feel as though they are really happening.' There's a connection here, she's sure of it. But what?

*

Still debating whether it's worth saying anything to the boss, she wanders over to Mack, who is finishing a phone call.

He gives her a tired smile and says, 'What's up?'

Rose sits on the desk.

'You know that Facebook group I mentioned?' she says. 'For people with sleep problems?'

'Yep.'

'Well,' she holds up her phone, which still shows the painting. 'This is the profile pic for one of the users . . . and it's also in Hannah's house.'

'So?' Mack's attention is already being tugged back to what he was doing. 'It could have come from anywhere. Could have been a joke present.'

Rose feels something deflate inside her. Maybe this is a waste of time and energy after all.

'But what if it turned out that Kirsty has this picture somewhere too?' she argues. 'Then it might be significant in some way?'

Mack frowns at the phone. He looks old and worn. 'You mean, he might leave it like some sort of calling card?'

'It's possible,' says Rose. 'Particularly as this painting is called *The Nightmare*, and the single thing we have linking these two women is that they both have, well, bloody awful nightmares.'

Mack looks up at Rose and hands back the phone.

'OK,' he says. 'But even if you're right about this, and it's some sort of reverse trophy situation, don't forget our guy was interrupted before he was able to finish the job.' He pauses. 'If he had to leave in a hurry, would he even have time to do this?'

'True. But look,' says Rose. 'We don't know what order he does this in, do we? Maybe he plants the picture first, while his victim's asleep? It's got to be worth having a look?'

Mack is reaching for his phone as he replies.

'I agree,' he says, 'ring my mate Devon, he's one of the CSIs who looked at the Perryman place earlier. He might still be there, if you're lucky.'

He gives Rose the number and she thanks him before hurrying back to her desk, dialling the number as she goes.

Devon is indeed still at the crime scene. After Rose explains to him what she is looking for, he promises he will call her back shortly.

She sits at her desk and drums her fingers, unable to focus on anything else. When the call comes, she snatches it up before it has properly begun to ring and says, 'Yes?'

'Hi,' says Devon, who has a deep, attractive voice, 'I've had a look and I can't see that postcard anywhere.'

'Ah, right, OK,' says Rose, shoulders sagging as a stale weariness sets in. She is about to thank him when she interrupts herself.

'Hey, wait,' she says. 'Can you check if she has a book on the bedside table? Worth looking to see if she was using the postcard as a bookmark, maybe?'

'Hang on.'

A few minutes pass and then:

'Guess what?' says Devon, excitement in his voice now. 'You were right. There is a card inside the book on her nightstand. Want me to bag it up as an exhibit?'

Rose has to stop herself from running to Rowland's office.

The other woman is having an irritable phone conversation, which she ends when she sees Rose at the door.

Rose comes in, hesitantly, still keenly aware of having been suspended yesterday.

'What have you got?' says Rowland crisply, and Rose begins.

It takes her a few minutes to explain her theory about the photo. Rowland googles the image as Rose speaks.

When she finishes, her boss nods, frowning. 'Yes, I know this picture,' she says. 'It's quite a famous one, actually.'

'But not exactly an attractive thing to have on your wall, is it?'

'Well, there's no accounting for taste,' says Rowland. 'Art is

144

very individual. But I agree that this painting being in the houses of both those young women is . . .' she pauses, 'odd, to say the least.'

Excitement suffuses Rose's chest. Finally, she has got something right.

'OK,' says Rowland decisively. 'You say one of the support group members has this as their profile picture?'

'Yep.'

'Right, take a look back at all their posts, see what you come up with.'

Is that it? She doesn't know what she expected, but it was more.

'Can we push Facebook on this?' says Rose. 'Track down that user?'

Rowland leans back in her chair. 'We can, but it is time-consuming and difficult.' She sighs. 'The law changed in 2018, supposedly to make it easier for international authorities to force them to release this kind of information. But in practice, it's still a bloody nightmare – if,' she makes a face, 'you'll pardon the pun.'

'Bugger!'

'Yes. We already had a Mutual Legal Assistance Treaty with America, but under the terms of the CLOUD Act in order to obtain data we must make a request to the US Department of Justice and they will then take it to a judge, and then, if we're lucky, things might start moving.'

Rose suddenly feels utterly wiped out by this rollercoaster day.

As she walks back to her desk, her phone rings. She glances at the screen, sees it is DS Moony. Why is she calling *her*? And what is her interest in this case anyway?

Rose's mouth feels dry and she runs her tongue over her lips.

She rejects the call and slips the phone back into her pocket.

21

Kirsty

Bobbing, sightless, in the black water. It laps at her limbs, which float free, useless. If only she could wiggle her fingers or toes, she could push to the surface and find the light again, but it's all too difficult. This reminds her of something, but the thought is a wispy thing that disappears like smoke as soon as it arrives.

But, wait, maybe the darkness is breaking up. Here come paler flashes in the gloom. The dark water is filled with geometric shapes that move in and out of her field of vision.

Clarity comes in a rush. She must have been on a boat that sank and now she is stranded in the sea. Yes, that's it! Someone will come and rescue her soon. They won't leave her in the sea. This probably happens all the time . . .

The geometric shapes soften around the edges and become more defined. She understands they are people, lots of people, moving around her. But why will someone not help her get out of the sea? It's cold here. She's frightened. The water isn't her friend. She isn't safe here.

Something tugs at her mind, like an insistent child's hand in hers. What is it? What does she need to do? Then a memory pierces the murky soup that fills her head.

She's in bed. She can hear her own heartbeat thudding in her ears and she needs to do something. It's very important that she does it, or something awful will happen.

But what is it? What is the THING?

Her mind thrashes to find the answer. Then she gets it! It's waking up! All she has to do is wake up and then the thing won't happen.

The man won't come.

But, wait, he did come.

Memories flood in, playing out as a series of scenes:

The terrible knowledge that someone is in her bedroom.

The relief when she thought, 'It's only a bad dream!'

Then the hideous, corrosive horror that followed. Because this time someone really was there.

Her frantic attempt to move stilled instantly by a suffocating density over her face.

Can't breathe, can't breathe.

And now she's in water, floating.

But he's coming back. She feels him, like a spreading shadow over her brain, staining her with the darkness. He needs to finish the thing he started.

He's here again.

She wants so badly to scream but all she can do is bob, bob, bob in the black water.

22

It's almost 9 p.m. when Rowland comes out of her office and shouts across the room.

'Kirsty Perryman is conscious,' she says, and there is an immediate ratcheting up of sound. She hesitates, as if making up her mind, then says, 'Mack and Rose, head over there and get a statement.'

Rose is grabbing her handbag and out of her seat before Rowland has even finished the sentence.

They make their way to the Queen Elizabeth General Hospital through slow moving traffic in companionable silence.

Sleet is falling on the windscreen and the sky feels ominous. Snow has been forecast for later, but only another light dusting. Just enough to make the journey more difficult.

'How's Caitlin doing?' says Rose after a while, and Mack takes a moment to answer as though choosing his words carefully.

'She's all right,' he says. 'But I had to let her know what the consequences of discussing my work might have been, however upsetting it was to hear. She knows I'm lucky to have hung on to my job.'

Rose winces at the thought and murmurs, 'Well, you're not the only one, Mack. It could so easily have been my fuck-up that caused the leak.'

He turns to her, a sad smile on his face.

'It wasn't, though, was it? It was mine.'

They drive in silence. The strange conversation with DS Moony hovers constantly at the edge of Rose's mind. She debates telling Mack about what happened in the pub that night. But how can she explain the parting shot from Moony?

'I think you know why, Rose Gifford.'

Mack finding out about her mother – she's not sure she could cope with that. It's too heavy a weight to bear. So she says nothing.

They pull into the car park of the hospital and drive around in circles until an elderly man hunkered down in the driver's seat of an old, immaculate Volvo painstakingly reverses out of a space, one inch at a time.

Rose pulls in and they leave the car, shivering at the drop in temperature since they left the station.

It's a vast modern building with a glass atrium and a Costa Coffee that is shuttered and dark at this time of evening. Rose thinks longingly of the coffee and muffin she might have had otherwise.

They ask at reception for the High Dependency Unit, where Kirsty has been moved from Intensive Care, and are directed up a level and along several long corridors with shiny floors.

A blonde, fresh-faced nurse with pink cheeks carrying a clipboard lets them in when they buzz for admission at the HDU. Smiling, she introduces herself in a soft Irish accent as Carly Jameson, the senior nurse in this ward.

They walk down a corridor with subdued lighting, past a series of rooms occupied by elderly patients, until they come to the nurses' desk. A tall, dark male nurse is talking to a middle-aged black woman, presumably a relative of one of the patients. She is crying quietly, and the nurse is speaking to her in a low, comforting tone.

'Let's go in here a moment,' says Carly, and they step into a small room with a couple of chairs and a box of grubby toys in one corner.

They sit down. Carly puts on a pair of glasses that are strung around her neck and examines the clipboard.

'So, as you know, Miss Perryman was admitted yesterday in a state of unconsciousness,' she says, glancing up and then reading from the paper in front of her. 'Her GCS was 3/15, which is very low. Sorry,' she pauses with a small smile, 'that's the Glasgow Coma Scale, something we use to determine how severe a coma is and how to treat that patient.'

'Thanks,' says Mack. 'Go on.'

She continues to read: 'She was not responding to verbal command or deep sensory stimuli. There were no motor reflexes, even after painful stimuli like prodding her feet with something sharp. Subconjunctival haemorrhages were observed in both eyes.' She looks up. 'So, this was pretty clear evidence of manual suffocation.'

'Can we see her?' says Rose. 'Is she up to being questioned about what happened?'

'Well, she was very distressed when she came around, and it took a while to convince her that she was safe. We had to give her a very mild sedative to help her sleep because she was trying to get out of the bed and became a little physical with one of our nurses. But we can see if she is awake now, if you like?'

'Yes, thank you,' says Mack, and the three of them get up at once.

Further down the corridor, they enter the room in which Kirsty is sleeping. Her round face is very pale against the pillow and her lips are slightly open.

They pause in the doorway and the patient suddenly jerks awake, saying, in a groggy voice like someone drunk, 'Mush shtay awake . . .'

Mack in the lead, followed by Rose and Carly, they enter cautiously.

'Kirsty?' says Carly, her voice loud in the quiet room. 'These people have come to see you, OK? They're police officers. Are you up to having a wee word just now?'

Kirsty peers at them, frowning, and then her eyes widen.

'Yes,' she says, her voice hoarse.

They come and sit down next to her on the two chairs in the room.

Despite the reddened eyes, dry lips and pale skin, she's still pretty.

Mack introduces them, but before he can say anything else, Rose cuts in.

'Why were you saying you shouldn't sleep?' says Rose. Mack flashes her a look, but Rose has a feeling Kirsty has a very short window for this conversation and wants to make sure they get to the point quickly.

Kirsty's eyes fill with tears, which she blinks away before replying.

'Because he's going to come back and get me then,' she says.

'Who are you talking about, Kirsty?' says Mack in a gentle tone. 'The man who hurt you in your home? Can you tell us anything about him?'

Kirsty shakes her head then swallows. Painfully, it appears, because she winces.

'Wears a balaclava. Black clothes. He kept coming and coming and then he was really there.'

Her eyes widened on the word 'really', which makes Mack and Rose exchange glances.

'What do you mean about him coming before that?' says Mack, leaning forward. 'Had he been in your property before the night of the attack?'

Kirsty closes her eyes and tears seep from beneath her eyelids onto her cheeks.

'You won't believe me,' she says, then opens her eyes and points at Rose. '*She* didn't believe me before.'

Rose shifts in her seat. 'I'm truly sorry about that, Kirsty,' she says. 'But we want to try and do everything we can to make sure we get this man and lock him up now he has attacked you. Is there anything else you can tell us about his appearance? Height or build?'

'He's really big,' she says. 'He straddled my chest, stopping me from breathing. Then he pressed something on my face . . .' she starts to cry in earnest.

Rose and Mack both glance anxiously at the door, expecting Nurse Carly to appear any second and throw them out. Rose continues hurriedly.

'Is there anyone at all, an ex-boyfriend, perhaps, who has been bothering you? Anyone who might have given you reason to be scared?'

'No, no, no, you're not listening!' says Kirsty, voice rising and so hoarse Rose winces to hear the painful effort involved. 'There's no one! He's a stranger and he gets in, even when everything is locked up! He gets into my sleep!'

'Kirsty,' says Rose evenly, 'can you tell us whether you are in a Facebook group called Sleepyheads?'

The pale woman in the bed frowns at her, then nods.

Mack and Rose look at each other, eyebrows raised.

'Why?' she rasps.

'Can you tell us whether you have been in contact with anyone there?' says Rose. 'Maybe a poster called Somnus?'

Kirsty shakes her head vigorously. 'That group's the only thing that's kept me sane,' she says. 'You don't understand.' Her voice almost disappears into a croak and she makes an alarming sound as though struggling to draw breath.

Mack starts to say something, and Carly materializes from nowhere at the door. She bustles in.

'Right, I think our patient needs another wee rest, OK, officers?'

'OK,' says Mack, and gets up. Rose remains in place a moment longer.

'Can you tell us why you think he's coming back, Kirsty?' she says. 'You're safe here, you know.'

'No,' Kirsty turns her head from side to side, still crying. 'He came back last night in my dreams.'

'Come on,' says Carly with brisk cheerfulness, 'you were only after having a nightmare and I promise no one can hurt you here.' She looks sharply up at Mack and Rose. 'I'll show you out, officers.'

*

As they are leaving the HDU a young nurse with short dark hair and large, protruding eyes is coming in. She stops in the doorway.

'Are you police officers?' she says. 'Here about the patient who was suffocated?'

Mack and Rose exchange an amused look. Is it that obvious? 'We are,' says Mack. 'Can we help you with something?'

The nurse looks around nervously and then beckons to them to come away from the double doors.

'The thing is,' she says conspiratorially, 'I don't know if I should even mention it.' She pauses. 'It's a little bit . . .' she bites her lip, '. . . weird.'

'If there is anything,' says Mack, 'that you think might be relevant to what has happened to this young woman, then I would urge you to tell us.'

'Yes,' says Rose, 'you never know what might be important and what might not until you've got all the details. We always say to people that they should tell us about anything, anything at all, that didn't seem right or worried them in some way.'

The nurse bites her lip and nods uncertainly.

'What's your name?' says Rose, taking out her notebook.

'It's Allie,' says the young woman. 'Allie Carter.' Then her words come out in a torrent.

'I was on duty last night,' she says, 'and it was about three in the morning when I heard funny noises coming from the patient's bed . . .' Her eyes dart around, minnow-like, and she runs her tongue over chapped lips before resuming. 'I looked over and, for a moment, I thought I saw someone there.'

'Oh yes?' says Mack. He and Rose, all alert, exchange glances. 'Did you go and check properly?'

'Well, this is the weird thing,' says Allie, bush baby eyes pinned to their faces. 'I went over to look, but there was no one there. There's no other way out of the ward, so I assumed one of the other patients had got out of bed. But everyone else in there is far too sick to go wandering about. I came on at ten and no one came past me.'

153

'OK,' says Rose slowly, her excitement fading away. 'Can you describe exactly what you saw?'

Allie blushes. 'I think it was a . . . a man in dark clothes but, like I say, it was for a split second. It was more a weird . . . shadow. And no one was there when I went to look. The patient was moaning and moving in the bed,' she says. 'All her vitals were all right, apart from a slightly elevated heart rate, and because I could see her eyes flickering really fast under her lids, I decided she was having a bad dream and that it was best to leave her.'

The nurse plucks at the hem of her tunic and can barely meet their eyes.

'Look,' she says, 'like I say, it was most probably just a trick of the light or something. It's a funny time, three a.m., isn't it? I shouldn't have said anything.'

'Do you have CCTV for this ward?' Mack says, and the nurse nods.

'Oh yes, we've had it through the whole hospital for a few years.'

'Right,' says Mack. 'Well, I think chances are that you're right and it was your eyes playing tricks on you, but my colleague and I will request the CCTV and watch carefully to see if there is anything suspicious, OK?'

Her mouth is set in a grim line as she nods. 'OK,' she says. 'I'm sorry if I've wasted your time. It was . . . odd, that's all. I'd best get back to work.'

She hurries off, head down.

They don't speak as they follow the winding corridor around and walk down the steps to the ground floor.

'Well,' says Rose, with a wry grin, 'I'm looking forward to hearing you tell the boss that we need to expend manpower looking for a "weird shadow" on the CCTV.'

'Quite,' says Mack in a voice laced with weariness.

They're almost back at the car when Rose stops so suddenly, Mack almost crashes into her.

'Look,' she says, 'let's go and find whoever deals with the

CCTV and have a look. They should be happy to show us, and a formal request will most probably be a waste of time. What do you think?'

'Good idea,' says Mack, and they turn back to the hospital entrance.

The Security Suite, as it is called, is housed in a separate building behind the main hospital. Mack knocks on the door and after a few moments a large man with a greasy ponytail and a shirt stretched tight over the mound of his belly pokes his head out and says, 'Yeah?'

Mack produces his badge and introduces them. The man, who says his name is Steve Cresswell, looks taken aback, but isn't so surprised he doesn't have brain space to let his eyes skim Rose all over before he asks how he can help.

'We're investigating the attempted murder of a young woman who is a patient here,' says Mack. 'One of the nurses thought she may have seen something on the ward in the middle of the night.'

Cresswell's eyes narrow. 'People can't simply wander into wards in the middle of the night, you know.'

Rose puts on her most sympathetic smile. 'No, we know that,' she says. 'It's probably nothing, but we ought to check. We could put a request in for the file but we thought we'd save everyone's time by coming along while we're here and taking a quick look. That all right with you?'

Cresswell's eyes crinkle slightly in an approximation of a smile. 'Don't see why not. Come on in?'

He opens the door so that they have to come close to him to enter and Rose gets a whiff of meaty breath and body odour, which makes her inwardly shudder. She's sure Mack is smirking and she gives him a sharp look that causes him to cough and mask laughter.

Cresswell pulls over the only other chair in the room and offers it to Rose, who smiles and says, 'I have to let my older, superior officer sit in these circumstances. It's the law.'

Mack gives her a look and takes the seat.

'So which ward is it you want?' says Cresswell, and Mack tells him. He begins to fiddle with buttons, a half-smile on his face.

'I'm a big fan of police dramas on telly,' he says, 'I like to think we're all on the same page, you guys and me.'

'Absolutely,' says Mack, deadpan.

'Right,' says Cresswell, 'here's last night. What time do you want?'

'Can we look at the period between, say, two forty-five a.m. and three fifteen?' says Mack, and Creswell presses some more buttons until there is an image of the ward from the far corner. All the beds are visible, including Kirsty Perryman's. She is asleep and quite still.

Rose looks at her watch. They ought to be getting back soon.

As if picking up on her thoughts, Mack says, 'Can you slowly move forward from there?'

'Sure,' says Creswell, and the image shifts. The two other patients do a speeded-up turn over in the bed. As the time capture shows the hour creeping closer to 3 a.m., Kirsty Perryman begins to shift. At this speed her head seems to thrash.

'Go back a bit from there,' says Mack, and they all peer closely at the image, now in normal time. 'There!'

Kirsty Perryman slowly turns her head from side to side and grips onto the sides of the bed, her face distressed and stretched as though she is crying.

They watch her do this for several moments and then she begins clawing at her throat as though fighting something or someone off.

Rose sits further forward in her seat. She looks at Mack again, her heart racing, but he is expressionless.

Then they watch the nurse Allie Carter appearing by the bedside and she gently touches Kirsty's hand and looks at the screen monitoring her vital signs for a few moments. Kirsty stills and then turns over in the bed, apparently deeply asleep again. Allie walks around the ward, peering at each bed as she does so, then stops in the middle of the room as if at a loss. They see her pull a cardigan closer around her shoulders and, with one more look around the ward, she disappears from sight, presumably back to the nurses' station.

Rose waits for Mack to speak first.

He turns to her and says, 'Well, I think we have everything we need, thank you, Mr Cresswell. Pretty clear no one was there. Shall we make a move, DC Gifford?'

Rose nods but says nothing as they take their leave and walk back to the car.

'Waste of time,' says Mack through a yawn, 'but at least we know we covered all bases and checked it out.'

'Yeah,' says Rose softly. 'At least we've done that.'

Mack is caught up with texts in the car on the way back to the station and doesn't notice that Rose is white-faced and silent, or that she is gripping the steering wheel hard to hide the fact that her hands are shaking. Grateful for the thick traffic, she tries to marshal her tumbling thoughts.

Because, unlike Mack and Cresswell, Rose saw something on that CCTV.

Something that couldn't possibly have been there.

23

Rose goes straight into the Ladies when they get back to the station and sits on the closed lid of the toilet with her head in her hands. She's sweating, and her stomach twists inside her. Touching her hand to her forehead, she winces at the heat there. Is she sick? This is not the time to come down with the flu.

But she's not sure whether this is a bug or a physical manifestation of the turmoil she is experiencing inside.

Pressing the tips of her fingers into her eyelids until she sees coloured swirls and blobs floating by, she tries to rationalize what she saw on the CCTV footage of Kirsty Perryman's bed. A trick of the light? An error of the digital film?

She's not even sure she can describe the appearance of whatever it was. It was more like a shadow, but a shadow flickering in a sickening way that made her think of insect wings, beating hard. It's like she can even hear the rhythmic noise in her mind, although there was no sound on the tape.

The darkness of the shadow . . . that was the other thing. You think you recognize degrees of darkness, from a blackout blind bedroom to the eye mask she wore in bed for a while. But this was entirely different. It was as though it had a depth and texture she had never seen before. A darkness that made her stomach heave with revulsion.

And suddenly Rose Gifford is so angry she can hardly bear

it. She balls her hands into fists at her sides and has to stop herself from thrashing about and beating the walls of the cubicle until they smash apart.

This is simply *not who she wants to be* . . .

She doesn't want to be a person who sees things others don't. She wants to be an ordinary policewoman. A sceptic. Not someone who thinks evil is a thing that can be seen flickering and dancing like a giant, ugly moth over a sleeping woman's bed. After all, just because she saw the same trick of the light that nurse saw doesn't mean she is her mother's daughter, does it? Or, rather, the person Adele Gifford always wanted her to be.

No one notices how quiet she is as the working day finally comes to a close. Her face feels stiff with the effort of keeping under control all the spiralling thoughts that are rushing at her, every which way.

She spends a good twenty minutes she doesn't have googling the symptoms of brain tumours. It feels as though it wouldn't be too bad if this were the explanation for everything that has been happening to her lately. They could cut it out of her. Give her some drugs or chemotherapy to make it go away. No more dead mother. No evil fluttering above a woman's bed, no nightmare form made visible in broad daylight.

But if it was something she had conjured out of her own head, what about the nurse, Allie? She was the one who saw whatever it was first.

Time to go home. Rose grabs her bag and coat and scurries out of the station before anyone can speak to her. As soon as she is in her car, she takes out her phone and stares at it for several moments before reaching into her bag and hunting for the business card.

With trembling hands, she dials the number.

It's answered immediately.

'DC Gifford?'

'Yes,' says Rose, wincing at the eagerness she hears.

There's an awkward silence and Rose fights the urge to hang up. But then the other woman speaks first.

'I heard about the attempted murder,' she says, followed by the suck and pop of her dragging on a cigarette magnified by the speaker. 'And that the victim had been complaining about nightmares in the same way as Hannah Scott.'

'Yes,' says Rose. 'There are big similarities. But there is something else,' she says, 'it's why I'm calling.'

'Go on.'

Rose stalls. She remembers the sickly lavender smell and Hannah Scott's lifeless body. Her arm itches and prickles and she longs to shred her nails against the skin there, to bring some relief from the turmoil inside her. She pictures Kirsty Perryman lying in her hospital bed, helpless against some entity that has been stalking her for months.

'Are you still there?' Sharply now.

She closes her eyes and begins to tell Moony about the visit to the hospital, from beginning to end. From the brief interview with Kirsty Perryman, to the nurse telling them in frightened tones about what she saw, to her seeing the CCTV and there being something very odd about it.

Moony doesn't interrupt and it's only the audible pulls on her cigarette that let Rose know she is still there. When she finishes speaking, she feels worn out and waits for a response.

'Interesting,' says Moony finally. 'Very interesting indeed. What did your colleague – Mack, I think he's called – what did he say?'

Rose looks up at the ceiling as though bracing herself.

'Well, he didn't seem to notice anything out of the ordinary.' This is a deeply painful admission to have to make and for a microsecond Rose thinks she might cry.

There's another silence.

'OK,' says Moony. 'I'd like you to come to my division tomorrow to discuss this further.'

Rose feels a thrum of panic. 'But I can't do that!'

'I'm going to square it with Rowland, don't worry,' says

Moony. 'I'll ask her to message you to confirm in the morning, and I'll text you the details.' Before Rose can gather a sentence together, Moony says, 'I'll see you at nine a.m.,' and the line goes dead.

As she puts the phone down in her lap, all she can manage is 'Shit', said very quietly.

24

In the car, Rose reads the address and punches the postcode into the satnav. It's a half-hour journey to a place she has never been to before, through Edmonton and not far from the Lee Valley stadium, which Rose knows was a venue in the 2012 Olympics.

Sure enough, a text from the boss came through at 7.45 saying, *Permission given to conduct research at UCIT. DS Moony to instruct.*

No getting out of it then.

Rose has caught the school run, and as she painstakingly attempts to join the A10, it feels like the whole of North London is sitting high in four-by-fours with grim expressions and a determination not to budge even an inch. Rose's outrage has burned down to a tired, sad feeling, as she contemplates the tiresome business of having to negotiate a new team of people. And who even is Moony? Rose has a feeling she isn't going to like the answer.

When Rose did her police training, she wasn't only looking for a career, she was looking for a sense of belonging that she had never experienced before, not at school and certainly not in her own home. For the last ten years, the Met has been her family.

But it hasn't come easily. She knows that she can be closed-off and she is living for a time when she is free of her mother's . . . what? Ghost? Is that what it is? Sometimes it feels as though the albatross that she carries around as a dead weight – the literal dead weight –is going to crush her. The only way she can cope is to keep a lid firmly on this side of her life and pretend it isn't happening.

She wishes she could tell Sam all this.

It takes more than half an hour before Rose is driving past the stadium and a cinema complex and then into streets with slightly dilapidated semi-detached houses. There is a patch of blue on the satnav coming up that signifies a reservoir in the distance, and the address is before that.

It's one of those November days where the grey sky bleeds into everything. Even the buildings seemed to be stained by a kind of weary gloom. The trees retain a few sad, ochre-coloured leaves that do little to lighten the grey.

The satnav tells her she has reached her destination as Rose drives over a humpback bridge and sees what looks like an old factory or mill building on her left. High gates in rusty mesh bar the way in and there is a battered sign saying, *Private Property of Thames Water Authority. Keep Out.*

In frustration, Rose reaches for her phone and looks again at the address she was given by Moony. It simply says UCIT, with a street address and postcode.

She gets out of the car, shivering as the biting air meets the exposed skin of her face, hands and neck. Walking down the road, Rose carefully checks door numbers. But all logic suggests the old water board building is the one she is after.

Rose goes up to the gate and on closer inspection, sees there is a basic intercom, with a single button. She presses it, waits, and then jumps when a loud buzz signifies that she can enter. Pushing the individual gate at the side it springs open and she walks through, looking up at the building in front of her.

The sun breaks through the clouds, turning the long, multi-paned windows at the front of the building to flaming rectangles. The building is made from reddish bricks, splashed all over with strata of graffiti that maybe cover decades.

There is a small car park on the other side of some scraggy low-cut grass and what looks like another entrance over there. Rose makes a mental note to ask if she can park her own car in there.

It's a more interesting-looking old building than Silverton Street nick, but it's in the middle of bloody nowhere. Rose can't see where the nearest shop might be, or tube station, should she have car trouble.

Internally grumbling, Rose walks into the main entrance and sees a reception desk that looks like something from the Second World War, behind which is a bank of electrical boxes of equal vintage. When a tall, large-framed young woman suddenly appears from a door to the right of the reception desk, Rose can only stare. The woman is dressed in a 1940s blouse and high-waisted trousers. Her hair is in a peroxide-blond Victory roll and her bright red lips are stretched in a toothy smile. She looks as though she has stepped out of one of those old wartime showreels Rose has seen on YouTube.

'Hi!' says the young woman, 'I'm Scarlett!' She must clock that Rose is eyeing her clothes because she laughs good-naturedly and says, 'Did you think you were seeing a ghost for a minute?'

Rose can't stop her expression closing over at this and she mumbles that she didn't, but Scarlett doesn't seem perturbed by her frostiness.

'I dressed like this before I worked here,' she says cheerfully, 'but I do kind of go with the décor!' She opens the door she came through. 'I'm guessing you are DC Gifford?'

'Yes,' says Rose, 'Rose.'

'The boss is expecting you,' says Scarlett as Rose follows her into a narrow corridor with a damp smell and uneven flooring. The ceiling is low, and the walls are painted bricks in a yellowish white. A battered sign with a finger painted in black on what was probably once a white background says *Office, this way*.

'What is this building?' says Rose as Scarlett clip-clops ahead of her in a pair of red and white spotted Mary-Jane shoes with a large bow, skilfully avoiding a small puddle of water on the ground.

'It used to be a pumping station,' says Scarlett, turning back to look at Rose with a smile. 'Then in the seventies it was a glove factory, but it's been abandoned for years. It's practically derelict. Probably ought to be condemned!' She says this so cheerfully, Rose wonders if they are having two totally different conversations.

This is a workplace?

They turn into another, wider corridor with a higher ceiling and the slightly claustrophobic feeling Rose has had since she came into the building eases.

'Here we are,' says Scarlett, when they reach a door that is modern and looks entirely out of place. She holds the card on a lanyard around her neck against a square panel and waits a beat, before pushing the door open. 'Welcome to UCIT,' she says and gestures for Rose to go first into the office in front of them.

Rose's sense of disorientation increases as she steps into the large, open-plan office. She feels a pinch of dizziness somewhere between her eyes and it must show because Scarlett, at her side, makes a small sound.

'Yeah, it's a weird room,' she says. 'There's something off about it. Boss says it's only the shoddy conversion, but I some-times wonder . . .'

'Wonder what?' says Rose, at her hesitation.

Scarlett drops her voice, so Rose has to lean in to hear her reply. 'Whether the building doesn't want us here.'

Rose turns to look at her, unable to hide her expression. 'The *building* doesn't want you?'

Scarlett nods earnestly, and Rose suppresses the weary sigh she can feel rising inside. What is she doing here? There must be more important work back at the station.

'If you look around,' Scarlett continues, 'all the angles are a bit off.'

Rose looks again and can see immediately that this is what has caused the slightly unnerving feeling. A friend of hers got into Feng Shui and suddenly became adamant that we all possess a sense of balance about rooms; and that if things are not as they should be, the effect will be very uncomfortable. Rose thinks she finally understands this, looking at the office stretched in front of her.

'Surely it's just been done badly, as DS Moony says?'

'Hmm,' says Scarlett. 'Maybe. I'm not convinced though.'

The other woman's phone buzzes then and Scarlett says, 'Ooh, 'scuse me for a sec,' before going over to the desk nearest the door, where a toy rabbit sits incongruously on top of standard-issue box files. There is also a large, colourful flower knitted from wool in a pot and several photos that she can't see from here.

Rose looks around, feeling the odd sensation she felt before passing almost as fast as it came.

The room looks like any reasonable modern office, but with huge windows along one wall that let in such murky light, it's as if they're underwater. She can see only three other people working in here, despite the size of the room. Each one has their own little island, quite distinct from the rest, with what looks like a briefing area over in one corner with a whiteboard and, incongruously, a sofa.

Sheila Moony is over at the far side, sitting back from her desk and talking into the phone, quietly but with animation. Twirling a pencil through the fingers of her free hand, she stares ahead and doesn't seem to have noticed Rose's arrival. Scarlett has become distracted by her own phone buzzing, so Rose is left to stand, feeling foolish.

A tall man in his mid-thirties with brown skin and short, cropped hair looks up from a desk over by the windows. He gets to his feet and approaches Rose with a smile. His eyes are warm and friendly.

'Hi,' he says, extending a hand. 'DC Adam Lacey.'

'DC Rose Gifford.' Rose shakes his hand, conscious that her

own is a little clammy. She catches a whiff of some kind of light, citrus aftershave that smells clean and fresh.

Lacey looks around and sees that Moony is off the phone but has her head down and is ferociously tapping away at her computer with two fingers. He hesitates, as if unsure what to do, then says, 'Come with me.'

They approach Moony's desk. There is a motorcycle helmet sitting on a pile of leathers. Moony's? Hard to imagine her as a biker, Rose thinks, especially as there is also a large, black handbag in crocodile leather Rose knows to be a Celine. She has no interest in handbags, but there had been a day last summer when she was round at Sam's and his sister Zainab had insisted on showing Rose the £2,250 object of her lust in a fashion magazine. Expensive handbags and motorbikes don't usually go together, but everything about Moony is hard to categorize.

On the desk there is a photograph of a smiling woman and man dressed in leathers and standing in front of two motorbikes. The backdrop is a baked red landscape, desert, maybe Australia. A bag of Haribo sweets sits open on the desk and Moony idly roots in the bag for one and pops it into her mouth.

She either doesn't see them standing there, or she is not interested in the fact that they are because she continues her two-digit assault on the keyboard, features drawstringed again into a scowl.

Adam coughs politely and Moony's head snaps up. Rose has absolutely no doubt that she had been aware of them all along and irritation zips through her. Is this a minor punishment for the other evening in the pub? In Rose's view, people who play these kind of mind games can frankly do one. She arranges her expression into one that is hopefully open without being eager, but with a smidgen of 'I know your game'. It's quite a challenge.

'Ah,' says Moony, giving Rose a blatant head-to-toe appraisal. 'Adam, I'm flat out this morning. Can you give Rose the intro talk?

He looks crestfallen. 'Oh really?' he says. 'But didn't you want—'

But Moony has turned back to her screen. The conversation is clearly over.

Adam gives Rose an apologetic smile and then gestures for her to follow him.

They go to his desk and he pulls up a second chair. His desk has a photograph of two young children, presumably his own, gappy-smiled and sun-hatted on a beach. A blue paper file sits next to his computer and Rose thinks she must have misread the title before he whisks it away into a drawer. She's convinced she saw the words: *ESP and remote imaging.*

He smiles at her and Rose tentatively smiles back. She tries to ignore the very slight tingle in her stomach as she catches another trace of his warm, clean smell.

Not the time, Rose, she thinks. Look where this got you last time.

'Look,' he says, 'first up, do you need anything? Coffee? Trip to the Ladies?'

Rose is actually desperate for a wee, so she smiles gratefully. 'I wouldn't mind both,' she says.

'Right,' says Adam. 'Here's a lanyard to get you back in,' he hands her a standard police-issue visitor lanyard. 'And the toilets are back the way you came, then sharp left down the first corridor, then right. How do you take your coffee?'

Rose makes her way out of the office and follows Adam's route, turning left into a corridor she hadn't noticed on the way in. This place is a regular Tardis, much bigger inside than it looks. The walls and ceiling are a sickly yellow institutional colour, the floor a shiny brown wood. Doors with numbers on them line the corridor.

There's a strange noise coming from somewhere nearby, a panicky shushing sound, like something is trapped.

She hesitates then gently turns the handle of the first room on her right. The door swings open and she steps inside.

The room is huge, with dark walls and two skylights above letting columns of winter light into the gloom. There is a single chair in the middle of the room. Black and white graffiti on one side of the room says, puzzlingly, 'Very, very, very' and a splashier one spells out the name 'Zerx' in yellow and green. The sound is coming from here, but she still can't see what it is.

A sour smell reaches Rose's nose then and she pictures someone in an old movie being interrogated in this room, on that chair, maybe losing control of their bladder. Shuddering, she hurries out and stares down the corridor. It ends in total darkness, a passageway into a void. This place is creepy, she thinks, hurrying to the turning Adam mentioned.

In the Ladies, which is old but clean and tidy, she uses the toilet and washes her hands. There are large industrial pipes snaking across the ceiling and a rusty old vending machine on the wall that once dispensed 'sanitary towels with belt'. Baffling. In its heyday the machine also offered tights and breath mints. Evidently everything the modern woman needed in 1950.

As Rose exits the bathroom, she hears a new sound, a rhythmic squeaking. Turning, she sees a woman slowly, painstakingly manoeuvring a large trolley. A metal urn takes pride of place and there are white mugs – the tin kind you might take camping – piled neatly alongside it. The woman, who is definitely beyond retirement age, smiles tiredly at Rose. She is wearing a faded overall with small sprigs of flowers on it and a headscarf covers her hair. Her face has a weather-beaten look and wispy grey curls peek out from under the scarf. Before Rose can say anything, the woman takes a turn down another, unseen corridor on the left.

She can't help feeling amused at the eccentricity of having an actual tea lady and she briefly wonders what other offices might be in this building. She hadn't remembered seeing any others listed outside, but it's doubtful the police would be paying the wages of a tea lady alone.

Letting herself back into the office, she is met by a bright smile from Scarlett, then makes her way over to Adam's desk, where two steaming mugs of coffee stand waiting. Not the mugs she'd seen on the tea lady's trolley.

'One of the perks of working here,' says Adam, raising his own mug to his lips, 'is that Moony is a snob about this stuff so you get really excellent coffee.'

'Oh, great,' says Rose, taking a sip and instantly feeling herself perk up. He's right, it is good. She sees now that there is a small kitchen area to one side with a proper filter coffee machine.

'You don't use the tea lady then?' she says. Adam's perplexed expression makes her lower her cup, uncertainly.

'I'm sorry?' he says. 'Tea lady?'

Rose's smile falters. 'The old woman? With the trolley?'

Adam is frowning. 'I'm not, um . . .' and trails off.

Rose, feeling as though she has already made a terrible faux pas, glances at Scarlett, who is hovering near a filing cabinet. If she had looked cheerful before, now she positively exudes delight as she beams over at Rose.

Adam starts to speak again, evidently as keen to fill the embarrassing silence as she is.

'Right,' he says, 'so do you know what UCIT stands for?'

'Something to do with, um, compliance?' says Rose. 'Although what that has got to do with my cases is anyone's guess.'

Adam's smile falters for a second and then he runs a hand over his scalp.

'Ah,' he says with a laugh. 'No, it's not that. We sometimes call it the cold cases team as a bit of an in-joke because of the nature of what we do.'

This whole conversation is making Rose want to scratch the itch that has started up with fiery heat in her arm, but she keeps her hands to her sides.

'UCIT stands for the Uncharted Crimes Investigation Team.'

Rose pauses with her mug to her lips.

'Um, sorry for being thick,' she says, 'but I don't get what you mean by "uncharted".' She thinks about Mack's words in the car and fights an almost overpowering desire to get the hell out of here.

Adam takes a long drink of his coffee, brow scrunched, as though gearing up for something difficult.

'Look,' he says, meeting her eyes again. 'When I first started working here, I thought I must have lost my bloody mind. I almost ran a mile. So it's a bit of an adjustment and you have to try and trust me when I say that after a while all this becomes normal.'

'OK,' says Rose, her unease increasing by the moment.

'What we do here,' he says patiently, 'is to look into cases that don't seem to fit into any of our . . .' he pauses, 'recognized ways of thinking.'

Rose cradles her cup and gives him a grin. 'I'm sorry, I'm still not getting it. What kind of cases?'

Adam puffs air out through his cheeks.

'OK,' he says carefully, 'it's probably best to start with an example. At the moment we are doing some research – because that's what we mainly do – helping Oxfordshire police with a misper. Young lad called Solly Thompson, who disappeared a year ago in Banbury. It didn't make the news. Unfortunately, the press gets more interested in, being frank, middle-class white girls than lads like Solly.'

'OK,' says Rose. 'So you're doing all the usual stuff? Surely that's a bread-and-butter case for Oxford?'

Adam pulls a face. 'Maybe it's easier if I show you.'

He turns to his desk and starts tapping away at his computer, opening various folders until he comes to one marked 'Thompson disappearance'. Then he opens up some CCTV footage that shows a young black boy of about fifteen in what looks like a newsagent's. There is the usual grainy black-and-white quality, but it's clearer than many Rose has had the misfortune to scrutinize for hours. The boy is looking at the sweets and crisps, then glances up sharply as though someone has spoken to him. Then it's as if he has been removed from the film. He's gone.

Rose peers closer at the screen and back at Adam, who is watching her carefully.

'What happened to the CCTV?' says Rose.

'Nothing,' says Adam. 'We've had it checked by the best technical people the Met can find, both in and beyond the Force.

The footage isn't damaged or doctored. Solly Thompson *literally* disappeared.'

Rose is unable to hold back the scoffing sound that bursts from her lips, but Adam levelly meets her eye.

'It seems,' he continues, 'that poor Solly isn't the only person this has happened to. There are reports going back four hundred years of people disappearing from that exact spot.'

Rose's mouth is literally hanging open now.

'I'm sorry,' she says, with a laugh of embarrassment. The feeling is for him, because he is clearly nuts. 'I'm still struggling here. What do you think happened to him then? Did a bogeyman take him?'

'No,' says Adam, with an exaggerated tolerance that is starting to get under Rose's skin, 'but that particular shop is located at the intersection of a couple of ley lines, and that particular spot has been associated with disappearances and strange happenings since records began.'

Rose goes to say something else, her cheeks hot, but it seems that Adam has finally run out of patience.

'Look, Rose,' he says, 'this is why it's better if Moony does this part. She doesn't pussyfoot about like me. The simple fact is, we exist to look into crimes that may have an esoteric or even supernatural explanation.'

Feeling oddly out of breath, as though she has just been running, Rose fights the urge to get out of her seat and flee. It's so strong her foot taps on the floor, beating out an anxious rhythm that reminds her of Leon Gavril's nervous energy in the interview room the other day.

'So, what . . . ?' she says. 'You're like the Met's version of the bloody *X Files* or something?'

She waits for Adam to laugh. To reassure her that no, it's nothing like a daft television show. This is the Met. This is the place she came to escape stuff like this.

Instead, he seesaws his head from side to side. 'We have heard that before,' he says, 'but we don't tend to get a lot of alien abductions in North London.'

172

She stares and he laughs, finally. 'That was a joke!' he says. 'What I mean is, we don't go looking for little green men. But we do, if I can be blunt, look into some weird shit.'

He pauses. 'That, basically, is what the uncharted bit means.'

'Weird shit,' mumbles Rose, and Adam smiles kindly.

Scarlett is back at the filing cabinet, and it's clear she is keenly listening to every word. She turns and says, 'Ghosts, ghouls and things that go bump in the night!'

'Excuse me, I just need a minute.' Rose is on her feet and heading towards the door. She wants to get into her car and leave, but either this is all a huge practical joke at her expense, or Rowland sent her here to do something, knowing exactly what this place was about. If Rowland has sanctioned this, then it's real. Everything she ever wanted from being a police officer is up in the air.

Her stomach is churning, heat blasting up her neck and face. She narrowly makes it into a cubicle in the Ladies before vomiting up foul coffee-smelling sick until she is empty and sweating. Rose wipes her mouth and exits the cubicle on shaky legs. She holds her mouth to the tap and takes a long drink, then splashes water on her face.

An annoyingly gentle tap at the main door to the toilets is followed by the entrance of Scarlett, unsmiling and looking concerned.

'Are you all right?' she says. Rose can't bear to meet her eye. She responds with a brisk nod.

'Only,' Scarlett continues, 'I wouldn't have thought it would be quite such a shock. Learning about what we do here.'

'Right,' says Rose. 'Well it is.' She busies herself with hand towels. 'I'm afraid I don't believe in this sort of thing and so I'm struggling with it.'

The small laugh from Scarlett takes her by surprise. It seems rude, from such an obvious people pleaser. She glances sharply at the other woman who looks startled, the smile gone from her face again.

'Oh,' she says, and a blush creeps up her cheeks. 'Only, I assumed, because of you seeing Hilda . . .'

'What are you on about, Scarlett?'

Rose is so tired, she can't be bothered with any more mad conversations today.

Scarlett is studying her face while playing with her necklace, a little gold bird of some kind against her skin that is blotchy with her obvious awkwardness.

'I don't know what she was really called,' says Scarlett, in a rush. 'But that's my name for her. The old tea lady. You saw her too!' Rose experiences the tipping sensation in the room again. 'You're the only other person who has ever been able to see her!' says Scarlett. Then, thoughtfully, 'I assumed that's why you're here. Because of what you can do. See the dead, I mean.'

25

The sheet is entangled with his legs and he rips it away and onto the floor. He sits on the side of the bed, his body slick with sweat under the dark clothes he likes to wear, head in hands.

His heart is beating so hard it's as though his body and not only his mind has returned from a trip. That happens, he's familiar with it to some extent, but it's more extreme and he takes a sip of water with a shaking hand in an effort to calm himself. It's beginning to take its toll, the travelling. He looks at his hands and watches them tremble, before forcing them under his thighs.

To be so close, twice, is almost more than he can bear. If only there were someone, or something he could consult, but he's all too aware that he is in uncharted territory and he is the lone pioneer.

He pads softly out of the bedroom and listens before going on soft feet down to the kitchen, where he begins to make chamomile tea. Despite having often recommended it to others. he's not sure whether it really does help sleep, which even for him is going to be elusive now.

Chamomile tea, lavender oil, vitamins, special lamps, routine, routine, routine. How many times has he patiently laid out the options to yet another desperate soul who claims they will do anything for a good night's sleep? And they are so grateful, they'll try anything.

These thoughts calm him because it's a welcome reminder about how wide a hunting ground he has. It's a big city, filled with people who toss and turn, and dream.

He gazes through the kitchen window at the back garden, which is half lit by the streetlamp in the alley behind. It's snowing. Delicate flakes are tumbling from a bruised, purplish sky and a fox the rusty colour of dried blood flashes along the back fence and disappears through an unseen hole.

He feels a warm sense of affinity with the creature that slinks around the sleeping city.

Calmer now, he sips the hot tea and makes himself go through the events of the last few days.

He'd spent weeks preparing for the moment when he was finally there, physically there, in her bedroom. Standing over her, watching her sleeping, he had felt like God. This time, he knew, would be even better than the last because he knew what to expect.

The house had seemed familiar after so many 'visits', and he knew all about the cat that hissed when he was nearby, the clever thing, and the way she kept the radio on all night long. But he hadn't known about that stupid little dog. What kind of person has a dog and a cat in the same house anyway?

It had all been going so well. He had left her gift and climbed carefully onto the bed. She was just waking up, the terror like a beautiful light in her eyes. With him sitting astride her arms, she couldn't do much except buck and kick. He lifted the pillow and pressed it down over her face, waiting for her to submit to the soft darkness. Telling her to let it happen.

Then that shitty little animal came barrelling into the room and tried to attack him. He had managed to shake it off and kick it, but it was barking so much that he couldn't stand the noise and needed to get away. She was still and he thought the job was done when he left, but he had been too distracted by that animal.

When he had learned, through listening in on the police scanner, that she wasn't in fact dead, he had resisted the urge to smash every window in the building. He was itchy and angry all day, snapping at people. By bedtime he knew he had to finish the job he started.

Easy enough to find out which hospital she was in. Easy enough to take on his night form and to visit her in her half state between life and death, so like sleep itself.

But it hadn't worked. Her distress had set off the all too familiar noise and activity of the medical staff and the moment had passed.

He will have to try again. It's intolerable to think about failing after all the work he has put into this.

26

'Where are you going?'

Rose doesn't need to push past Scarlett as she heads for the door of the toilets, because the other woman moves out of the way. But Scarlett can probably sense that Rose would have shoved her out of the way had the need arisen.

Her skin is on fire and she finds she can only take small, shallow breaths. She makes her way back to the main entrance, not without a wrong turn or two along the way, during which time she is fully prepared to see any manner of twisted image her sick imagination cares to throw at her.

Have to get out.

Out. The word ricochets around her mind as if in an echo chamber.

The air is a blade against her burning skin, and she huddles by her car, hands shaking as she tries to find her keys in her overstuffed bag. Where are they? Where are the fucking *keys?*

Rose is on her knees and she can feel the rough, cold ground through her trousers. Yanking the bag open in front of her, she rummages inside, desperate fingers trying to feel the cool metal she so needs to feel.

It's only when she has been through every pocket at least three times, she realizes that she put the keys in her pocket earlier instead of her bag. Why did she do that? She never does that. She isn't thinking straight. Still, she has them now and she can open the car and get the hell—

'Where you off to, then?'

Moony is standing at the gate, a cigarette hanging out of one corner of her mouth as she flicks a plastic lighter to spark it up, her eyes narrowed and on Rose.

'I have to go,' Rose says. 'Sorry. I don't think I'm the right fit for here.'

Rose opens the car door but Moony hurries over before she can get inside.

'Wait a minute, DC Gifford.' Her voice is hard, and Rose forces herself to meet the other woman's gaze. Moony looks like she is gritting her teeth, her jaw set and her small, bright eyes fixed on Rose in a way that makes her squirm even more inside. She wants to claw at the rash on her arm and it feels like a superhuman effort not to do so.

There's a moment of silence. Rose can hear the sound of distant traffic and a dog barking somewhere nearby. But it's so much quieter here than what she is used to. It only adds to the strange, disconnected feeling of all this.

'This something you do, is it?' says Moony. 'Disobey orders and flounce off?'

'No, I, don't, I . . .' Rose is momentarily lost for words.

'Well, explain to me what you think you're doing, then?'

Rose's mouth has gone dry and a headache, leftover from the earlier adrenaline, begins to squeeze her temples.

'I can't explain it,' she says quietly, then blurts, 'Only—'

'Only what?' Moony pulls on her cigarette, her round cheeks sucking in then releasing again.

'Only I'm not into this sort of thing, that's all. What you do here, I mean.'

As soon as she says it, she knows it is a mistake. Moony's expression hardens further.

'Right,' she says, in an icy-cold voice. 'Not proper police work, is that it?'

'I didn't say that.'

'No, but you thought it, didn't you?'

Rose has nothing to say to this.

Moony surprises her by letting out a sharp laugh and throwing her cigarette to the ground.

'Well, DC Gifford,' she says, 'I'm your superior officer so you'd better get your arse back inside that office, because there is work to be done. Police work. Isn't that what you are? A police officer?'

She doesn't wait for a response but turns and begins to walk towards the entrance again.

Rose swallows down the bitter shame rising in her throat. She thinks it must be nice to have a day that didn't involve a dressing down by a superior. She never used to have them. Now they seem to be a daily occurrence.

Feeling about twelve years old, Rose follows the other woman back into the building, trying to pep-talk herself as she goes.

She can do this. All she has to do is spend the day here, as requested, and then she can return to Silverton Street where she can be the version of herself she works so very hard to be.

Neither Adam nor Scarlett look up when they come back into the office, for which Rose feels immensely grateful. Scarlett is on a call and Adam is frowning at his computer screen.

Moony gestures for Rose to sit on the visitor chair next to her desk. The motorbike helmet is by her feet and she sits carefully, so she doesn't accidentally kick it.

'Adam!' says Moony, crossing her arms and facing Rose. 'Come on over.'

Adam gets up and comes to stand by the desk. He glances at Rose and she isn't sure if there is something sympathetic in his expression or if it's simply the way he looks. There is something reassuring about having him near, even though he is a stranger.

'Right,' says Moony. 'Repeat everything you said to me on the phone last night. I want every single detail.'

*

Describing what she saw out loud for the second time feels easier than it did the first. Maybe she will be able to get through today after all.

Maybe – and this thought is so unusual she is momentarily stunned – it's actually a relief. To not be totally alone and trapped inside a particular reality would be a huge relief. It's such a revolutionary and frightening idea that her heart immediately begins to speed up.

'Are there any other details you can tell us about the case?' says Moony. 'It was the locked room aspect that alerted me to this in the first place, but I gather there have been developments on that?'

Rose fills her in on the replacement key issued to Sofia Nikolas and the theory about how someone got through Kirsty Perryman's front door. She mentions, too, that Perryman had an alarm that had somehow been bypassed.

Adam is clearly lost in thought, his fingers idly stroking his chin and his eyes no longer on Rose. Moony says nothing.

Rose hesitates.

The man who comes in the night . . .

'The thing is,' says Rose, forcing herself on, 'both victims talked about nightmares before the attacks. Sleep paralysis episodes, specifically. They both claimed a man in a balaclava "visited" them beforehand.' Rose makes air quotes around the word 'visited'.

Moony sits forward, placing her hand on the desk. Rose notices once again that although she doesn't wear make-up or other jewellery, she has several knobbly silver rings on her small, chubby hands. They give the disconcerting impression of knuckle-dusters.

She tells Moony and Adam everything she can think of relating to the reported dreams of the two women. As she does so, she can feel herself calming down. This is police work. It doesn't feel any different. As long as she isn't going to be seeing ghosts everywhere she goes here and, perish the thought, her bloody mother can't get here.

When she is done, Moony and Adam look at each other and then Moony slaps the table. Her rings clunk against the surface.

'I knew there was something strange about this case,' she says triumphantly. 'I had this weird hunch the moment I heard about it. What do you think, Adam?'

'I don't know,' says Adam. 'It's a strange one. Might be nothing – the dream thing could be pure coincidence.'

'Oh, before I forget,' says Moony, and turns to rummage in a file on her desk. 'This is what I thought about first of all. Couple of women who supposedly got literally scared to death. Have a read.'

Rose takes the files, wishing she could discreetly leave them on the chair.

'Remind me of the details?' says Adam.

'Two odd ones,' says Moony. 'First is a woman called Mary Donovon. She was eighty-six years old, lived in a small village in Yorkshire. Had a heart condition, which killed her. Her daughter, one Clare Morton, is convinced that her mother was literally frightened to death in her bed.'

Rose looks up, a sarcastic smile tugging the corner of her mouth. 'Right,' she says. Seemingly unbothered by her response, Moony continues.

'And then we have Ronata Betts, known as Ronnie. Sixty-three and from a town about ten miles from Mary Donovon. Also had a weak heart. Also died in her bed.'

'And she was *frightened to death* too, I suppose?' says Rose.

This picture shows a younger woman with dyed black hair standing proud from her forehead. She has pencil-thin eyebrows drawn on and large, dark eyes, which are open and staring in the same manner as the other picture. Her mouth is open slightly and drooping, as though she died as she was literally about to cry.

Rose looks up. 'And she was *frightened to death* too?'

'I don't know,' says Moony in an easy tone. 'But I can tell you that her boyfriend, a long-distance lorry driver, went to the police right before Ronnie died, claiming she was being scared by someone while she was sleeping in her bed at night.' She pauses, clearly relishing the look of surprise Rose tries unsuccessfully to hide.

'. . . and I think that might sound a bit familiar to you,' says Moony. 'Anyway, have a read.'

'Thanks,' says Rose, doubtfully.

'. . . I'm wondering whether it's some form of astral projection?' Adam says.

'Go on,' says Moony, sitting forward a little.

'Well,' says Adam thoughtfully, leaning his hip on the side of the desk. 'Rose says that the alarm was on in the second victim's house, so the assailant must have been able to disable it. I'm wondering whether he was using astral projection to stake out the property in the period before he went in and carried out the attack?'

Moony makes a face. 'If that was the case, surely the victims wouldn't be able to see him. I've never heard of that happening before, have you?'

Rose has been looking back and forth between the two other police officers while they speak, feeling redundant and, once again, deeply uncomfortable about where this discussion is going. What the hell is astral projection?

Her feelings must be writ large on her face because Adam flashes her a grin.

'You're wondering what we're talking about, right?'

'Well, um . . .'

Adam laughs. 'Honestly, it really does take some adjustment, working here, but you'll get used to it, I promise.' Then, 'Astral projection is an advanced form of meditation that allows lucid dreaming, which some people claim they can do. There are reports of people travelling outside their sleeping bodies, as it were, and roaming about freely.'

Rose can't help screwing up her face.

'OK,' she says, 'but you don't believe in that, do you?'

Adam exchanges a look with Moony, whose expression remains impassive.

183

'I didn't,' he says. 'No. Thought it was a load of absolute nonsense.' He pauses. 'Then I met a man called Kenny Wiggins.' He grimaces. 'Horrible old bastard.'

27

They are in Rose's car, she and Moony, in a traffic jam on the North Circular.

Adam had argued vociferously that it should be Moony and not he who accompanied Rose to visit this Mr Wiggins, who lives near the Brent Cross Shopping Centre. Apparently he'd been telling Moony 'every day for the last two weeks' that he needed the afternoon off to go to his daughter's school concert and, while it had looked as though Moony was all set to renege on their agreement, she eventually gave in and curtly informed Rose, 'You're driving.'

None of this makes Rose feel any less sense of trepidation about this Kenny bloke, whoever he is. The fact that they have been sitting in near silence since they got into the car doesn't help either.

Moony evidently doesn't do small talk, which is fine with Rose, because she doesn't either. But as the traffic crawls forward and a miserable rain begins to spatter the windscreen, Rose can't help comparing this uncomfortable atmosphere with the ease she shares with Mack when they are out and about like this.

'So,' she says when the discomfort becomes too much. 'Can you tell me about this Kenny Wiggins? Why we're going to see him?'

Moony stops looking at her phone and drops it into her lap with a grumpy sigh as though Rose has been indulging in non-stop chatter since they got into the car.

'It's not easy to describe our Kenny,' says Moony. 'I'll let you form your own opinion once you've had the pleasure of meeting him. But for a while he was one of the best informants my old division in the Met'd ever had, despite his . . .' she pauses, as though searching for the right word, '. . . rather unorthodox methods.'

Rose glances over questioningly. The other woman has a wry smile playing around her lips and a bright mischief in her eyes.

'Which were . . . ?'

'Well, he says he got information using astral projection,' says Moony. 'Which is why we're going to see him.' She pauses, as though expecting something from Rose, but she remains quiet and waits for more information. She's also concentrating on driving. The traffic is beginning to move again but the rain is battering the windscreen. It drums on the roof and streams down the windscreen, almost overpowering the wipers, which are making a frantic *thwick-thwick* sound.

'Kenny did a few stints in prison for burglary, starting from a young age,' Moony continues, louder now. 'When he came out after his last stretch, we caught him in the process of planning his next job. But he gave us some very valuable intel about a bigger heist, and so we cut him a deal.' She stops to rummage in her bag, from which she extracts a bag of Haribo sweets and pops two in her mouth. Rose isn't offered one, which prompts a stab of irritation even she realizes is disproportionate to the crime. But there is a weird rudeness to this woman, as though she is constantly daring Rose to argue with her. She pledges to herself that she won't give Moony the satisfaction if she can help it.

'Over the next few years, he gave us pieces of information that proved very useful, mainly in relation to thefts and raids on jewellery shops. Then he made the mistake of telling one of my colleagues, with a certain amount of glee, that he got this intel through his *dreams*.' She laughs at the memory. 'We were all, "OK, Kenny, whatever you say, as long as you deliver the goods, we don't care what you tell yourself." He took offence and flounced off for a while. But then something came up and we needed his help, so we went back. He found it in his heart to forgive us and after that case was wrapped up he tipped us off about a terrorist cell planning an attack on the Stratford Westfield.'

Rose can't help glancing over at Moony, who is looking out of the window, frowning.

'That's quite a leap,' she says, 'I mean, in terms of the type of crime.'

'Yeah,' says Moony, 'that's what we thought too. We felt duty-bound to check it out, and thank God we did. We found two suicide vests and a small homemade nail bomb in the property we investigated and made five arrests. Kenny said – and I'll always remember this – "Now do you believe me?"'

'What did he mean?' says Rose.

'Well,' says Moony, 'Kenny lived in the same street, but he'd never been inside that house and had no personal connections with the terrorists.'

'But that doesn't mean anything,' says Rose. 'He could have found out in any number of ways. Could have overheard them at a bus stop or something.'

'True,' says Moony in an easy tone. 'But it was only after the event that we found out he'd been laid up in bed with not one, but two broken legs, sustained after falling from a ladder cleaning windows. He hadn't been out of his house for almost two months and those men only moved in three weeks previously. Told us, rather triumphantly, that he'd "projected himself around the neighbourhood" to make the time pass quicker.'

Rose remains silent. This doesn't seem like compelling evidence to her, but she can't be bothered to pick away at this point. An uncomfortable thought nudges at her: could Moony be *that* credulous? Darting a glance at the squat figure next to her, frowning and eating yet another Haribo, she has to concede that the woman has a no-nonsense air about her. At any rate, she's nothing like Adele Gifford, Rose's gold standard for loopy behaviour.

The road they are after is one that runs parallel to the North Circular but can't be accessed directly. Coming off at the next exit, they painstakingly weave through back streets until they reach the address. They park and get out of the car hurriedly, because of the rain, and make a dash for the front door. Rose has a quick look around while they wait for an answer to Moony's knock.

The row of three semi-detached houses stand alone, like the sole survivors of an air raid that claimed the rest of the street. A gasometer close by dominates the horizon, a hulk of rusty bones that look menacing against the black and grey sky.

Wiggins' house is an ugly 1950s property with pinkish, scabby pebble-dash on the outside. Grey net curtains cover some of the windows, while another has a droopy Spurs scarf pinned across it.

Getting no response from the doorbell, Moony raps hard on the door. Both women are scrunching their shoulders up to their ears as if this might offer protection from the rain that is soaking them to the skin.

The door opens by about four inches and half a large pink face with piggy eyes peers out at them.

'Afternoon, Kenny,' says Moony cheerfully. 'Any chance we could come in for a chat?'

Wiggins doesn't open the door any further. Before speaking he does a strange movement with his mouth, a disconcerting full cupid's bow, as though masticating the words before they came out.

'I might be busy,' he says in a gravelly voice.

'You *might* be,' says Moony, which feels riskily sarcastic to Rose when the rain is beginning to snake its way inside her collar and into her jumper.

But Wiggins gives a small chuckle and the door opens.

188

Inside the house, a wall of smell hits Rose, almost making her gag. The pungent animal nature of it immediately makes Rose think of pet shops, but there is an undertone redolent of boiled meat and vegetables.

'You'd better come through,' says Wiggins over his shoulder, and they follow him down a hallway of dirty magnolia anaglypta walls, with a series of cages at one end, which may account for the smell. But when Rose gets close, all she can see inside are leaves and twigs.

They walk into a kitchen diner where a pan is boiling hard on a standalone cooker, its sides streaked with yellow grease. Some abomination is cooking there, judging by the smell. When Rose sees what is lying on brown paper on the kitchen counter, it's all she can do not to cry out in horror.

The dead rat is several inches long. Its grey fur forms small dark points, as though wet, and pinkish-grey feet curl up in the air, stiff. Tiny black eyes stare sightlessly up at the ceiling.

Rose cannot prevent her gaze from scuttling between the rat on the counter, whatever is boiling away on the stove, and Wiggins. He gives a slow smile, relishing her discomfort, then goes over to stir the pot.

'Have we interrupted lunchtime?' says Moony cheerfully, and Rose feels a lurch in her stomach.

'I'm just getting ready to feed my girls,' says Wiggins, 'but it can wait. Can I offer you some tea?'

'Oh, no need,' says Moony hurriedly, 'but thanks. We've come to pick your brains, if that's all right? This is my colleague, DC Gifford.'

Wiggins lets his eyes travel around Rose's face and then down the full length of her body before giving a grunt, possibly of approval. What a vile man. She almost wishes she could arrest him simply for being horrible. And whoever 'the girls' are, she sincerely hopes she won't meet them.

He gestures for them to sit at a white-painted table with three chairs that have greasy grey and pink cushions. Copies of the *Sun* and a stack of empty Domino's pizza boxes take up most of the tabletop. Rose shoots a nervous look at the floor, in case the 'girls' are already out and on the lookout for their lunch.

Rats? Spiders? Snakes? *Please, not snakes.*

'How can I help you, ladies?' says Wiggins.

Moony tells him that she wants to ask him about his 'particular skills'. While his attention is focused on the boss, Rose observes Wiggins in all his glory.

He is grossly overweight and has a large, almost bald head with yellowish-grey hair sprouting like a monk's tonsure down his thick neck. He's clad in a t-shirt of indeterminate colour that doesn't quite meet his grey tracksuit bottoms, exposing an expanse of pink belly that hangs down in folds. Scales of psoriasis or some other skin complaint form a silvery pattern on his arms and Rose finds herself itching and shuddering in response. A faint cheesy smell comes from under the table, where his feet are planted uncomfortably close to Rose's in their white socks and black sliders. She moves her own further back under the chair.

'I thought you lot didn't believe in my nocturnal exploits,' says Wiggins in a prim voice, drawing his lips in tight. His full, pouty lips are the shape certain women pay good money for, and the effect in his doughy face is disconcerting. Meaty hands rest on the table and Rose notices that he has extra-long, yellowish nails on his index finger and thumb. A guitar-player, or maybe it's just another part of his look.

'Oh, come on, Kenny,' says Moony, smiling a little. 'That's all water under the bridge. We carried on using your services, didn't we – at least until the intel stopped coming.'

Wiggins pulls a doleful face.

'Well, that's the trouble with moving in other realms. You can't do it forever without getting weakened eventually. I don't know why. I can't seem to do it any more. It was actually making me quite sick in the end.'

The thought of Kenny Wiggins roaming about people's bedrooms at night is so awful, Rose feels a sense of relief that his powers have deserted him.

But none of this is going to help them catch Hannah's killer. She decides to get to the point.

'When you do this . . . astral projection thing, can other people see you?' says Rose, feeling Moony's eyes on her. 'I mean, the part of you that's . . .' she struggles for a word before settling on, 'travelling'. Surprisingly, it's getting easier to use these terms, she is finding.

He regards her with watery blue eyes. 'Not usually,' he says mysteriously.

Moony picks up on the shift in tone and sits forward. 'What do you mean, "not *usually*"? Have there been times when people did see you?'

Wiggins drums his fingers on the table, frowning.

'It was very rare,' he says thoughtfully. 'Only happened a couple of times.' There is a brief exploration of a nostril again before he continues.

'Sure I can't get you some tea?' Rose detects a gleam in his eye, as though it's a challenge rather than an offer.

'Go on then,' says Moony. To her horror, Rose finds herself nodding mutely in agreement. It's clear he wants to drag out his moment of feeling like he has all the power. If that's what it takes to get answers, so be it.

Wiggins heaves himself to his feet with much sighing, as though he hadn't volunteered in the first place, and goes to the sink, where he fills an ancient-looking kettle that is streaked with crusty limescale. Taking two mugs from a mug tree, he carries on talking.

'The first time it happened,' he says, 'I was, um, how shall I put it, I was doing some *research* in a warehouse down Tilbury way.' His eyes dart from Rose to Moony and he runs his tongue over his lips.

'Don't worry, Kenny,' says Moony, 'we're not here for anything other than a bit of help. Nothing you say is going to get you into trouble.'

'That's good to hear,' says Kenny. He pours water into the mugs, then goes to the fridge for a carton of full-fat milk. After unscrewing the top, he sniffs and makes a face that isn't totally reassuring.

The two mugs of tea are placed down on the table. Rose forces herself to take a sip and almost gags. The tea has a milky sheen and delicate fat globules floating on the surface.

'So, I was wandering about,' says Kenny, sitting down again with a huff, 'doing my thing, and there was a security guard who had fallen asleep on the job, the lazy bastard. He was head back, snoring like a locomotive, and twitching the way dogs do when they're dreaming. It was fascinating to watch so I stood there for a bit, but then he woke up and let out a huge gasp, and for a split second he met my eyes and I swear he could see me.' He's smiling at the memory. 'Bloke almost shat himself! Anyway, I was as shocked as him and sort of froze, thinking I'd been caught, but when he came fully awake he shuddered and looked around, and it was obvious he couldn't see me any more.'

'So,' Moony says, lifting the cup to her lips and then putting it back down again. 'Why do you think he saw you?'

Kenny shrugs. 'No idea,' he says. 'But I reckon it had something to do with the space between being asleep and being awake, which was all part of the lucid dreaming that I had mastered. It's like there's a split in the two dimensions of dreaming and reality, and in that moment of waking, they cross.'

'Dreaming isn't a *dimension* though,' Rose finds herself saying. 'It's simply part of being asleep. It's something our brain does to, I don't know, tidy up all the nonsense of the day.' She wishes she had a more scientific explanation to hand, but this is the best she can do.

Wiggins looks at her with an expression that is uncomfortably close to sympathy.

He doesn't reply. Instead, he lets out a snort of laughter and directs his next comment to Moony alone.

'That's the kind of thinking I've come to expect from the average plod,' he says.

'So,' says Moony, eager to get him back on track, 'did it ever happen again? Someone seeing you in that astral state?'

He purses his lips and rearranges himself in the seat.

'Only once, but it wasn't quite the same thing.' His voice is flat now. 'There was an old lady I came across one night, mad as a box of frogs, who thought she was talking to her dead husband. She seemed to sense something but couldn't see me exactly.'

Rose's skin tingles unpleasantly as she thinks about the black flickering thing above Kirsty Perryman's hospital bed. Her head has started to ache and she sorely wants to get out of here.

A silence falls, during which Wiggins continues to explore his nose and Moony appears lost in thought.

Then she springs to her feet.

'Right-oh, Kenny, thanks for your time. We'll let you get back to your girls.'

As Rose makes her way out, her eyes return to the dead rat, which she had almost managed to forget about. Now she's horrified all over again.

'What's that in the pan?' she says, before she can stop herself.

Beside her, Wiggins grins, revealing small, grey teeth.

'Oh that's just a mutton stew for me,' he says. 'This beauty is for Khaleesi, my boa constrictor.' He pauses. 'Want to meet her?'

28

Rose beats a hasty retreat back to the car and her hands are shaking as she pulls open the door.

Moony takes her time getting in next to her, despite the icy rain that continues to lash from a slate sky, and when she does, Rose is sure she is going to see a smirk on the other woman's face. Instead, she is looking thoughtful, chewing her bottom lip. She gets into her seat, making a performance of it, with sounds of great effort.

They drive off in an awkward silence and then rejoin the thick traffic on the A406. Everyone has their headlights on, dotting the gloom with smeary orange.

Finally, Rose cracks.

'Well,' she says, 'he was quite something, wasn't he?'

Moony doesn't respond but emits a gentle belch, which she makes no attempt to hide.

'He's a one-off, to say the least,' she says. Then, 'But I'm not sure you having a stick up your arse while we were there was particularly helpful. Are you like that with all interviewees?'

Rose's mouth opens and closes in speechless response. She shoots a glance at the woman next to her.

'What are you talking about?' she says, and the heat rising within her makes itself felt in her voice. 'He's a total fruitcake! Not to mention, creepy as hell!'

Moony reaches into her bag and extracts another couple of Haribo sweets, which she chews ruminatively before responding.

'I admit he's not exactly David Cassidy,' she says, bafflingly, 'but he has delivered the goods on more than one occasion. I don't think it was the appearance and personality of our Kenny that was the problem.' She pauses. 'I don't even think it was the rat popsicle.' Then, 'Blimey, I hope I never have to say those two words together again.'

Rose almost laughs, despite herself.

'No,' Moony goes on, sounding thoughtful. 'I think it was the nature of the discussion.'

'Well, that certainly didn't help,' says Rose forcefully. The whole encounter was horrible and weird, and she wants to go home and douse herself in the hottest water she can stand. Not that this would be much in her shower, admittedly, but still.

Moony turns to her now and Rose takes her eyes off the road to meet her gaze. She notices that the other woman has two slightly different coloured eyes. One is brown, and the other very dark blue, and it is oddly disconcerting.

'Why exactly *are* you in such denial, Rose?' she says equably. The effect is as though someone has lit a fire under Rose's seat. Her face and neck instantly flush and she wants to claw at the unbearable itch that has sprung up on her arms. 'I mean, you heard what he said. Sounds like people with certain sensitivities might be able to see astral projection and you can't deny you saw something in that hospital.'

She makes herself take in a steadying deep breath before replying.

'I'm not in *denial*, as you put it,' says Rose, and her voice is too loud for the space. 'I just don't believe in this . . . crap' – oh, the relief in getting this out – 'that you clearly do. I don't even know what I saw. And . . . and I think my time would be much better spent back at Silverton Street, getting on with my actual job' – she couldn't stop, even if she wanted to – 'instead of wasting time playing at being Ghostbusters!'

She finds she is breathing very heavily. Sweat prickles along her brow.

'Feel better for that, do you?' says Moony after a beat.

Rose maintains a mutinous silence in response.

'Because,' Moony continues, 'it's fair to say that you aren't the only person feeling let down today, DC Gifford.'

'What is that meant to mean?' says Rose. She wants away from this woman. Now. Out of this claustrophobic car and away.

'I *mean*,' says Moony, whose own tone remains infuriatingly even, 'that I expected more open-mindedness from you, all things considered.'

Rose's stomach lurches so hard she has to swallow bile.

Here it is, she thinks. *Now we're getting to it.*

'Meaning?' she manages.

'Oh, come on, Rose,' says Moony. 'I know it was a long time ago, but have I changed that much?'

'*What?*' Rose hasn't even registered that they are off the North Circular and approaching the Great Cambridge Roundabout. She tries to focus on this well-known seventh circle of hell, despite the clamminess of her hands on the wheel and the buffeting wind against the car, which adds to the feeling of being attacked both inside and out. 'I'm sorry,' she says, 'but I have no idea what you're on about.'

There is a pause and when the other woman speaks, her voice is maddeningly gentle.

'I think it was around August time?' she says. 'Domestic disturbance called in from an address in High Barnet?'

Rose's blood turns to sluggish ice, slowly rolling through her body.

It can't be her. Surely . . . ?

'Do you remember putting on my hat?' says Moony. 'I was new to the job, but I remember thinking it wasn't a very healthy environment for a little kid. But the reason I remember it most now, in the job I'm in, is that you had an expression in your eyes that I have seen many times since.'

Rose can barely catch her breath, but she manages to push out the words, 'What expression?'

'Haunted,' says Moony softly. 'You looked literally haunted. As though there were other sounds you could hear that you were desperately trying to block out.'

Her face stings as if she has been slapped, and her ears seem to ring in sympathy.

Peering through the bars of the stairs. The shouting and then the exciting, clean sound of radios and authoritative voices. The kind policewoman with the hat.

'Oh for goodness' sake,' says Moony, irritably. 'It doesn't matter to me what kind of place you grew up in. I just happened to see your name and wondered, that was all. Gifford isn't such a common name.'

'Is that why you asked for me?' she says in a tiny voice. They are back at the UCIT building and the car crunches into the unevenly surfaced car park and pulls into a space.

'I suppose it is,' says Moony. 'But you've made your feelings clear, so now you've brought me back, you can bugger off to Silverton Street.'

She gets out of the car without another word and closes the door. It's hard to tell whether it is the wind that causes the shake, or the force with which it was closed.

Rose is too stunned to move. With the engine still running and the wipers frantically trying to clear the rain, she watches Moony's stout figure walk away until she disappears inside the building, as if she has been swallowed up.

29

Driving back to Silverton Street on autopilot, Rose is battling with a range of complex emotions.

She is aware that she ought to be feeling mightily relieved. After all, she can go back to MIT14 and tell her boss that nothing of interest emerged from her day's research. Maybe that will mean the end of having to spend time with DS Sheila Moony. Perhaps one day, meeting Kenny Wiggins will be nothing more than a funny anecdote. She pictures herself telling Sam— no, *Mack*, telling Mack all about it.

So why then, does she not feel relieved? Why does she feel chastised and petty, and as though, yet again, she hasn't done her job properly? Maybe it's because she knows that she was only let out of the station on this jaunt today to get her out of the way.

Maybe it really is time to think about that transfer.

Miserably she glances at her phone, lighting up on the seat next to her. Mack has replied to her message letting him know she's on her way back.

The traffic has slowed at lights, so she scoops it up and reads the message:

Great. Any idea of ETA? Briefing in five minutes. Development, I think!

She feels a stab of affection for Mack and his insistence on proper punctuation and full spelling in his text messages. She has missed him.

She is lucky because the briefing has been delayed and she gets back as Rowland is starting. Her boss gives her a nod, but Rose sees several friendly smiles. Mack gives her a little thumbs up and mouths: *OK?* She nods and grins. Looking around the room at her colleagues, she feels a wash of affection for these people who live very much in the real world.

Things have moved on since she was in the day before.

A business card advertising the services of one Hand-E-Man – *Call Russ on 088824 3671* – has been found in both houses.

A call to a grumpy Sofia Nikolas has already confirmed that a minor job was carried out by this man a couple of weeks before Hannah was killed.

'Right,' says Rowland. 'Update me, please, on this Russ character.'

Mack stands up to address the team.

'No reply on that number and it turns out it's a burner,' he says, as a murmur of frustration goes around the room.

'Hmm,' says Rowland. 'We need to get him in. What else do we have?'

'We don't have an address, sadly,' says Mack. 'But Sofia Nikolas says she thinks it was someone Leon Gavril knew.'

He exchanges a look with Rose, who makes a face.

'Might have known he was mates with that scumbag,' she says, and someone laughs behind her.

'Hang on,' says Rowland, 'isn't that a rented property through a landlord though? Wouldn't the landlord be the one to organize repairs?'

'Yep, ordinarily,' says Mack. 'But Sofia says their landlord stopped responding to messages when he went off to Pakistan to sort out his mum's funeral. Last month they had a problem with a leaking sink and Gavril tried to fix it, but, reading between the lines, he made it worse, so he ended up asking this other guy.'

'Typical man who thinks he knows how to fix things when he hasn't a clue,' says Ewa in a heartfelt way then blushes as everyone laughs.

'Look,' says Rowland, glancing at her watch, 'don't bother trying to ring Gavril. He's not going to rush to help out the police, so he probably won't even pick up. Go over there in person and ask him about this Russ guy.' She looks around the room. 'I don't need to remind you of this, but I'm going to do it anyway, because I'm like that.' She pauses, before continuing. 'I've been thinking about what it would be like to wake up in your own bed, in the middle of the night, to find someone there, in the room, standing over you.' Rose feels a shiver at her words and she clearly isn't alone. The men seem to shift a little and some of the female staff glance nervously around.

'Then everything is darkness because that person is pressing a pillow over your face,' says Rowland in her clear, measured voice. 'You feel the life draining away as you struggle for the final breaths you will ever take. That's what happened to Hannah Scott, people, and it happened to Kirsty Perryman – only she's still with us. I have a strong feeling the same person is responsible for both these crimes and I want to see him thrown away like the piece of rubbish he is. OK?'

She looks around the room as people mutter, 'yep,' and 'OK, boss.' Then, 'So let's double down on all efforts. Look harder at the CCTV around both properties. Look into any other ways the two women might be connected. This feels like a much-needed break, but it could be nothing. Thank you, everyone.'

Before she leaves, she looks at Rose and says, 'Quick word, please.'

Rose follows her into the office and Rowland closes the door.

Searching her face for clues, and finding nothing, Rose says, 'So . . . ?'

'So,' says Rowland, taking a sip from a purple metal water bottle, 'did anything useful come out of your morning at UCIT?'

Rose snorts a sarcastic laugh and immediately sees from her boss's stony expression that it is the wrong response.

'Well,' she says, 'it seemed like a waste of time to me. I mean, do you know what they do over there?'

'I do.'

'And?'

'And what?'

'Don't you think it's all a little . . . stupid?' Rose's heart has started to pound for some reason. She pictures Rowland saying something along the lines of, '*I think you know why, Rose Gifford*,' and a sour burst of bile rises in her throat.

Rowland sighs and sits back in her seat. 'I admit it's unorthodox,' she says, 'and doesn't fit with my own . . . world view, but they have had some successes and are respected by the Commissioner. We don't advertise what they are about for obvious reasons, so please don't talk to anyone about today.' She pauses again, scrutinizing Rose's face. 'So you got nothing helpful at all?'

'We interviewed a guy about something called astral projection,' says Rose. 'They seem to think the killer might be doing some sort of "other realm" visitation to these victims before he strikes.'

Rowland sits tapping her pen against the desk, eyes fixed above Rose's head.

After a few seconds she slaps the pen down on the table with a bang.

'I'm not sure how useful this has been,' she says, 'but hopefully it will stop Moony bothering me. She had a bee in her bonnet about these nightmares, but I don't think it's relevant. We'll get on with things our way. Off you go, Rose.'

They set off in the car and Mack waits a beat before asking the question he has clearly been dying to ask.

'So,' he says with evident relish, 'tell me all about your

mysterious morning with DS Moony then. I have no idea what could possibly have been more important than what we are doing.'

Rose feels as though a heavy coat is being lifted from her shoulders as she lets out a laugh, which comes out more high-pitched than she intended.

'Oh my God!' she says. 'I feel like I stepped into some kind of alternative reality today. I hardly know where to start!'

'Well, have a go,' says Mack affably, leaning over to offer her a piece of gum, which she takes with gratitude. She hasn't eaten or drunk anything for hours and her mouth feels stale and dry.

She starts with describing her arrival at UCIT and Adam's description of what they do. Leaving out the tea lady part, she goes on to describe the visit to Kenny Wiggins' house and the mad interview there. She also omits to tell Mack about the conversation with Moony on the way back, and the way she was dismissed.

He listens to the whole thing with only raised eyebrows and then lets out a low whistle at the end.

'Well,' he says, 'that sounds like quite the morning.' He pauses. 'I heard a rumour about UCIT, but was never sure I believed it.' He looks thoughtful. 'I have come across Adam Lacey,' he adds. 'I don't know much about her, Moony, but I worked a case with Lacey back when I was with Vice, and he's a great bloke.'

'Yeah,' Rose laughs, 'but he's as nuts as she is, clearly! Ley lines? I mean, come on!'

She glances at Mack, searching for something in his expression that isn't there.

'Don't you think it's a load of old shit, then?' Her voice sounds pleading, despite herself. 'Astral projection? Supernatural stuff?'

Mack takes ages to reply. Then, finally he speaks. 'I guess I'm surprised that resources are being spent this way when we're so stretched, yes. But I also think there must be a reason why they are being sent in that direction.' He pauses. 'Can only be that they get results, however *out there* they sound, don't you think?'

Rose grunts in reply, not trusting herself to speak.

'Anyway,' says Mack with a barely concealed yawn. 'You're back in a different kind of madhouse now, kiddo, so no harm done.'

No harm done. Only, thinks Rose, a bomb going off under everything she has been trying to hold together for so long.

Haunted. That was the word used by Moony. And it was true. Adele Gifford may have been lying to all those punters, but Rose had to learn ways to ignore the flickering shadows she saw slinking around the house, and the whispers that snuck into her ears at night and made her pull the duvet up tight around her head. She was haunted then, and she still is.

A feeling of such intense loneliness wraps itself around her insides that she has to swallow hard and concentrate on the road.

Arriving at the same blue front door with chipped paint of only a few days ago is a strange sensation.

Everything looks identical, from the moody grey clouds threatening sleet overhead to the closed blinds on the windows. Rose feels a dragging sadness that something has fundamentally changed since they were here before. Her whole view of the world, and who she has tried to be, has shifted. And it hasn't even led to them catching the killer.

Mack knocks on the door and a few moments later, Leon Gavril opens it.

His face immediately falls into a sour grimace.

'The fuck you want?' he says. He is dressed in one of those vests that showcase the muscles, despite the five-degree temperature of the day. A baby girl – evident by the fact that the few thin wisps of hair she owns have been pulled into a savage sprout on the top of her head with a pink bobbly band – is over his shoulder and making unhappy sounds.

'It's good to see you too, Leon,' says Mack easily. 'Is it all right if we come in? We're trying to track someone down and think you can help. You're not in any trouble.'

'Oh, I'm not?' says Gavril, in a voice dripping with sarcasm. 'Then in that case you can fuck off.' He goes to close the door but Rose stops it with her foot, which he glares down at before looking stonily into her eyes.

'Come on, Leon,' she says. 'The only reason the CPS aren't right this minute scheduling your possession with intent to supply trial is because you agreed to cooperate with us. So unless you want to come back down the station to re-assess all that, I suggest you talk to us, OK?' She smiles at him. 'I think the little one just threw up on you, mate.'

'What?' He pulls the baby away and looks at his shoulder, which is dotted with beige-coloured sick. 'Oh, man . . .' he says and turns to go into the house.

Rose and Mack exchange amused looks and take this as an invitation to follow him inside.

'Go in there and wait,' barks Gavril, vaguely gesturing to a door on the left.

They enter a small living room with a cream sofa and chairs and laminate flooring. The space is dominated by a huge photograph of the baby, whose tiny head is encased in a pink headband with a bow. Rose idly wonders how ostentatious the headgear will be when the child actually has some hair to play with. The baby looks startled but her brown eyes and long nose make it clear who her daddy is.

'Poor kid,' murmurs Rose, and Mack stifles a laugh with a realistic cough as Gavril comes back into the room, wearing a grey t-shirt. He has a bottle for the baby and settles himself into a chair to feed her.

'All right if we sit too?' says Mack.

Gavril shrugs and keeps his eyes fixed on his daughter, who is greedily pulling on the bottle with her lips, making a high-pitched whistling sound.

They sit down on the sofa. There is a coffee table in

front of them that is covered in dirty plates and fast-food containers.

'Missus away?' says Mack.

'None of your business,' says Gavril. 'Tell me why you're here, then get lost.'

'Right,' Mack continues. 'Fair enough. Can see you've got a lot on your hands, so we will come straight to the point. We're looking for a bloke called Russ and wondering if you can tell us where we might find him.'

Leon glances up, then back at the baby, who is lolling drunkenly, eyes glassy. 'Never heard of him,' says Gavril.

'Are you quite sure?' says Rose. 'Because the thing is, Leon, Sofia told us that you do.'

At the mention of Sofia's name, he glances up and flashes a guilty look around, almost as if expecting Kate Morley to come into the room. But judging by the contrast between the neat decoration and the man-pad eating arrangements, Rose is sure she is away, maybe even permanently.

'I'm not messing about,' he says, expertly lifting the baby girl and placing her over his shoulder to burp her. 'I can't think who you mean. Who is he?'

'A handyman,' says Mack. 'He came round to fix the sink after . . . after you'd had a go at it.'

Rose glances at Mack. They shouldn't deliberately wind people up, but it's hard not to when you have someone as easy to rile as Leon Gavril.

Gavril's face sours even further as he rubs surprisingly gentle circles on the baby's upper back.

'Oh right, him,' he says as the baby lets out an enormous burp. For a split second all three adults are united in amusement until Gavril remembers that he hates the other two and fixes his face back into its scowl. 'I know him from the Green Dragon. He does bits and bobs around the place when he's here.'

'When he's here?' says Rose. 'Where else does he go?'

'Dunno,' says Gavril. 'Festivals and stuff, I think. Sells t-shirts and, ah, other stuff.' His expression tightens.

'Don't worry, Leon,' says Mack, quite kindly. 'All we need is some info on this guy and we'll leave you in peace. Do you have a full name for him, address, anything like that?'

Gavril screws up his face in concentration.

'I think he's called Meeny? Meehan, something like that. No idea where he lives, but if he's in town he's often at that pub I mentioned, the Green Dragon. On Barrons Lane.'

'Yeah, we know it,' says Mack. 'Thanks for your help, Leon. We'll see ourselves out.'

He grunts in response as the baby projectile vomits all over his shoulder and the back of the chair.

'Better out than in, eh?' says Rose cheerfully, and is met with such a sour look that it's all she can do to suppress the laughter that rises up inside her.

Back in the car, Mack rings the station and asks Ewa to look up Russell Meehan AKA Meeny on the PNC. She says she is just finishing something urgent and will get back to them shortly.

The Green Dragon pub, their next port of call, turns out to be one of those pubs that is less old-fashioned London boozer and more boxy 1950s monstrosity with no character whatsoever.

The clientele at this time of the day consists of a bunch of old men staring grimly into pints or looking at newspapers. A couple of smartly dressed elderly men are playing draughts at a table off to the side. Magic FM is on the radio and Mariah Carey is warbling away about all she wants for Christmas.

'It's barely November,' mutters Mack. 'When in God's name did this become such a thing.' It's not really a question, so Rose doesn't answer.

From behind the bar they are being eyed by a tall, skinny man with glasses and thin wisps of hair over a freckled crown. Rose puts him in his late forties.

It's obvious he knows who they are and yet again, she marvels at the way certain types are able to tell. Is it the suits? The cynical look in their eyes?

'Help you?' says the man, without a smile.

Mack does the introductions, then says, 'We're trying to find someone we believe is one of your locals,' he says, 'and wondered if you could give us a steer on where we might find him?'

'I can try,' says the man, his 'troy' revealing a Northern Irish accent.

'Great,' says Mack. 'He's called either Russ Meehan or Meeny. I'm told he comes in here fairly often.'

The barman's body language visibly relaxes.

'Oh *him*,' he says. 'Yeah, I know him, all right. Think it's Meehan. He's a character, all right.'

'In what way?' says Rose, and he turns an appraising eye her way. She sighs, inside rather than out.

'He's an odd fish,' says the barman. 'Thinks he's some kind of intellectual, but no one has a clue what he's on about half the time. He's got himself a slap a few times when people haven't taken kindly to some of his banter.'

'What sort of thing does he talk about?' says Mack.

'Oh all sorts,' says the barman. 'I try to tune him out most of the time. I heard him going off on one the other day about how he can move a beer glass with his mind.'

Rose and Mack look at each other and then back at the barman.

'When was he last in?' says Rose.

'Not for a while,' says the barman. 'Maybe a month or so?'

'Any idea where he lives?' says Mack.

The barman screws up his brow as he thinks. 'Hmm, you're on your own there,' he says. 'Sorry.'

Mack nods. 'OK, here's my card. If he comes in, or if you have any thoughts about how we might find him, give us a call, eh?'

'Sure,' says the barman, but the card proffered by Mack stays on the bar and Rose is fairly sure it will go in the bin the moment their backs are turned.

They don't get a chance to speak before Mack's phone rings.

'Brilliant,' he says, 'text me the details.'

He turns to Rose with a grin.

'Our Mr Meehan is indeed on the PNC, for an attempted burglary five years ago. Served two years in Pentonville. Also a string of minor public order offences. C'mon, kiddo. Let's go.'

30

The address is an estate off the Caledonian Road, a couple of boroughs away, in Islington. It's one of those North London areas where elegant three-storey terraced streets lined with Lexuses and BMWs sit cheek-by-jowl with 1950s properties exuding only an air of poverty and neglect.

This address is very much the latter, and they park the car near a patch of grass adorned with what is ostensibly a play area, but is currently filled with a group of young men in hoodies who are perched, crow-like, on the battered, rusty equipment. The men scatter as soon as Rose and Mack exit the car, melting off into various walkways as though they were never there.

'Something we said?' says Mack with a laugh. 'Are we that obvious?'

'At least it means they'll leave the car alone,' says Rose. 'Possibly.'

They go through a pedestrian walkway into the main estate, looking out for the names of the blocks as they go. The buildings are two storeys high in brown, grubby brick. Walkways are fenced in with wire mesh, most likely to stop people being thrown off.

Meehan's registered address is next door to a property that is streaked with black marks from the ground-floor window;

evidence of a recent fire. They knock at the door and wait, but there is no reply.

'Let's have a look round the back,' says Mack, and they make their way to the alley that leads to the rear of the block.

Meehan's flat has filthy blankets across the windows and an air of abandonment.

Rose's arm begins to prickle, and she scratches at it absent-mindedly as they attempt, without success, to get through the back gate into the small yard.

The neighbouring property on the opposite side to the fire-damaged one has a neater look about it, apart from a pair of rotting Halloween pumpkins on top of the fence, which seem to watch them with grotesque jagged eyes. The house has cheerful yellow curtains in the window and a tidy yard containing some pots with lustrous plants, which must surely be fake this time of the year, and a small child's slide, beaded with rain but clean. Something moves at an upstairs window and then passes out of view.

'Hmm. I'll go back round the front and try again,' says Mack. 'You stay here.'

Rose waits at the back and then a door opens in the property next door. A stout elderly woman with an ashen complexion and dyed black hair in a stiff, almost conical up-do, appears at the garden gate and regards Rose with suspicion.

'Are you from the council?' says the woman.

'No,' says Rose, 'we're police officers.'

The woman rolls her eyes. 'There's no point coming now, is there! It stopped at three o'clock in the morning and they told me the council were the only people who could deal with this.'

Rose frowns. 'I'm sorry,' she says. 'I'm not sure . . . ?'

'The noise!' the woman says before she can finish the question. 'It wouldn't stop! Music all hours of the day and night! I look after my granddaughter and neither of us got a wink of sleep! She's making up for it now, bless her, but I can't do that, can I? I'm dead on my feet!'

Her eyes are sparkling with exhausted tears and Rose feels a pang of sympathy for the woman.

Mack reappears at her side as she asks, 'Do you know your neighbour's name?'

'Yes,' says the woman, all the pep of her temper appearing to have ebbed away, so her voice is softer. 'He's called Russ something.'

'And do you know where he is?' says Mack, before hurriedly adding an introduction for himself and Rose.

'Well, I expect he's in there, after the night he had,' says the woman. 'I haven't noticed anyone going out. And he usually slams the front door so hard it shakes the whole building, so I'd have heard.'

Rose and Mack exchange glances, each thinking the same thing. Either Mr Meehan is hiding in there, or he is incapacitated. Whichever it is, they have reasonable grounds to force entry. First, Mack decides to have one more go at rousing him. His banging on the door and shouts of 'Police! Open up!' should be enough to rouse the dead. After a few moments of this, Mack moves away to make the phone call, which he conducts in a quiet voice.

While he does so, Rose gently questions the woman, whose name is Marion Griffiths, about Russ Meehan. Griffiths is only too happy to oblige, and by the time Mack comes back to report that Rowland is sending backup, Rose has learned several things.

Meehan has had a very disordered life since coming out of prison and spends a lot of time playing loud music and apparently taking drugs. He is, according to Griffiths, 'much more intelligent than you would think,' and, 'seems like he comes from a good background by the way he talks', but he also has 'some strange notions'.

'In what way?' Rose had asked, to which the other woman replied, 'Oh, he goes on about all sorts of rubbish if you let him. Claims he's a pagan, whatever that is. Then he started going on about witchcraft, so I try not to have anything to do with him if I can help it.'

*

It takes half an hour for three uniforms from Silverton Street to arrive, with mutterings about 'traffic'. They've had to park on the road and some confusion ensues about where exactly they need to be. By this time Rose and Mack have both drunk welcome mugs of strong tea from Griffiths and are stamping their feet at the bitter cold.

Bulky in their stab vests and helmets, the uniforms finally appear, brandishing the battering ram known as the Big Red Key.

Mack shouts a warning through the door: 'This is the police! We're entering this property by force, so stand back!' Then there is an explosion of sound as the door splinters open.

The uniforms barge into the house, their heavy boots thundering down the hall, and Rose and Mack follow behind. Rose hears one of the uniforms say, 'Fucking hell!' and once she is past his broad back, she can see what he is looking at.

They are in a gloomy living room with a kitchenette off to one side. A grey patterned blanket over the windows gives the room a strange, subterranean feel, but it's what is on the wall that has stopped everyone in their tracks.

'Is this guy a bloody devil worshipper or something?' says Jerome, the biggest and bulkiest of the uniformed officers.

A massive five-pointed symbol inside a circle has been daubed on the wall in red paint. Creepy.

'Well, that's certainly a pentangle,' says Mack with a grimace. Rose shivers and glances down at a dusty glass coffee table, on which sits a large book with the same symbol. *The Magick Bible*.

She moves out of the room and into the hallway, which smells of skunk, fried food and damp so badly she wrinkles her nose. This place is making Kenny Wiggins' home seem like a des res in comparison.

'Mr Meehan?' she calls up the stairs. 'It's the police. We're coming up, OK?'

Mack and the three uniforms fall in behind her as she climbs the stairs. Underfoot, the worn, faded runner that passes for stair carpet is gritty with dirt and loose in places.

Another, even more unpleasant smell hits the back of her throat as she reaches the top and she grimaces and puts a hand over her nose. Vomit? And possibly worse.

Turning into the first room on the left, she sees it is a dumping ground filled with boxes, carrier bags stuffed with papers, and a couple of guitar cases. One of those long flags you see at festivals or outside cafes in the summer is pressed into a corner, looking like a crushed green wing of some giant bird.

Mack is ahead of her, entering the only other bedroom up there.

She hears him suck in his breath, and then say, 'Oh, no.'

31

The atmosphere is sombre back at Silverton Street. Conversations are muted as people gather in the briefing room, where a tight-faced Rowland waits.

'So our suspect was found at five p.m. today with a needle in his arm after taking a fatal overdose of heroin. SOCO's initial examination of his flat has revealed a pair of gloves that seem to link him to Hannah Scott.'

She sticks an enlarged photograph onto the board showing a pair of black gloves, then points to the picture of the hairbrush found in Hannah's room.

'The brush that was used on Hannah Scott's hair post-mortem has some sticky residue on it that has come from hair products. I'm told it's quite common for handles of brushes or hairdryers to get like this.'

There's a small frown between her eyebrows at this, as if she finds it hard to imagine, while Rose pictures her own hairdryer's grubby handle.

'Anyway,' Rowland continues, 'this means we have been able to get a very good print of the glove worn by the killer.'

It wouldn't be the first time, Rose thinks, that a criminal believed simply wearing a pair of gloves was enough for them to 'leave no trace'. She knows of cases, even if she hasn't individually worked them, where the distinctive weave of a glove had been used to convict. Sometimes, the thin latex sort from the chemist could even transfer a fingerprint through the material.

'Not only could we potentially match the weave of the glove,' continues Rowland, 'but here' – she uses her laser pointer to indicate one fingertip of the glove – 'there is a tiny bobble of material where it has got caught on something.' She looks around the room. 'This exact shape is present on the glove we found at Meehan's property.'

A small 'whoop' goes up from the team, but Rowland's expression quickly quashes it.

Everyone is quiet once again.

She puts up another photo, this time of a handful of postcards showing a painting Rose instantly recognizes.

'We also have these cards,' she says, 'which were found at both crime scenes. And tech have confirmed that Meehan was a member of that Facebook group, which both our victims were in.' She glances at Rose when she says this, but that's the only acknowledgement of her role.

'So, together with the fact that he had been a handyman at those properties, it's looking pretty conclusive,' says Tom from the back of the room. 'Meehan was our man.'

Rowland sighs and runs a hand over her chin. 'It looks like it,' she says. 'Which is of course very good news indeed. But . . .' She pauses and Mack finishes her thought.

'But it's a bloody shame he never had to face justice, isn't it?' he says. 'He took the easy way out.'

There is a murmur of agreement around the room.

'What about Kirsty Perryman?' says Mack. 'Do we have any forensics, or is it all circumstantial in relation to her?'

Rowland looks over at him. 'For now, we have no forensics as such, but the team are still on this. We will have to wait and see.' She turns back to face the team. 'So I guess that's it,' she says. 'Well done, everyone.' But her tone is flat and it doesn't feel like they have just cracked a case.

Someone suggests the pub then, and Rose goes to collect her things, passing Sam on the way. They both stop.

'It feels weird, doesn't it?' she says, and he nods.

'Yeah, I know what you mean.' His expression is sombre. 'Something unsatisfying about it ending this way.'

They are looking into each other's eyes and a comfortable understanding passes between them. Tentatively, Rose says, 'Coming for a drink?' He hesitates, then smiles.

'You bet.'

By the time they are on the third round in the Dame Alice, everyone has got over the strange way the case has been concluded and is in celebratory mode.

Even Rowland has stayed and is currently in deep discussion with Tom at the bar, while Rose is crammed on a corner bench seat next to Sam and Ewa, whose normally quiet demeanour has been heightened by the double vodkas she has been drinking.

Mack, across the table, is talking about the moment they entered Meehan's weird flat.

'. . . when I saw that Devil-worshipping thing on the wall, I got such a shock,' he says. 'I mean, I've seen some things in my time, but that was new to me. I half expected to find a goat sacrifice going on in the next room.' This gets a laugh from everyone.

'What else do we know about him?' says Ewa, then hiccups and apologizes with an embarrassed glance around the group.

'Not a whole lot as yet,' Mack says. 'He had a history of substance abuse, from what we know so far. Mental health issues too. We're waiting for the rest of the background on him to come in.'

'It's an unusual way to kill someone,' says Sam, raising a half-drunk pint of Guinness to his lips. 'I mean, your usual woman-hater tends to use more . . .' he hunts for the word. 'I want to say *violent*, but suffocating someone is still a violent act. Not sure what I'm trying to say here!'

'No,' says Mack, 'I know what you mean. There's something very neat and tidy about putting a pillow on someone's face.

And the whole postcard and brushing the hair thing . . .' He grimaces, then says, 'Yeuch,' with feeling.

As Rose goes to get another round in, she enjoys the pleasant blurring the drink and company are bringing to her tangled thoughts. As she pays for drinks, she sees the door open and two people walk in.

It's Deputy Assistant Commissioner Martin Thomlinson, with another colleague, heads together in deep conversation. Rose can't stop herself from swivelling to look at Rowland, turning her whole body to do so.

Rowland clocks her first with a quick frown, then she sees Thomlinson and her expression looks open and vulnerable for a moment. When her eyes pass back to Rose, there is something incredibly close to hatred there. And it isn't for him, it's for her: Rose.

Oh God. She may as well have yelled, 'Hey, look who's arrived! It's the married man who dumped you!' across the crowded bar.

Turning to the tray of drinks in front of her, she hesitates before picking it up. Then she downs her own vodka in two gulps and orders another to take back to the table.

It's 11 p.m. and Sam is attempting to get Rose into an Uber, but she keeps thinking of things she wants to say to him.

'What's that lovely lentily thing your mum makes . . . is it Moong Dahl?' She slurs and stumbles slightly, so he has to catch her arm. 'I really want to eat that. Do you think I will be able to find it? Or can I come to your house and get some?'

She starts laughing then, because this suddenly feels immensely funny. Sam smiles indulgently and assures the driver she is not going to be sick. Rose, however, has turned away from the cab and is stalking off down the road.

'Hey, wait!' he calls after her as she crosses the road to the minimart, where she stands at the entrance, looking in.

'Rose, what are you doing?' he says, next to her. 'You're going to get a bad rating from that driver after this.'

When she turns to him, she finds that her eyes are brimming with tears she wishes she could squash back into her eyes.

'Oh, Sam,' she says, 'I mucked it up, didn't I? With you, I mean? You're so lovely.'

Even in her drunken state, she can see his discomfort, but somehow, she is reaching for him. Snaking her arms around his neck, she buries her face in the wool of his coat.

'Rose, don't do this,' he says, gently removing her arms and placing them back at her sides. His face is kind, but still, the humiliation hits her in a hot wave.

'I can't even give you a hug?' That wave is turning to sour anger, so the words come out much harsher than she'd intended. 'I thought we were mates. That's what you said, isn't it?' She puts on a deep voice: *'Let's be friends.'*

'We are, but . . .' he makes a sound of exasperation and takes a step back, both palms raised. His cheeks are flushed, and it seems to Rose that he has never looked better.

'I can't be doing with these constant mixed signals from you.' He stops and his shoulders slump. 'Anyway, I'm with Lucy now.'

A silence falls, broken by a rowdy group of lads crossing the road towards them. The one at the back, a scrawny guy with a floppy beanie and a long beard says, 'Oi, you cunts, I'm not having that!' and gives Rose and Sam a look of curiosity before passing.

'I need to go,' says Rose, and starts to walk away quickly.

'Rose!' Sam calls behind her. 'You've had a hell of a day. Let me get you into a cab, OK? We can probably flag one down or go to the rank down the road.'

Rose spins around to face him and hisses, 'I'm a policewoman. I don't need a fucking chaperone.'

She hears him quietly say 'OK' as she stalks down the street, attempting to hold her head high.

32

Rose gulps down water from a pint glass at the kitchen sink, drinking so fast that it slops down the front of her shirt. She knows she is going to have the mother of hangovers tomorrow.

Speaking of mothers, she looks anxiously round the room and hopes she won't have to put up with that tonight on top of everything else. Climbing the stairs to bed, she feels as though her feet have weights attached to them.

Once in bed, she attempts to get comfortable but all she can see is Russ Meehan's thin arm, banded with ropy veins and flung out on that dirty sheet covering the couch. The needle was lying flaccidly where it was still inserted into the vein. A thought comes to her that causes an electric bolt of adrenaline, waking her up even more.

That'll show you, Moony. It was all down to a sad misfit with a disordered life and some broken part of his brain caused him to do bad things. No supernatural goings-on. Nothing but regular police work that led them to him.

And yet . . .

Those women were genuinely convinced that someone had been coming to them in their dreams. How had Meehan done that?

Rose turns over in bed.

It doesn't matter. Forget about it. Go to *sleep*.

The hangover begins to kick in around 4 a.m., when Rose becomes aware of a terrible pounding at the back of her skull, like someone is repeatedly hitting it with a blunt instrument. Her eyes feel glued together and the inside of her mouth so sticky and gross, she can't bear to try opening her lips.

Padding downstairs with a blanket around her shoulders, she gulps down paracetamol and orange juice. It's 5 a.m. when she comes to, curled up on the sofa. She doesn't remember sleeping but suddenly she is disorientated. Something damp is on her arm. Yanking up her sleeve, she sees that she has scratched her arm so badly that she has drawn blood.

Wrapping the baggy cardigan around herself, she huddles into the smallest shape she can make, a ball of misery. The thought of going to work is appalling, not least because she made a tit of herself with Sam.

Then there's Rowland. Rose is acutely aware that her days at Silverton Street are numbered. She looks around at the depressing living room, stuck in the 1980s with its ugly bookcases that never held a single book, only cheap ornaments, and now empty.

It is time to make a change. Maybe she will take a couple of days off; start throwing stuff out.

This thought galvanizes her and she decides she is going to call in sick. She has never done it before, but since the case is closed, she won't be missed as much.

Rose goes into the kitchen to retrieve her phone, which she neglected to charge. As she looks inside her large shoulder bag for it, she sees the two slim folders she was given by Moony the other day. She hesitates for a moment then takes her phone to the charger in the kitchen, plugs it in, and types out a message about having been ill. It's blatant, when she was seen drunk last night. But she finds she doesn't care that much. Instead, her gaze keeps being dragged back to her bag and those two files inside it.

Meehan is dead, isn't he?

The case is *over.*

But something feels wrong. It has felt wrong ever since the briefing when Rowland laid out all the evidence that damned the man they had found dead. Rose is adept at ignoring the things that scream inside her, at ignoring her deepest instincts. Her arm prickles in response.

Maybe she will have a little look, then she can throw those files away and try to forget about them.

She pours a large mug of coffee, then goes to the table, gets them out and begins to read.

33

Kirsty

Kirsty comes through the front door and Joy bustles ahead of her, chatting as she does so about how she has filled the fridge and put the heating on in advance.

'Now,' she says, turning to Kirsty with a frown, 'are you absolutely sure you don't want to come back to my house tonight?'

Kirsty smiles. 'No,' she says. 'I just want to be in my own bed again. In my own home.' She is exhausted by the simple journey from hospital to home and longs to lie on the sofa and watch rubbish television. She is already missing the presence of the little dog and has been thinking that she might get one of her own. Not a puppy. Maybe a rescue dog. Something with a bit of attitude.

The news that the man suspected of attacking her is dead has given her back her life. She is still having flashbacks, and the dreams haven't completely stopped. But that's all they are now. Dreams. She knows that none of it is really happening. She is safe, at last.

The tiny worm of doubt that the police didn't have a conclusive case against him for the crime against her can be ignored. The nice Family Liaison Officer, Carol, who visited her in the hospital today, told her that the investigating team believed there were enough links between her attack and the murder of Hannah Scott for them to presume that the same man was responsible. And anyway, someone had been round to make her house more secure than ever before. No one was getting in here without her permission, not ever again.

It takes another hour before she can convince Joy to leave her on her own. When the other woman – so kind, but so noisy – finally goes, with an insistence that she can come back the minute she is needed, Kirsty lies back on the sofa and looks around with a heavy sigh.

She feels like she has been to hell. But at last she is free and she won't even have to stand up in court and be in the same room as that man, which she had been dreading. How could she have ever explained the things that had happened before that night? Whatever the police think, she knows that the man – she didn't want to hear his name – had found a way to visit her in her dreams before he came to attack her in the real world. Joy doesn't believe this either, but Kirsty is tired of talking about it. He is dead. Whatever he was, whatever kind of real-life monster, he is gone.

It's still only ten o'clock when she decides to get ready for bed. Being in hospital was exhausting and all she wants is to float into soft oblivion in her freshly changed sheets.

But first she decides to rearrange her bedroom. There is a symbolism in this. It will be the start of the new her, the one who sleeps like a normal person and doesn't turn the process into something that absorbs all her waking hours too.

Kirsty drags first her dressing table, then her chest of drawers with difficulty towards the bedroom door, where she wedges them to make room to move the bed, the all-important bed.

She is sweating and her arms ache as she pulls the bed, an inch at a time, across the room and into a new position behind the door.

She doesn't need to be able to face the door from her bed. It's probably bad Feng Shui anyway, she thinks, panting as she flops onto the bed.

A few minutes later, she has moved the other items into their new spaces. It doesn't feel quite right like this, but she is too tired to do anything about it. Her hands trembling from all the exertion, she begins to undress for bed.

After brushing her teeth in the bathroom, she comes back into her bedroom, frowning at the realization that it doesn't look right like this, that she won't in fact be able to do anything but put it back to how it was. But that will have to wait until the morning.

Climbing into bed, Kirsty's heart begins to pound. Old habits die hard and she has missed out too many stages of her ritual to be able to relax. She switches on the radio and lets the low murmur of voices burble into the room, keeping her eyes fixed open until they become too heavy and she finally succumbs.

Heart pounding, she awakes with a cry.

It takes a few more seconds for Kirsty to realize that daylight is seeping through the curtains in a pale winter wash. It's not the night any more. Turning to look at her clock radio, she sees it is 8.30 a.m.

The night is over. She slept all the way through. No night-mares. No strange visitors.

She is free.

Relief is a flood of sweet warmth from her crown to her extremities that makes her want to cry and laugh all at once. She lies there for a few more moments, savouring the feeling of total freedom. Work have been brilliant, and she has another four days before she needs to go back. Maybe she will think about doing something different. She can do anything now.

Kirsty has a leisurely shower and uses the expensive shower gel given to her ages ago that she had forgotten she had. Luxuriating under the hot water she stays there until it begins to run cool, then pads through to her bedroom and puts on a onesie so comfortable that wearing it feels like being given a hug.

When she opens the fridge, she smiles to see what Joy has put in there. There are half a dozen eggs, some bacon and a pint of milk, along with the sort of old-fashioned butter she would never buy and some raspberry jam. A loaf of nutty brown bread sits on the side. Not the white sliced stuff Kirsty favours, but she is so appreciative of the gesture that she makes two thick slices of toast and smothers them in butter and jam. She makes a cup of weak, milky tea in her favourite mug with the funny little poodle on the side and sits down at the table, where Joy has thoughtfully put her post into a neat pile.

There are a couple of bills, which she can't be bothered to look at now, so she slings them to one side, and several Get Well Soon cards from old friends and people at work. Funny, she thinks, she probably wouldn't have known what to send when someone wasn't ill but had been almost murdered in their beds, but some of the older people in her life clearly had no such qualms.

Once she has finished the post, she remembers that something woke her earlier and that it was most likely the sound of the letter box. The postman doesn't usually come that early, but now she is being all organized, she will check and deal with whatever it is straight away.

In the hallway, she yawns as she sees that there is a postcard on the mat, on top of a flyer from a local Indian restaurant. The postcard looks like it was hand-delivered.

She picks it up then feels an unpleasant jolt at the picture.

It's an old-fashioned painting, showing some horrible goblin thing, which is sitting on a sleeping woman's chest and staring defiantly out, like it is looking right at you.

Why on earth has she been given this? It doesn't seem to be advertising anything as far as she can see. She peers at the information about the name of the painting printed on the back.

The Nightmare.

34

**WEST YORKSHIRE POLICE –
RESTRICTED WHEN COMPLETE**

Statement of: Michael Pearse

Age: 59

Occupation: Lorry driver

This statement (consisting of 2 pages, each signed by me) is true to the best of my knowledge and belief and I make it knowing that, if it is tendered as evidence in court, I shall be liable to prosecution if I have wilfully stated in it anything which I know to be false, or do not believe to be true.

I am the above-named person and I am making this statement in regards to the death of Miss Ronata Betts, known as Ronnie, on 5 August 2010.

I have been the partner of Ronnie for two years. On the night in question I was coming back from a two-day job to Calais and I entered the house using my own key at around midnight.

I had left a message for Ronnie at Doncaster services telling her I would be home late, and she replied to say she was excited to see me but would go to bed and I could wake her up on my return.

When I came into the bedroom I could tell that something wasn't right because the bedcovers were dishevelled, and she was lying very still in them. I called her name then in a panic, in case she'd been taken ill, but she was not responsive and that was when I realized she was dead. I called 999 and an ambulance came a little later, but I am not sure what time that was.

The reason I am making this statement is because it is my belief that something happened to my Ronnie and I want it on record. As I told the police officer at the front desk, she looked like someone who had been given a scare and her mouth and eyes were open like someone who had had a terrible shock.

I often had stints away and Ronnie used to get nervous when I was on the road because she didn't sleep well and in the time before she passed she kept saying that a man was coming into the room at night and scaring her. I didn't believe her at first and I will regret that until my dying day. She had very bad dreams as a rule and used to often have to take sleeping pills if I was away, but these dreams were getting worse and worse. Before I went to Calais she got upset and said to me, 'Mick I really think the man is going to get me at some point because he is so scary', and I comforted her as best I could but as I say, I thought this was just her imagination.

But when I saw what she looked like in the bed it was my belief that someone did get in despite the home security measures that were in place and that he somehow caused her heart to fail from fear.

This statement is true to the best of my knowledge.

There is a note from a PC Simon Burns pinned to the witness statement that says:

Death confirmed natural causes by Leeds Infirmary on 6 August 2010. Thorough search of property showed no possible access points for intruder. Case will not be passed to Coroner at this time.

The other sheet of paper in the file was a print out of a crime report, dated January 2011.

It was a perfunctory account of several visits to a police station from August 2010 to January 2011 by a woman called Mary Donovan.

The interesting part came at the end, in the officer's notes.

Mrs Donovan has been in several times over the last few months with a claim that someone is coming into her room at night and 'standing over her' in a threatening manner. We have had conversations with her daughter, a Clare Morton of Haxby Farm, Longleigh Lane LS29 6QR who appears to believe what her mother is saying.

I have been round to look at the property and advised on security. There was no sign of any break in and the security was otherwise good. Ms Morton has subsequently informed us that her mother is now deceased, following a heart attack. The matter is now closed.

35

By nine-thirty the next morning, Rose is looking up at the sign reading THE NORTH on the M1.

There has been a weather warning for Yorkshire and the west of the country, with a suggestion of heavy storms. As Rose bears down on Loughborough, there's a gentle tap of rain that her wipers smear across the window as the wind begins to wallop the sides of the car.

After a stop at a service station off the M1, Rose drags her weary body back into the car. It's raining hard, and visibility is very poor. It feels as though every other vehicle is a massive lorry, which whips up a deathly spray and makes her little car feel as though it is immersed in thick fog. She has to crawl along at 50 mph, peering through the gloom with tired, gritty eyes. Her hands are clawed around the steering wheel so that she has to keep giving them a shake to get rid of the numbness.

The first address is in a village called Monxton, which is about ten miles from Leeds. Even though it is only two o'clock in the afternoon, it feels like twilight and the sky has a sinister violet tinge to it, as though building itself up for some truly apocalyptic weather.

*

While the rain has died down, the wind is so strong that when she parks and attempts to get out of the car, she is momentarily unable to open the door. It's like a burly bloke is leaning his weight against it for fun.

She looks around at the slightly depressing estate. There is a row of shops, including a dry cleaner's and, bizarrely, one that sells trophies and celebratory cups, along with a shabby bakery and a Lloyd's chemist. Behind the shops is a terrace of two-storey houses in a dirty grey stone with dark-edged windows that seem to glower in the fading light.

Rose feels a wild stab of anxiety that she might have driven for four hours for nothing. Michael Pearse, after all, is a long-distance lorry driver. He could be halfway across the continent at the moment. She could have passed him going the other way on the M1. She hasn't even made a plan about where to stay tonight, having thought she would find somewhere cheap in Leeds city centre later.

But she is here now. If there is the tiniest chance that they've got it wrong and Russ Meehan wasn't the man who attacked Kirsty Perryman and murdered Hannah Scott . . . if he is still out there, then she's going to hunt him down. Speaking to local police is no good. She knows exactly what kind of mindset she will meet there. Her own. At least, her own until this whole crazy case happened.

No, she must speak to the people directly involved if there is any way she can. It's all she has left. Doing her job to the very best of her ability.

It feels like all the carefully constructed walls she has built around herself since she was a young girl are crumbling. The world doesn't work the way she wanted to believe it did, outside of that house infested with ghosts.

Saying this even in her head makes her stomach swoop like going fast over a humpbacked bridge.

She tries it out loud:

'I'm Detective Constable Rose Gifford and I see dead people.'

She begins to laugh and soon she's uncomfortably close to losing control. Wiping her sore eyes, she leans her full weight into the car door to open it, and steps outside.

Rose tries to tidy her windswept hair behind her ears as she knocks on the door of the last address she has for Michael Pearse. There is an England flag in one of the upstairs windows and the front door has a sign that says, *Love me, Love my Doberman.* Rose shifts uneasily and waits as a cacophony of barking explodes inside the house, along with an ominous thump as something hurls itself at the door.

'Shut it, Prince!' The door is open now and a teenage girl stands there, somehow holding onto the collar of a massive beast that is barking wildly and revealing an array of terrifying yellow teeth. The girl has fair hair in a high ponytail and a stripy onesie with slipper Uggs. Despite the slightly orange foundation and the false lashes, she looks very young.

'Yeah?' she says as the dog lurches again. 'Stop it!' she yells, yanking on its collar.

'I'm sorry to bother you,' says Rose, 'but I'm actually looking for a Michael Pearse. Does he live here?'

The girl's eyes narrow. 'That's my dad,' she says. 'Why do you want him?'

Rose experiences a flood of intense relief that's rear-ended by a sudden conviction he isn't going to be at home.

'I'm a policewoman, from London,' says Rose, and the girl's eyes widen, so that she suddenly looks very young. 'There's nothing wrong,' Rose adds hurriedly, 'but I wondered if I might talk to your dad about a statement he gave a few years ago?'

The girl stares at her, mouth slightly open, and Rose feels a wave of intense weariness. At the very least, she was hoping for a cup of tea.

'I'm DC Rose Gifford,' she says when the silence starts to become awkward.

'I'll get him,' says the girl, almost comically polite. 'He's napping, but he said he wanted up about now, so it's no bother.'

Her accent, to Rose's ears, sounds warm and welcoming, despite her initial reservations. 'Come on in,' says the girl, then again, 'I'll go get him.'

She gestures vaguely towards an open doorway from which Rose can hear the sounds of a television playing, then skips up the stairs two at a time.

To Rose's relief, the dog has lost interest and padded off down the hallway to what she assumes is a kitchen, judging by the loud lapping of water that can be heard.

She goes into the small sitting room and looks around at her surroundings. The television is so vast it almost takes up an entire wall. It's currently showing something Rose recognizes as a big Netflix series about screwed-up superheroes. There are two ancient leather sofas and a real-fire-effect gas fire is belting out heat, so condensation runs down the windows in rivulets.

The girl had been doing homework on the coffee table by the looks of it. A textbook on *Macbeth* lies next to a lever arch file and a plate of half-eaten toast.

Rose takes her coat off and fans her red face with a hand. She's sweating and desperately thirsty.

There is a murmured conversation from upstairs and then the thumping of feet coming down the stairs that seem to shake the small house to its frame.

A short, overweight man in a rumpled black t-shirt and grey tracksuit bottoms comes into the room. He has a bald head and a red face. He is looking at her with so much suspicion that she gets to her feet with a broad smile and extends her hand.

'Hi,' she says. 'I'm so sorry to drop in like this, but I have driven up from London today and I am working on an enquiry that I believe . . .' she falters. What does she believe? That is a question that would take a very long time to answer. She changes tack.

'I mean, I wanted to have a quick word in relation to a statement you made in 2010 to West Yorkshire police about a Ronata Betts?'

Pearse's entire body clenches, reminding Rose of a dog that has a scent in its nose. Something eager blooms across his face then, and discomfort prickles about her flimsy basis for this visit.

'I did,' he says, then to the girl behind him, 'Make us a brew, Chlo, OK?' They both look enquiringly to Rose and she smiles and says she would love one, thanks.

'Come and take a seat,' he says. *Tek a seat.*

Rose sits on one of the sofas, which is covered by a fine layer of dog hair, and crosses her legs. It is ferociously hot in here and her head is swimming with the heat and tiredness.

'Have you found owt new, then?' says Pearse, his eyes fixed on Rose's face.

'Well,' says Rose, 'I have to admit that this is an unofficial visit and I can't offer you any new information, owing to the fact that I wasn't privy to the original investigation.' She tails off, suddenly aware that there would have been no investigation.

Pearse's shoulders visibly slump.

'So why are you here?' he says.

Rose hesitates, choosing her words carefully before she speaks. 'Mr Pearse . . .'

'You can call me Mike.'

'Right,' she says, 'Mike . . . I'm here because we have had a couple of crimes in our neck of the woods that have . . .' she pauses, '. . . a rather strange aspect to them. One of my colleagues brought to my attention the statement you gave about Ms Betts. As I was in the area, I thought I might ask you a few questions. Is that all right?'

Pearse, Mike, stares at her and the girl who is presumably his daughter comes into the room with a tray neatly laid out with a teapot, mugs, milk in a jug and a packet of sugar lumps. There is also a packet of Ginger Nut biscuits. Rose's mouth waters at the sight.

'Thanks, love,' he says to the girl. 'Best go up and get on with your homework upstairs.'

'But, Dad . . .'

'No buts,' he says firmly. 'On you go.'

The girl heaves a dramatic sigh and gathers up her things before eyeing Rose then leaving the room. Mike closes the door and begins to pour the tea. He has neat, precise movements for such a bulky man, Rose thinks, as he hands her a cup and beckons for her to add milk and sugar. Thanking him, she takes a sip of the tea, which is strong and reviving. The biscuit packet is offered and Rose refuses, worrying that she might not be able to stop if she starts.

He takes a sip of his own tea and then regards her.

'What do you want to know exactly?' he says after a moment.

She puts down her cup and rummages in her bag for her notebook.

'I'm interested in why you went to the police about Ms Betts's death,' says Rose, notebook on her knees and pen poised, 'when a verdict of natural causes was delivered at the inquest?'

Mike Pearse sits back in the chair and rests his chubby hands on his thick thighs. He has attractive eyes and may have been a looker, once.

'It was the visits,' he says matter-of-factly.

'Visits?'

'Yes,' he says. 'Someone was frightening her for ages before she— before she passed on. At first I kept telling her it were nowt but bad dreams.' He gives a short, sad laugh. 'She were a terrible sleeper, Ronnie. Up and down all night.'

Rose has another sip of tea and her stomach rumbles so audibly that she blushes.

Mike smiles and proffers the packet, with an encouraging jiggle.

'Go on,' he says. 'Sounds like you've come a long way and you might need these.'

She thanks him, takes one then says, 'So go on, why is it that you think all this wasn't just in her head?'

He sighs audibly.

'Look,' he says, 'I'm not daft. I didn't believe in all the woo-woo stuff that Ronnie were into.' He wiggles his fingers at, 'woo-woo'. 'But,' he continues, 'there was something about the way she described it to me that didn't seem like it were all in her head. I mean, dreams don't usually involve someone actually touching your face? And the week before she died, someone really had been into the house.'

'Oh?' Rose's attention pricks up at this. 'I didn't see that on the report.'

'Well, that's because I only found out after, and when I went back, I pretty much got the bum's rush.'

'How did you find out?'

'Her neighbour mentioned it to me. She's moved away now, but she said Ronnie was convinced that stuff had been rearranged in her room.'

'Why didn't she tell you?' says Rose, and his face seems to collapse in on itself. His eyes fill with tears.

'Because we had a row before she died,' he says, closing his eyes briefly before continuing. 'I said I thought she needed to see someone – you know, someone professional. And she were upset with me. Thought I didn't believe her.'

Rose nods. 'I see,' she says. 'But I have to ask you, what changed your mind?'

Mike sits forward a little in the chair.

'Because,' he says fiercely, 'she died looking as though something had literally frightened her to death. I don't know about you, but I don't think any nightmares are as severe as that. I think someone was in her room. And I think the shock killed her.'

Ten minutes later, Rose dashes back to the car as the wind whips her hair across her face and into her mouth. The rain is icy cold, colder than any rain she has experienced before, and she shivers as she sits in the car and digests what she has learned.

There wasn't much that Pearse could tell her that was useful. But his utter determination that Ronnie Betts had some manner of night visitor was hard to ignore. Sure, she thinks, it could be denial mixed with guilt that he wasn't there.

But what if someone had found a way to stalk her through her nightmares? Rose knows this is insane. Yet . . .

What if she was practice for the real thing? For the murder of Hannah Scott?

But why the long gap? It doesn't make sense.

If, though, there is even the slightest chance these cases are connected, Rose must see this through. Grimacing at the wind howling outside the car, she turns on the engine. There is one more place she needs to go.

36

Rose swears, repeatedly and loudly, as she attempts to peer through the windscreen and not crash the car because she very clearly hasn't reached her destination, despite what the bloody satnav is saying.

It's a place called Haxby Farm, at the end of Longleigh Lane. She's looking for a turning off this winding B- road lined with stone walls, which feels as though it may simply fill with water like some terrifying water slide before too long.

The rain is so heavy that the windscreen wipers can't keep up and there are only tiny moments of visibility that instantly pass. She crawls along at twenty miles an hour, knuckles rigid on the steering wheel, silently praying that a tosser in a Land Rover or a tractor doesn't suddenly come careering around a corner, killing them both.

As the satnav repeats the assertion that she has arrived, Rose longs for London, where a single postcode might encompass ten houses. Surely half of Yorkshire is contained within the one she wants.

Rose is a very good driver. She has never felt genuine fear before on the road. But as the car is buffeted by winds and the rain lashes as if on a personal vendetta, she realizes that this is no longer safe. She must find somewhere to stop and assess what to do next.

A little beyond the next bend, she spots a passing place. With a sigh of relief, Rose pulls in and looks to her right. There's a gate, and in the field beyond she glimpses something moving. With a leap of hope, she sees it is a farmer, struggling with a piece of machinery by the hedge.

As soon as she climbs out of the car, she is instantly soaked to the skin, but she pushes against the force of the wind and approaches the gate.

'Excuse me!' she yells and waves an arm.

The farmer, a good-looking man in his thirties with curls plastered to his scalp and dark eyes, looks over and then jogs towards the gate where she stands.

'Help you, love?' he calls out, the wind almost snatching away his voice.

It's all true, she thinks. About them being nicer here.

'I'm lost!' she yells. 'Can you tell me where I might find Longleigh Lane?'

'Yer on it, love,' he bellows back. 'Where d'you need to be?'

'Haxby Farm? Am I close?'

He smiles and pushes his hair back from his face. 'Yep, it's hard to see, but the entrance is back that way, about two hundred yards on the right. There's a bus stop you'll see first, then get ready to turn.'

Rose thanks him.

'Take it careful though!' he calls. 'Dangerous weather, this.'

'Thank you!' she says. 'And I hope you get this, um, sorted.'

He grins as he hurries back to the mysterious thing he was doing. Rose climbs back into the car, shivering as she starts the engine and performs a hair-raising three-point turn.

The instructions are spot on, and Rose feels an intense relief when she sees the turning. There is even a sign, which she hadn't spotted on the way past the first time.

The track is slick with ruts and mud. Rose longs for a 4x4 as her car complains and whines. She crawls and bumps her way up the lane. It's so dark here, and the track appears to be sided by high hedges. It feels like she is in a tunnel without end, and she is grateful when the track opens out.

There is a barn to her left and some farm machinery stacked up on the right. The house itself is made from grey stone lit by a few floodlights. A yellow Labrador appears from somewhere and comes running over, barking hysterically. She likes dogs generally, but not when they appear to be guarding properties, like the two she has encountered today.

As she contemplates whether it is safe to get out of the car, light spills from the front door of the house and a woman appears, watching her.

Rose pushes open the door and speaks gently to the dog, which immediately presses up against her legs with an adoring look on its face. She pats it on the head and begins walking toward the woman at the door, wishing she wasn't quite so dishevelled and damp.

'Hi,' she says, 'I'm sorry to turn up like this, but I'm looking for Clare Morton?'

'That's me,' says the woman. She has a weathered complexion, with tired eyes and thick black hair pulled back into a bun. Dressed in a patterned fisherman's jumper and jeans, her arms are crossed a little defensively. 'How can I help you?'

It's so wild that Rose can barely get the words out. Thankfully, Clare Morton's demeanour changes as she registers the miserable state Rose is in.

'Look,' she says, 'it's filthy out here, come inside and we can talk out of the rain.'

'Thank you,' says Rose, embarrassed at the way her teeth are chattering as she enters the brightly lit, narrow hallway. The dog comes in after her and the woman shouts as it bounds through into the house, spraying drops of water as it goes.

'Bloody animal,' she says. 'So what's this about? Not the best time to be travelling up here, what with this storm.'

'No,' says Rose apologetically, 'I'm a stupid southerner and a little out of my depth with all this *weather*.'

Clare Morton smiles, a new warmth in her eyes.

'So,' says Rose, quickly recovering her professionalism. 'I'm a policewoman. My name is Detective Constable Rose Gifford and I'm with the Met. This is not official business – well, not really . . . but I wondered if I could talk to you about some questions you raised over the death of your mum?'

The woman flinches, as though this were the very last thing she'd expected Rose to say. A hand snakes to a thin gold chain around her neck.

'I'm not sure how I can help, but you'd better sit down and warm up, since you're here,' she says.

Rose thanks her and takes off her sodden shoes. She places them neatly next to pile of shoes of varying sizes, from a pair of toddler-sized pink trainers to some very large men's walking boots.

'Come on through,' says Clare Morton, just as a high-pitched voice yells, 'Mumeeee!' and some very heartfelt crying follows.

'Oh bloody hell, what now.'

Rose walks behind the hurrying woman and comes into a kitchen whose instant warmth and light envelop her, making her even more aware of how wet she is.

There is a range at one end of the room, which adds to the rustic effect of the whitewashed stone walls. A kitchen table is covered in cups and children's plastic plates, with colouring books and a big box filled with a jumble of coloured pens and pencils. Two small children, maybe six and seven, stare at Rose with wide eyes. They both have the same Celtic looks as their mother, although the smaller boy has been crying and his face is red and blotchy. The little girl has a defiant look as she holds an Innocent Smoothie drink out of the boy's reach.

'What's going on?' says Clare. 'Why all this mithering?'

'She won't let me have my drink!' The novelty of Rose's arrival isn't enough to distract the boy from the injustice that has been done to him and he begins to wail again, his mouth a small pink O.

'He spilled it on my picture!' says the little girl.

'Oh, for goodness' sake,' says their mother. 'I've had enough of the pair of you today. Go and watch more telly, I don't even care any more.'

The children exchange delighted glances and the boy does a cute little fist pump as they clamber off chairs and scurry out of the room. Rose can't help grinning.

'I think those two may go far,' she says.

'Or become master criminals,' says the woman with a wry look, and Rose laughs. The tension has eased and a great slap of sheer exhaustion hits her in the face in its wake.

'Let me make you a hot drink and get you a towel, and then you can explain why you're here, OK?'

'Thank you so much, Ms Morton,' says Rose.

'Call me Clare, please.'

A few minutes later, Rose has a tea in front of her in a large earthenware mug and has towelled the worst of the rain from her hair. She's still freezing cold, but as she takes a grateful sip of the tea, she feels the violent chills start to subside.

Clare places her hands on the table as though preparing for something difficult.

'So,' she says. 'Go on.'

As she did with Michael Pearse, Rose chooses her words carefully. She tells Clare that there are aspects of a recent case in London that appear to chime with the claims she made regarding the death of her mother.

When she finishes, Clare puffs out air through her cheeks.

'Look,' she says, staring down at her small hands, which have roughened red skin on the knuckles. 'I always had this fear that something scared my mother that night. That someone got into the house. But there was no proof. She always had these tall tales, you see . . .'

She drifts off.

'Go on,' prompts Rose.

'Well,' says Clare, 'she was a funny old thing, my mother. Had some strange ideas about this house.'

'Oh?' says Rose. 'What kind of ideas?'

Clare pulls a face and then gets up to close the door to the kitchen. 'Last thing I want is our Katie hearing this, because she already has an over-active imagination,' she explains. Then, 'My mother used to believe the house was haunted.' She is blushing as she says it. 'I feel stupid even saying this to a policewoman like you,' she adds with a self-deprecating laugh.

'Please don't worry. I hear all sorts of strange things in my job.'

If only you knew.

'Right,' says Clare and begins to pick at some hardened candle wax on the wooden surface of the table. 'Well, I had no time for this nonsense. When we bought this farm and my mother came with us, we fell in love with the place. But she used to have terrible nightmares. She found out summat that upset her, and then she got some really crazy ideas.'

'What did she find out?' says Rose, cradling the warm mug in her hands and attempting to pull its warmth into her cold core.

'A girl died here,' says Clare with an anxious glance at the closed door. 'She climbed out of the top window onto the roof and threw herself off.'

Rose grimaces. 'Nasty,' she says. 'But what was it that your mother thought was happening before she died?'

Clare brings her arms in around her body, as though hugging herself, and her eyes cloud with sadness.

'She had been going on about her dreams, which started off being regular nightmares about that girl. Then it changed and she said a man was getting into the room and standing over her bed.'

A new chill squirms up Rose's spine. She waits for Clare to continue.

Clare gives herself a little shake. 'The thing is,' she says, 'I know it was all in her head, but sometimes . . .' she swallows, '. . . sometimes it seemed so realistic, what she were saying, that it gave me a bad feeling.'

Rose nods. There is silence for a few moments.

'But you believe she died of natural causes?' she asks.

Clare looks up, chewing her lip. 'Well . . .' she says, and then, with heat, 'I have to, don't I?'

'Why?' says Rose gently.

'Because we have to live here,' says Clare, eyes sparkling. 'And with ourselves. Because if there was more to it, and we did nothing . . .'

A crash from the other room followed by a scream has Clare on her feet, swearing under her breath as she leaves the room.

There is a sound of wailing with a thin, plaintive voice in protest above it and she can hear the rumble of Clare's gentle chiding, quickly becoming more frustrated.

The small windowpane in the kitchen suddenly rattles so hard that Rose jumps, and she shivers anew as she contemplates the idea of driving to wherever the nearest hotel is likely to be.

When Clare comes back into the room, pink-cheeked and with hooded, weary eyes, she is talking into a mobile phone.

'Shit, really?' she says, and eyes Rose in a colder way.

Then, 'Aye, OK then, love. What time, do you think, in the morning?' She nods and grimaces.

Moments later she hangs up and seems to brace herself before turning on a weak smile.

'Well, it turns out a couple of trees are down on either side of us on Longleigh Lane. We're going to be cut off until the morning, so you'll have to stay here.'

Rose gets to her feet.

'Oh,' she says. 'No, really, I can't impose like that. Is there any way at all I can get past?'

Clare waves a hand airily. 'Forget it,' she says briskly. 'You're going nowhere tonight.'

When Clare shows her to a small bedroom built into the attic space, Rose feels an intense yearning to be alone. It's horribly awkward, being an unwanted guest. She has no dry clothes and

Clare, being a kindly soul even though it is clear she would rather Rose wasn't there, has given her a pair of worn, soft pyjamas to put on for the evening while she dries Rose's clothes over the kitchen range.

Rose says she will catch up on a few emails, but Clare laughs and says, 'Good luck with that.'

Sure enough, the WIFI doesn't appear to be working.

She rereads the papers given to her by Moony, then dumps the envelope on the floor next to the bed.

Sighing, Rose lies back on the small bed and looks around her. The room has old-fashioned flowery wallpaper and lilac curtains. There is a bed covered in a colourful homemade blanket and a plain yellow duvet cover. A chest of drawers and a rickety chair painted white with an embroidered yellow cushion sit across the room. The bedside table is also painted white and looks as though it has been there for many years.

Rose's arm begins to itch, and she scratches it absent-mindedly.

Her fingers tingle with the desire to get on with some work online, but with a sense of resignation, she goes instead to the small bookshelf and picks up a battered copy of something called *Lace* by Shirley Conran, which she's never heard of, but looks like it might pass the time.

The evening drips away, somehow, after an uncomfortable meal of fish fingers, chips and beans where the two children stare at her as though she is a fairground oddity.

Rose is too bone-weary to care. After washing up, which she insists on doing, she takes herself off to the room at the top of the house.

She gets into bed by half past nine and can feel her eyes drooping before she has even turned off the light. The storm still rages and up here in the attic, it's like being buffeted about in a boat instead of in something rooted to the earth with concrete and steel.

But it's not enough to keep her awake. Soon, she is asleep.

37

He likes to come back here, when he can. Back to where it all started.

Sometimes he wonders if he will ever feel as alive as he did that first time, the night when, with his gentle whispers alone, he guided Helena out of her restless bed, where she tossed and turned in the throes of bad dreams, and encouraged her to open the dormer window.

It's only as an adult that he can analyse the reasons for it. Then, it had simply felt exciting and shiveringly transgressive in a way he couldn't describe.

Now he thinks it was about the fact that he'd never had any power in that family. Always the least important one, the one they left to 'get on with it' as his parents were so fond of saying. The one who could be ignored while all the fuss happened around his sister, with her endless needs.

It required a chair, the white one with the wicker seat they'd had all his life, for her to clamber on. He remembers her pink nightie being rucked inside her knickers and he gently eased it out so she would look nice. He wanted her to look her best on such a big night.

Things like that matter. When you are going on such an important journey, you need to look your very best.

When she was standing on the chair and reaching her arms up through the window, he had almost backed out. But then he saw the stars above her head, a wash of diamonds against the velvet black, and it was beautiful, all of it. It felt right.

A few more whispered words from him. Then he watched her pale feet, so much smaller than his, disappearing through the window.

The old lady living here had been the reason to come back. He hadn't been able to believe it when he saw her address on the paperwork.

He had no desire to push *her* out of a window. He wasn't a monster. But he craved something else. He wanted to watch that transition from sleep to death happening in front of him this time.

And now he is back, but there is someone else here. Someone he is not expecting to see at all.

38

Somewhere in the middle of the night, Rose becomes aware of dark shapes that flicker across the room like bats. Only she can't see them, or touch them, because she can't move. All she knows is that a terrible evil is around her, and then she awakes with a cry.

Grasping the glass of water with a trembling hand, she drinks it down. Her heart feels like it is going to ram its way out of her ribcage, and she is covered in sweat.

Switching on the light, she sees it is 3 a.m. A long time until morning.

By six there is the sound of piping voices from downstairs and Rose takes herself wearily to the big bathroom she used the night before, where she washes and uses the toothbrush given to her by Clare. Her eyes are shadowed and red, and her face looks pinched in the old spotted mirror above the sink.

Was any of this worth it?

Downstairs, the noise of the children and the radio on the windowsill are an assault.

Clare regards her and goes to pour tea from a large green pot, which Rose gratefully accepts, along with the thick slices of toast and marmalade she is offered.

'The road has been cleared,' says Clare. 'My Jamie rang earlier.'

'Is that your husband?' says Rose, and a shadow passes over Clare's face.

'Yep,' she says wistfully. 'Lucky bugger. Getting *stranded* in town.'

Rose doesn't know what to say, so remains quiet and then accepts a second cup of tea.

It's time to leave.

Rose thanks Clare profusely for her kindness, mentally making a note to send some flowers when she is back in London.

'Before I go,' she says, eyeing the little girl who is hanging on her mother's hand and watching her, '. . . that, um, family, you mentioned, who were here before. Do you know what happened to them?'

'Stop pulling, Katie!' she says, throwing a distracted look Rose's way. It's clear she wants Rose to go so she can continue with her job of thinly veiled crowd control. 'What? Oh, well both the parents died within a short space of time . . . cancer, in both cases, I think. And there was a brother. He was a doctor in town at Mum's surgery.'

'Oh yes?' says Rose. 'What was his name?'

'Oakley, I think. Yes, that's it,' says Clare. 'Doctor Oakley.'

The name pings in Rose's brain. Hannah's GP was called Oakley. Surely a coincidence?

Rose's car splats mud as she revs her way down the drive, and she has a horrible feeling she might get stuck there forever, but finally she is on the main road again and driving to wherever it is going to take to get a signal.

Her mind is churning with everything and she desperately wants to ring Mack. But what can she say? It's all too ridiculous. And he wouldn't approve of this mission of hers up north. Especially when she is meant to be off sick.

*

She keeps snatching up her phone, looking for a signal, and is quite aware that she might happily arrest someone for doing the same, in normal life. But nothing about this is normal.

Finally, as she comes towards the village before the one Michael Pearse lives in, she is able to pull into the car park of a pub.

She dials the number Pearse gave her the day before. After ringing so long that she was convinced it would go to voicemail, a groggy male voice says, 'Yup?'

'I'm sorry to bother you, Mr Pearse,' she says, 'but it's DC Rose Gifford here again – we met yesterday?'

'Oh, aye?' fully awake now.

'I have a quick question about Ronnie. Do you happen to know what her GP was called?'

'Oh yes,' he says, 'he was brilliant. Tried to help her in all sorts of ways. He was so supportive right the way through it all.'

'And his name?' Impatience cuts through her voice but she can't help it.

'Dr Oakley,' he says. 'Can't remember the Christian name, but definitely Oakley.'

Despite the tiredness that lurks in the background, Rose has never felt so awake in her life as she does right now, in this car park, ringing Mack.

When she hears his familiar greeting on the other end of the phone, she launches straight in:

'I know this is insane, but do we know if Hannah's doctor, James Oakley, is also Kirsty Perryman's?'

Mack must be outside, as she can hear a siren going past.

'What?' he says. 'What are you on about?'

'I'm in Yorkshire,' she says, then as he starts to speak, she cuts in, 'No wait, listen!' She transfers the phone to the other ear. 'Oakley lived up here, with a sister who killed herself. And years later, he was the GP for two women who died after reporting a man coming into their room and frightening them.'

'Are you sure?' Mack's voice is suddenly energized. 'Murdered?'

Rose pulls in a breath. She has to work hard not to have her words tumbling all over each other.

'Well, that's the thing,' she says. 'These cases weren't recorded as suspicious deaths, but the women's families felt something wasn't right. Like these two people were literally frightened to death.'

'Rose,' Mack says very quietly, as if not wanting to be overheard using her name. She feels something sink inside her at his tone. 'Kirsty Perryman rang us this morning, hysterical because she'd been sent one of those creepy postcards. That *Nightmare* painting. It's got Russ Meehan's fingerprints all over it. He must have sent it right before he overdosed.'

Rose is silent, her bubbling excitement suddenly stoppered.

'Look,' she says. 'If Oakley knew Meehan – and I think he did – he could have somehow got that postcard into Meehan's hands. I mean, why wear gloves to the crime scene then send that card without them? It doesn't make any sense.'

Mack is listening again, and she loves him because she can tell that, despite how nuts this all is, he isn't laughing at her.

'Mack, look,' she says carefully. 'I know how it sounds! But the things these people said match what Hannah Scott and Kirsty Perryman said about their assailant. I had to come up here and check it out. I just had to.'

There is a long pause, finally brought to an end by a slow release of breath.

'All right, kiddo,' says Mack. 'I'm still not clear on all this. But I have to tell you that we've had a stabbing at the Wood Green multiplex overnight, so no one is going to be interested in spending time on a case that is closed.'

Rose winces, guilt at skiving off work a physical weight in her stomach.

'But if you think this Oakley is worth looking into,' says

Mack, 'I will cover for you if needed. Do what you have to do today and tomorrow too if necessary.'

'Thank you,' she says quietly.

'Hang on a minute though,' he says. 'Didn't Kirsty tell us the man in her room was huge? As I recall, Oakley was a slight sort of fella.'

'Yeah,' she says. 'I think we gave Kirsty's description far too much credence,' she says. 'If any of us wake up with a man over the bed, he is going to take on monstrous proportions. Our brains simply register a predator. Someone who'd woken suddenly to find an intruder would be too disorientated to be accurate about details.'

Mack is clearly being called away. She hears a muffled conversation in the background.

'Look,' he says, 'do what you have to do, kiddo – but hey, be careful, OK?'

Once off the phone, Rose searches for Kirsty Perryman's number. It rings so long it almost goes to voicemail, but as Rose is about to leave a message, a querulous voice says, 'Yes?'

'Is that Kirsty?'

'Yeah, who is this?' She sounds as frail as a woman twice her age.

'It's DC Rose Gifford from Silverton Street. We met a couple of times?'

Silence.

'Can I ask you something, Kirsty?'

'If you must.'

'Thank you,' says Rose. 'Look. We're tying up a few loose ends on the case and I hope you won't mind me asking for a few details for our records?'

'Like I said, go ahead.'

'I only wanted to know,' says Rose carefully, 'who your doctor is?'

A pause.

'It's Dr Hussein at the Cowley Road practice.'

252

'Right,' says Rose, suddenly floored. Her body sinks into the seat, as though she is a very great weight. 'How long have you been there?'

'Oh, years and years,' says Kirsty. 'Why do you want to know that?'

'As I said, I'm filling in paperwork,' says Rose. She runs a hand over her face. 'Did you see her every time? Ever seen any other doctor there?'

'No, I don't think, I—' she stops abruptly. 'Although, there was that time they had a locum in. He was nice.'

'Oh yes?' A flare of hope ignites inside her.

'Yeah, he was really sympathetic about my sleeping problems. They usually only give you short shrift, you know? But he actually listened.'

Rose's heart is pitter-pattering in her chest.

'Remember his name?'

'No idea, sorry.'

'What did he look like?'

A pause. Then, 'He was ordinary, you know? Glasses. Beard, I think. Quite nice looking. Why?'

'Like I said, tidying up a few loose ends. Nothing to worry about,' says Rose, trying to keep the excitement from her voice. 'I'm grateful for your time. Anyway, I wanted to ask how you've been?' This was about as far away from why she was calling as it was possible to be, but after her poor start with Kirsty at the station, she is eager to change the woman's perception of her.

'Well, I had a good night's sleep in my flat,' says Kirsty, then her curt voice audibly wobbles. 'But some sick bastard trying to freak me out isn't helping my recovery at all.'

'Ah,' says Rose. 'You mean the postcard? I heard about that.'

'Yes!' says Kirsty, sounding close to tears. 'This really awful painting was on it. It's called *The Nightmare*, apparently. I mean, what sicko would even do that?'

Rose feels a strange settling inside. Like something in motion has stilled.

She's right about this. Russ Meehan didn't stalk and kill those women.

James Oakley, with his kind eyes and his beard and his supposed Hippocratic fucking Oath. He did it.

Now she just has to work out a way to catch him.

39

When Rose pulls into a space in the scruffy UCIT car park she sits for a minute or two, thinking about the last time she came here. She feels about ten years older.

Maybe it's because she has had to let go of something so heavy that she feels strangely frail and heady in its aftermath. It's so hard to admit, but she knows that fear of who she was, so long held close, had turned into a brick wall of prejudice over the years.

She wonders if this is the thing that has been missing in her as a police officer. Maybe Rowland knows that half of Rose's mind has been taken up by a Herculean act of self-denial.

Her arm itches on cue and she raises her sleeve to see the raw, red skin.

But if Rose believes that her own, seismic change of heart will mean that she'll be welcomed with open arms by DS Sheila Moony, she's mistaken.

Scarlett meets her in reception and if she is less effusive in her greetings this time, Rose recognizes her own coldness on the previous visit may have played a part.

Today Scarlett is wearing a pair of wide-legged cream trousers and a silky top with a wide collar over a lilac cardigan. Her hair is down and hangs in soft waves around her face.

'Your hair looks great,' says Rose as they walk down that gloomy corridor with its greenish-tinged light. Hair is usually a good start, she thinks. Sure enough, Scarlett turns to her with a broad smile. 'How do you get it to look as good as that?'

'I spend too much time and money on it,' she says. 'The fact that my wife is a hairdresser helps too!' she says.

Rose laughs. 'Well, I could do with sorting this mess out sometime,' she says, giving her hair a tug.

'It's actually lovely,' Scarlett says kindly. 'You're a busy person and it just needs a little TLC.' She pauses. 'Like we all do.'

In the office, Rose experiences that odd disorientation again but is relieved she didn't come across any dead tea ladies or other assorted phantoms on the way.

Adam gives her a warm smile when he sees her, which she returns, but Moony, head down over her desk, doesn't look up.

Adam slightly raises his eyebrows at Rose in a gesture she takes to mean anything from 'Don't worry, it's only her way' to 'You're in for a bumpy ride.'

When Moony still refuses to look up, Rose says her name, and the other woman stagily pretends to have only just seen her.

Rose experiences a stab of irritation. Should she have taken this straight to Rowland? Life has become incredibly confusing. She shifts from foot to foot then decides she is going to brazen it out.

Plastering an open look onto her face that she isn't feeling, she says, 'Right, so thanks for agreeing to see me.'

'I've got twenty minutes,' says Moony, stony-faced. 'Take a seat.'

Rose grabs a chair and sits down next to the desk. Again, there is a motorbike helmet and some leathers stashed next to it.

Before Rose can say anything, Moony speaks.

'Have to say, I'm surprised to see you back here.'

Rose feels her treacherous cheeks flushing. 'Well,' she says, 'let's say that my mind has been opened a little more since I saw you the other day.'

'I'm glad to hear that, DC Gifford,' says Moony, 'because I don't have time to deal with a certain type of police officer. I've met enough of them in this job, let me tell you.'

'What kind?' says Rose, even though she isn't sure she wants to know the answer.

Moony sits back in her seat so it bounces squeakily. She's got fancy cowboy boots on today with her plain jumper and jeans. They are swirled with red and black, as if flames are licking up her ankles. She drums her stubby fingers, knobbly with those knuckle-duster rings, on the table and eyes Rose as though mentally sizing her up. It's not particularly pleasant and Rose wonders what she is like in interview.

'The kind who take such a blinkered view of the world that they end up allowing bad people to get away with doing a whole load of bad things.'

Rose meets her gaze evenly.

'That's not me,' she says. 'So we're all good.'

Moony has the merest hint of a smile around her lips and she looks at Rose a moment longer, then slaps her hand against the desk. Her rings make a loud retort against the wood.

'Good,' she says. 'Then you'd better fill me in on why you're here.'

Rose begins by telling Moony that the investigation into Hannah Scott's murder had been concluded following the death of Russ Meehan. Then she describes how, after reading the case files Moony had given her, she set off for Yorkshire. She pauses when she gets to the night-time part, skipping forward to the morning and the discovery of the Oakley connection. Adam has migrated over to the table while she is speaking and listens intently until she has finished.

'Wow,' he says, 'interesting. But what about the forensics that put Meehan in the frame? Wasn't there something about a glove—'

'I reckon Oakley knew him,' says Rose. 'Someone like Meehan, with all his drug and mental problems, would have had contact with a lot of doctors. What if Oakley knew he had a connection to the household and planted it there?'

Moony, looks thoughtful. 'It's possible,' she says. 'Have you called it in?'

'I told my senior officer, but they've had a stabbing in the last two days and the fact that the case against Meehan was so overwhelming means this is not going to be given any time. I mean,' she pauses, 'I'm not even meant to be here. I should be there, dealing with the rest of our caseload.'

'But you're here,' says Moony. 'So presumably you feel very strongly that this doctor is to blame.'

Rose summons up her confidence, even though her stomach is churning. 'I do.' She pauses before continuing, hotly. 'And the bastard has sent a postcard to Kirsty Perryman too – *that* postcard. No useful fingerprints on it, but it's like he's still toying with her. He might even go back to finish the job.'

Moony looks up at Adam.

'Thoughts?' she says, and he makes a face.

'I think our starting point should be a visit to our not-so-friendly GP to see what he has to say for himself.'

'Good plan,' says Moony, and she starts to speak again but Rose cuts her off.

'One thing I should mention,' she says. 'I think I've experienced this sleep thing myself, or something like it.' Her heart beats uncomfortably hard in her chest.

'Oh?' says Moony. 'What's it like?'

'Horrible,' says Rose, with feeling. 'I was absolutely convinced that a malevolent presence was leaning over me. I think what these women experienced was a step up from that, but what I felt was bad enough.'

'Well, in that case I think it's very clear what we have to do,' Moony says, excited now. Rose catches a glimpse of the closest thing to a smile she has seen to date.

But Rose doesn't like the way the woman is eyeing her.

'What?' she says, as a feeling of unease begins to grow inside.

'We're going to trap him,' says Moony, clapping her hands together. 'And when I say *we*, I mean you.'

40

Rose finds herself standing outside James Oakley's surgery, sweating inside her jumper and trying to calm her breathing.

She can't say she is looking forward to this. But she's going to do whatever it takes.

'Whatever you do, don't give away that we're on to him,' Moony warned her. 'Get him interested in you, but keep it cool, OK?'

Rose has always liked the idea of undercover work. The notion of shedding her essential Roseness and becoming someone else is an attractive, exciting idea. It's probably why she was rather good at drama at school, even if she never had the courage to appear in any productions.

So, after she fills out the temporary patient form in reception and takes a seat, she rubs her eyes in order to look as tired as possible. In truth, this isn't much of a stretch. She has barely had a good night's sleep in living memory. Acting sleep-deprived isn't going to require an Oscar-worthy performance on her part.

But when the man she's come to see appears at the edge of the waiting room and calls out, 'Rose? Rose Gifford?' she looks up and experiences a moment of doubt about this whole venture.

He smiles as she approaches, but it's mixed with mild puzzlement.

'Hello again,' he says in that pleasant, calming voice. How often have vulnerable people sat opposite him and allowed themselves to reveal the very worst, the most shameful and unpleasant parts of themselves? Never knowing the cold heart beating beneath that smart V-neck jumper and shirt.

'Is this a police visit?' he says as he leads her to the consulting room.

Rose gives him a rueful look as they go in and sit down.

'It's probably unprofessional of me, but no, it isn't,' she says.

'OK.' His expression remains friendly but perplexed.

Rose rubs her chin and gives a self-deprecating laugh. 'The thing is, Doctor,' she says, 'my job is so full-on, you never quite organize yourself to do the things grown-ups are meant to do, like sign up to your local surgery.'

He laughs, showing small, even teeth. Rose thinks of predators that look benign but will rip your throat out in a moment.

'So when you actually need a doctor, it all becomes a huge hassle.'

'I see,' he says, smiling. 'But why me? Why not go down to your local surgery? Whereabouts is that?'

Rose tells him, watching him carefully.

'I can recommend Dr Meredith there,' he says. 'Known him for some time.'

'That's great,' says Rose, 'and I promise to get that sorted, but I thought you seemed, well . . .' she feigns shyness. Thankfully, the excruciating nature of having to be nice to this creep has flooded her face with heat, so it looks particularly convincing. '. . . especially sympathetic.'

Oakley sits back in his chair, comfortably.

'Fire away,' he says. 'How can I help?'

Rose looks down for a minute as though finding this suddenly harder.

'The thing is,' she says, 'I don't know if it's the stress of the case we were working on, but ever since reading up on parasomnia, I can't seem to sleep!'

Looking up, she sees he is watching her, his expression oddly blank. For the briefest of moments, so quick she thinks she may be imagining it, it's as though no one is there behind his eyes. But she may be projecting this, she tells herself.

'It's very common,' he says. 'And unfortunately there isn't an awful lot you can do beyond all the basic advice about going to bed and waking up at the same time, avoiding hard exercise before bed. That kind of thing.'

Rose looks crestfallen.

'I think I might need some sleeping pills,' she says. 'Only to get through this immediate period. I can't focus on my job.' Then, as if as an afterthought: 'Especially not with all these nightmares.'

'Nightmares?' he says. Does she imagine a quickening in him at this, like an animal raising its nose to prey? 'I thought it was insomnia that was the issue?'

'It's that too,' she says with a weary sigh. 'But when I do sleep, I get these horrible nightmares. Very vivid and violent ones. I don't think doing the job that I do helps,' she says.

'No,' says Oakley, with what could be mistaken for genuine sympathy. 'I can't imagine it helps at all.' He turns to his screen and begins to tap at the keyboard. 'I'm going to prescribe you some Zopiclone,' he says. 'But only for a few days, because you don't want to get addicted to that stuff. In the meantime, try to do relaxing things before bed. Don't look at screens. And try lavender oil – some people find that helps.'

These last words send a chill down Rose's neck and across her shoulders like rain dripping inside her collar.

'Lavender oil,' she manages to say. 'Thanks. I'll certainly give that a go.'

Getting up to leave, she smiles in a grateful way. Inside, she is thinking, *I'm going to get you, you bastard.*

41

A few minutes later he walks back into the waiting room and calls out the name of the next patient, a Mrs Morgan. She's one of his regulars, a middle-aged woman with health anxiety that mainly arises from her incessant googling of harmless symptoms.

He arranges his face into the usual pleasant mask as she begins to describe the sensation of a tender vein at her temple, and how she is concerned that she has a condition called arteritis.

Oakley lets her speak, because that is why she is here, to be heard. For years she'd been a carer for an aged mother who has recently died, and it is clear that loneliness is the main reason for these visits. He doesn't care. He is used to sitting here and letting patients' words wash over him. The sympathetic manner goes a long way in this room and half the people here are like Mrs Morgan anyway. There's nothing much the NHS can do for them.

But the job has served him well for his nocturnal activities. He learned such a lot about sleep by listening to patients' accounts of their more baroque nightmares. And it was a patient who first introduced him to the world of lucid dreaming. It took practice to do even the basic stuff, becoming aware of his surroundings while he was still asleep. The first time he actually left his body was a very special moment. He can still remember so vividly how it felt to rise up and look down at his own sleeping form, curled in his bed and vulnerable. When he found that he could pass through the wall and into the bedroom of the sleeping family next door, he had felt like an all-seeing god.

They were an unattractive lot; the man a loud oaf who seemed to spend most of his time shouting in the garden and barbecuing things, the woman a ratty-faced drudge who never picked up after their large dog in the street, and a couple of teenage boys who were barely this side of delinquent.

But they were helpless, lying there. Although he couldn't touch them, he could wander around their home quite freely, as and when he wanted.

He kept practising this and perfecting his craft, uncertain where it might lead – until the day Ronata Betts told him that she believed some spirit was visiting and touching her in her bed. Her words had lit a spark in his mind, which grew into something bright and full of potential. What would happen if he were to project into the bedrooms of people who were living in a constant state of exhausted hyperactivity? Night after night their brains were telling them that someone was there, someone was sitting on their chest . . . He wanted to see for himself what it would do to them if they sensed him there.

It was so much easier than he thought. And when the shock of it killed Ronata Betts, he had rediscovered the omnipotence he had felt as a child when, merely by whispering to his sleepy sister, he had caused her to cross over from one plane to the next.

There have been other cases since then. The old woman who lived in his childhood home. The man with chronic lung disease who was so overweight he couldn't move out of bed who he had tended as a locum in Birmingham.

Moving to London and meeting Juliet had put an end to those activities. With her in his life, he had no need of them. It was only in the dark days after she'd gone that he returned to his old ways.

It was Hannah Scott who'd reignited the spark. She'd come into the surgery, all sleepy-eyed and needy, and it started him wondering. What if he was really there, at the end, in the room? What if he didn't only scare a sick old person to death, but actually made it happen with his own hands?

It had been the most incredible thrill of his life.

Russ Meehan had been the one who'd told him about the Facebook support group. All those desperate, exhausted people flocking to share every detail of their miserable nights. Russ had told him about Devil's Claw and other herbal remedies that enhanced sleep states. Useful if you want to lucid dream, and particularly useful to him when he set out to enhance night terrors in others. Hannah Scott had clung to every suggestion he offered that might help her sleep, and who reads the small print on a herbal remedy?

When he had seen an invoice from Russ at Hannah Scott's house for work done, it had brought a jolt of shock at his sheer luck. No difficulty, then, in passing one of Russ's cards to Kirsty Perryman as a suggestion about it might make her feel safer. He'd had a feeling it would come in handy if the police started making enquiries.

Poor Russ. He feels bad about him but, let's face it, he had been the perfect scapegoat. Getting caught was never an option and it was all too easy to set the guy up. With a drug habit like that, he'd never have made it to fifty anyway.

All he had to do was whisper to him in his sleep, urgent but gentle murmurings while he was in that liminal place. He talked about the pain Russ was in, and how there was a way he could relieve all of it. Quickly and easily. He didn't even have to dirty his own hands.

Amazing how suggestible people can be. Like that girl, the one who took a photo of a key with her *own phone* and never even knew that she had done it.

It's all too easy, he thinks a little wearily.

Then, as if from nowhere, he is overwhelmed by a slap of

bone-deep fatigue. This has been happening a lot lately, and it's not only from lack of sleep. He's never struggled with that before.

The truth is that something isn't right. His skin is flaky, and he has a permanent bad taste in his mouth. He's also seen traces of blood in his urine. He needs to get that checked out.

But does it matter, ultimately, if something is seriously wrong? Sometimes he thinks he has had enough of it all.

Juliet's face floods his mind and the impact is such that he has to sink back against the desk. He imagines her gentle voice, scolding him for neglecting his health, urging him to look after himself.

The sense of loss is as sharp now as it was the day she slipped quietly away, lying in bed next to him nine months ago. They'd had ten happy years together, as unlikely a couple as they may have been, with her almost six feet one and statuesque, towering over his slight frame. She was also fifteen years his senior. But ever since they had met at a conference on paediatric care where she had been a keynote speaker, they had been inseparable.

She knew about his foibles around sleep, his deep fascination with it. It had been Juliet who bought him that postcard – *The Nightmare*. He doesn't know why he left copies with those women. It simply felt right. And as for sending a final one to Kirsty – well, it tickled him to do so. He'd made the decision to let this one go. It was too much trouble. But he wanted her to know she would stay in his thoughts.

He had trusted Juliet with even the darkest part of him. When he told her of the crimes he had committed, she had cried at first. Then she had held him close and made him promise that, as long as they were together, he wouldn't do it again.

As long as they were together, he hadn't.

When she became ill, he'd spent so many long nights beside her as she tossed and turned in damp, twisted sheets. The nocturnal wandering was the only thing that got him through those difficult times.

And when she had gone, releasing him from his promise . . . well, he had to do something to fill the screaming emptiness inside.

But things are moving to a whole new level now. This policewoman, coming into the surgery because she too has a parasomnia. A trap?

No, he thinks. There is simply no way to connect him. Who could guess about *this*?

He thinks of her Thomas Hardy cheeks, so flushed and pretty, and those sleepy eyes. And his weariness lifts a fraction.

Maybe his time is nearly up. But he can still go out with a bang.

42

Rose is struggling to recall a more uncomfortable meeting than the one she's enduring. Her conclusion: this is hands down the worst.

She is in Rowland's office, along with Sheila Moony and Mack. It's hard to meet Mack's eye, because he looks even more uneasy than she feels. He keeps darting glances at her as if he isn't entirely sure who she is any more.

Moony has outlined Rose's theory about James Oakley and requested that the case be looked at again. She managed to say 'astral projection' without batting an eyelid, in contrast with Rose's squirming a few days ago.

When she finishes, Rowland lets out a heavy sigh and sits back in her chair. She looks tired and there's a stain on the sleeve of her suit. It looks like egg yolk, but Rose isn't sure.

'Look, Sheila,' she says, 'I have respect for what you do over there . . .'

Rose hears a gentle snort from Moony and she and Mack exchange amused looks of shock. It's a relief to feel that they share a bond still.

Rowland either pretends not to notice or decides to let it go. She continues: '. . . but as far as I can see, you have no evidence that this James Oakley is the man who murdered Hannah Scott and attacked Kirsty Perryman. It's all a little . . .' she hunts for the right word, 'nebulous.'

'Absolutely,' says Moony. 'We've got jack shit at this precise moment.'

This has the effect of wrong-footing everyone, including Rose, who briefly meets eyes with her boss and then turns her gaze back to Moony.

'And that's why,' Moony continues, 'I want to formally request that I can have Rose for a couple of days to dig deeper into this. We need to find a way to investigate him without bringing him in and alerting him to the fact that we're on to him.'

Rowland is silent, apparently deep in thought.

'What do *you* think, Rose?' she says at last.

Rose breathes in slowly, buying time. She wants to get this right.

'I'm not going to lie,' she says, 'I thought this was a load of heebie-jeebie rubbish when I first came across it. But . . .' oh God, here we go, 'during the course of this investigation I've had my eyes opened about things I didn't want to have to admit were true. And one of those things is that I may now be on Oakley's radar when he does his . . . whatever it is.' She still struggles with the term 'astral projection'.

'Shit,' says Mack, sitting up straighter in his seat. 'Are you suggesting using yourself as bait?'

She smiles at him, gratefully. 'It probably won't work!' she says.

'So what exactly is his MO?' says Rowland.

'It may sound insane,' says Rose, 'but he is finding his way into people's homes at night using this *thing* that he does to gain access. Then I think he gathers information about the property to break in and kill them in person.'

'You're right,' says Rowland curtly. 'It does sound insane.'

Rose holds her breath.

'But on the other hand . . .' A hopeful lift inside. '. . . One thing that has always bothered me is the way Sofia Nikolas had that copy of a key cut.'

'It was such a strange thing to do,' says Mack.

'Sofia and that bloke, Gavril, have they been ruled out as suspects?'

Rowland sighs. 'Yes, I think so,' she says. 'I mean, we know he was up to his toe-rag activities elsewhere at the time of death. As for her, well she was never a likely candidate to do it alone.'

But Rose is still thinking about that key. Something Gavril said in the interview is tickling the back of her mind.

She closes her eyes for a second to picture it. Him sitting with those meaty thighs apart, the fingers drumming on them. The desperate look that occasionally flashed into his eyes.

'*She was a terrible sleeper. Always having nightmares.*' And then, '*They were both a bit nuts about this stuff, her and Sofia.*'

'Did we ever ask Sofia about her sleep habits?' says Rose.

'No,' says Mack. 'I don't think so. Why would we?'

'Well, yeah, why would we?' says Rose, feeling her heart rate increase. 'But I think Gavril said she sometimes sleepwalked.'

'Go on,' says Rowland. Both she and Moony are watching Rose carefully.

'What if,' Rose says, 'he somehow *suggested* to her that she take the photo? I mean, you hear about people cooking three-course meals and so on in their sleep without even knowing they did it, so taking a photo wouldn't be too great a stretch.'

'That's true,' says Mack. 'There was a case not long ago where a guy successfully defended himself against a sexual assault case because he was literally asleep when he did it.'

Rowland is silent for a long time. Then she gets up decisively from her desk.

'OK,' she says, 'I can't in conscience release you on this when we're so busy, unless Mack agrees. Mack?'

Mack looks at Rose and manages a weak grin.

'I think we'd feel pretty shit if we let the person who did these crimes get away with it,' he says. 'Far as I'm concerned, this is worth checking out.'

Rowland lets out another heavy sigh.

'OK, DS Moony,' she says. 'You can have her for two days. Do what you have to do. But that has to be it.'

'Great,' says Moony. 'Two days it is.'

As they come out of the room, Moony murmurs, 'It's not the days we're interested in.'

43

'Right,' says Moony, one be-ringed hand tapping a rhythm on the table, 'we're going to find out every single thing about this James Oakley that we possibly can. I'm hoping that we'll know what he has for his breakfast by the time we're done with him.'

She launches into a ripe smoker's cough, then reaches for the can of full-sugar Coke on the desk and takes a swig.

It is 8 a.m. and Rose is at UCIT, blinking gritty eyes and drinking the very good, very strong, coffee that Adam has made for her in a large chipped mug. She had slept heavily for once, but felt disorientated when she woke with a start, having dreamed about swirling Dementor-like shapes circling above the bed.

'I'm heading off to court at nine thirty to get a PO – ex parte, of course,' says Moony. 'I don't think we'll have any trouble getting it, but in the meantime, do as much research as you can using publicly available information.'

Rose hopes she is right. An ex parte Production Order allows the police to dig into a suspect's finances, employment and phone records without the suspect knowing.

She stops and looks over at Scarlett, whose blond head is bent over her notepad while she writes. Her hair is in a simple ponytail today and she is dressed in an understated way, in black trousers and a fluffy purple jumper, one Conversed foot swinging as she writes feverishly on the pad.

'Scarlett,' says Moony, and her head bobs up.

'I'd like you to follow him today. See where he goes, what he does. He's likely to be in surgery all day, but I don't want him going off for a sandwich without you knowing where he is.'

Scarlett's cheeks flush with evident pleasure at being given this task and she nods eagerly.

'Adam,' says Moony, 'I want you to focus on his phone records. See if you can place him anywhere near those two victims. Obviously, given that he works not far from either of them, it's not going to be the thing that nails him, but we can still build a picture of his movements.'

Finally she turns to Rose. 'You can use your charm on the BMA and GMC, see if they'll tell us the places he has worked. It may be that they won't do it until we have the Protection Order because of bloody GDPR, but we can try. And look at his social media profile. If he is a member of that Facebook group – and I'd bet my Harley that he is, it's going to be almost impossible to find him. But have a look and see what you can find, anyway.'

'Yeah,' says Adam. 'If he's as clever as we think he is, he will have made a fake ID and probably accessed it via a VPN, so we can't trace it.'

Virtual Private Networks are the route of choice, Rose knows all too well, for anyone wanting to access the internet without revealing their location or identity.

'But, hang on,' she says as a thought occurs to her, 'I think some institutions block or log attempts to use them? The NHS might be one of them?'

She remembers a case where a small-time drug dealer was caught out after attempting to access the dark web via his day-job computer at BT.

'True,' says Moony thoughtfully. 'But it would take time we don't have to find that out.'

'There is another way,' says Adam. 'We could hack his computer. One of the guys from our usual tech company could do it for us. We wouldn't need a court order, but you'd have to clear permission from higher up.'

'That won't be a problem,' says Moony mysteriously. 'What exactly are we going to do with his computer?'

Adam explains, 'Our tech guy will send an email with a virus hidden in it, which will allow us to see everything he's doing on that computer.' His eyes linger on Rose and he gives her a slightly puzzled smile. She looks away. Hot *and* clever, she thinks. Stop it, Rose!

Moony nods. 'Right, we'll do it. I'll get someone in, but it will still take time, so let's get on with everything we can do in the meantime.'

The briefing breaks up soon after and Moony gets ready for court. Rose watches out of the corner of her eye as the other woman emerges from the Ladies in full leathers, carrying the crash helmet she'd noticed by the desk. She looks, small, round and fierce, like an armoured granny. The large and expensive handbag evidently goes into one of the huge panniers on the side of the bike. What a funny little woman she is.

'Right,' she says, 'I'm off. I don't expect to have any objections to this, but wait for my call before going anywhere we're not meant to be. I don't want any slip-ups that could jeopardize a case against this creep, OK?'

A murmur of agreement and she is off.

The call comes in at 9.50. The judge has granted the order, which means they have the right to call in all his phone records, employment history and financial records.

Rose manages to get a rather reluctant secretary at the General Medical Council to provide her with a list of places Oakley has worked since he qualified as a doctor. There is a buzz of satisfaction when this list confirms he is the same doctor who worked at a large practice on the outskirts of Leeds, which would have served the villages where Ronnie Betts and Mary Donovan lived.

He has worked at a few other places since then, including a practice in Hemel Hempstead, before ending up in the capital. His brief stint as a locum at the surgery where Kirsty Perryman is a patient is also confirmed, which seems to have been a one off.

At 2 p.m., she looks up from her desk, having barely noticed that she hasn't eaten or drunk anything for hours. Her neck is stiff, and her eyes are sore. She yawns and catches Adam's eye as he grins at her from his desk.

'Know the feeling,' he says. 'I think we could do with about twice as many people as we've got for this. I'm trying to do an Extraction Report here and my eyes are starting to cross.'

At that moment Moony holds up a hand to signify that they should listen. She is on the phone.

'OK, Scarlett,' she says. 'Good work. Now he's back for afternoon surgery, you're probably safe to go get a sandwich and take a break. Thanks.'

She puts the phone down and wanders over to where Rose and Adam's desks face each other.

'So he was at the practice all morning,' she says, 'but he went off for a drive at lunchtime, according to Scarlett.'

'Where'd he go?'

Moony walks over to a large map of North London pinned to the wall. Rose and Adam follow.

'So the surgery is here,' she says, putting a pin into the address. 'And he took a drive all the way over here . . .' she puts a pin into the map, '. . . in East Barnet.'

Rose feels a lurch in her stomach as she comes closer to the map.

'What did he do there?' says Adam.

'That's the odd thing,' says Moony, 'he drove onto this street here and parked. Scarlett thinks he was looking at a property across the road.'

'Staking out the home of a new victim, maybe?' says Adam.

'Possibly, 'says Moony, then, 'Rose? What's up? You've gone pale.'

Rose swallows. 'Yes,' she says, attempting a grim smile. 'It's . . . that's my road. I live there.'

The biggest smile Rose has seen to date spreads across Moony's face.

'OK,' she says. 'You're hooked, little fish.'

So now it's a matter of waiting for Oakley to break into her bedroom while she is sleeping and try to murder her, and they can get him.

Easy as pie.

She closes her eyes and feels a wild stab of nostalgia for the days when all she had to deal with was one ghoul in her own home.

44

That evening, Rose goes back to her house and looks around, thinking of ways someone could break in. She has to make it easy, without making it so easy that it is obviously a trap.

The locks are all in good condition. It might be a dump, but Rose is a police officer and she knows what happens when keys are left under pots and broken window catches aren't mended. Trying to do the opposite feels like tearing off an inch of her own skin.

In the end she decides on the method that Oakley most likely used to get into Kirsty Perryman's flat. She moves the hall table, which probably dates from the 1970s and has been there all her life, so it's a little nearer to the door. The keys to the house can now be seen by someone peering through the letter box. All it would take is a long hook, and they could easily be secured.

As she does this, it occurs to her that the entire plan is stupid.

For a start, every scrote in this patch of North London now has the means to break into the house, not just the person she is after. They could have a free-for-all – not that she owns much.

Secondly, what if Oakley has no interest in her? The other women were stalked for some time before he struck in physical form. This experiment could take weeks, and Rowland's given her two days.

But Moony has been very clear. There is going to be someone outside Rose's house, keeping watch, for as long as they can stand it, however long it takes. The plan is that each of the three members of UCIT will take a stint, even Scarlett in the early evening. She fought for this quite hard, surprising Rose with her forcefulness.

Although she isn't a police officer, she argues that she can provide a pair of eyes to give the others a break. She will, she promises, call Moony, Adam or 999 the very moment she sees anything suspicious.

Rose's two days at UCIT come to an end and they are no closer to being able to arrest Oakley. He has so far failed to open the email containing the hacking virus, which was organized on the first day.

He has clearly watched enough police shows to know that leaving one's mobile phone on when going off to commit a crime is a bad idea, and so they have no activity beyond his home address on the nights of the two attacks.

It's all very dispiriting, and as Rose reluctantly gets into her car at the end of a long second day, she looks at the strange old building in the gloomy November light and muses how it will be a culture shock to go back to Silverton Street to carry on as though none of this ever happened. And the big question is, will it have been for nothing?

Rose hits the ground running the next few days, when she and the Silverton Street team have to deal with a stabbing in Turnpike Lane, outside a nightclub after a drunken fight. They quickly establish that it's not gang-related, and the perpetrator is picked up and charged, based on CCTV evidence.

She is low key with everyone about what she did at UCIT. It's secret work, but that's not the only reason for her silence, even with Mack. Her earlier instinct, to mock and look for someone to share her scepticism, has faded. She now feels protective of the people there and the work they do.

Rose is so tired when she gets home from work that she sleeps without any problem. Knowing someone is sitting outside in a car, watching the house, is an unusual sensation. She is aware of her mother, standing sometimes by the window, when she wakes in the morning, but it is only for a second, and she isn't sure whether it's a dream.

Her shift cycle comes to an end and she is entitled to a few days off.

It has been agreed that the UCIT team will continue to monitor the house for another week. After that, Rose will make her property secure once again.

On the final day, there is a knock at the front door at about 8 p.m. and Rose can see the distinctive form of Scarlett behind the glass.

Scarlett has been doing the early shift, watching to see if Oakley is in the area, rather than actually protecting the property.

A spasm of discomfort passes through Rose. Neither Moony nor Adam showed any desire to come into the house so far, so what is Scarlett doing? Rose has already had a grim day, trying to tackle some of the rubbish in the attic. Her plan is to clear out the junk in this house one room at a time. Although the old woman hadn't shown up to make the process even worse, it had been a dusty and unpleasant job that had involved almost putting her hand directly onto a huge spider and getting a cobweb in her eye.

Knowing she can't leave the woman standing there, Rose attempts to fix the right expression on her face as she opens the door. She is going for open and friendly, without being overly inviting, but it's clear the latter has won out by the way Scarlett's smile falters.

'Hi, Rose,' she says, 'signing off duty!' She does a little salute then winces. She is dressed in so many layers, topped off with a thick quilted coat and a black hat, that her arms are slightly distended at her sides, like an over-wrapped toddler. Before Rose can respond, she says, 'Look I'm really sorry but I need to pee! They only let me do this one other evening and I brought my She-wee, but I forgot it tonight.'

'Your what?' says Rose, still reluctant to let her in.

'She-wee,' says Scarlett. 'It's a funnel thing and you can pee into a bottle with it!'

Rose grimaces. 'I'll take your word for it,' she says. 'You'd best come in.'

As Scarlett steps into the house, Rose feels the same stab of shame she felt on the rare occasions she brought a friend home from school.

Back in Year Seven there was a girl called Maisie Bennett who came by after pestering Rose about it for weeks. Rose had been around to Maisie's house, in the wealthy suburb of Hadley Wood, and it had been like stepping into a different world.

Maisie lived in a large, detached house with a double driveway and a garden that seemed to go on forever. Her bedroom was painted in a pale lilac colour and had flowery fairy lights hanging on the double bed. There were more books crammed into the white bookshelves by her bed than in Rose's entire house, and her dressing table held a neat array of toiletries that were neither own-brand or from Asda. She had instantly loved this bedroom so much it hurt her chest.

Maisie's mum was a pretty blond woman who smiled a lot and made them an exotic dinner that consisted of chicken with olives and pasta. They'd had fancy chocolate ice cream for pudding, with strawberries that Maisie's mum just happened to have in the fridge. It didn't seem like they had been bought specially, because she sort of discovered them there and seemed surprised. To forget that you had a whole packet of strawberries almost blew Rose's mind more than anything else about that visit. She'd spent the evening in awe, and when Maisie's mum drove her home later, in a high-up car that was clean inside, she hadn't said a word the entire journey.

When the evening was finally reciprocated, Rose had made them both beans on toast because Adele had a client. They'd eaten in front of the television in an awkward atmosphere. Maisie kept looking around with wide eyes and saying things like, 'But what is she *doing* in there?' Rose had tried not to let on what line of 'business' Adele was into, but it was clear the very next day when she saw Maisie whispering with Janine Nowack that the secret was out. Later that day, a girl called Tabitha, the biggest bitch in the year, had asked Rose if she could commune with her dead guinea pig because she missed him. Rose had been aware that her brief period of feeling normal in secondary school had come to an end.

So it feels like that now, as Scarlett comes into the house smelling of some kind of light, flowery perfume, with a slight undertone of cigarette, her energy bringing colour into this drab hallway despite the uncharacteristic dark clothing.

There is only one bathroom, upstairs, so Rose tells Scarlett where to go and then waits awkwardly at the bottom of the stairs, before realizing how weird this is going to look and going to stand in the kitchen instead.

A few minutes later she hears the rattle and whoosh of the ancient pipes and Scarlett comes down the stairs and into the kitchen.

Rose has, quite deliberately, avoided being alone with Scarlett since that first day at UCIT when she saw the phantom tea lady trundling along with her trolley. This past fortnight Rose has had to open up a part of herself that she had wanted hidden all her life. She still isn't ready to have conversations about it.

But Scarlett is looking at her with such a sympathetic expression on her face that Rose has to wonder whether she bumped into the ghost of Adele Gifford on the upstairs landing and had a little chat. Either that, or it's because she lives in this weird house that looks like the home of an old lady rather than a woman of thirty.

'Well,' says Scarlett, 'thanks for that. I'll get back outside.'

Rose manages to hide her surprise that no unwelcome discussion is forthcoming and shows Scarlett back to the door.

'OK, well thanks,' says Rose on the doorstep. 'You know where to come if you need to pee again!'

Scarlett gives a smile, but it is a troubled one rather than her usual hundred-watt flash of red lips/white teeth.

'Thanks, Rose,' she says. 'But can I ask—' She bites off the end of her sentence and her face fills with colour.

Please please, thinks Rose, don't have seen Adele. Please don't ask me about it.

'What?' says Rose, teeth gritted, and Scarlett looks away, clearly getting the picture.

'Nothing,' says Scarlett awkwardly. Then, 'Look, Adam is on his way. Take care, all right?'

Rose closes the door after saying goodbye and leans her back against it while looking up the stairs.

'Keep out of the bloody way, Mother,' she hisses under breath.

Unfortunately, it is turning out to be quite the evening for unexpected visitors because an hour and a half later, the doorbell goes again.

Rose comes into the hallway cautiously and sees the outline of a tall, broad man outside the door. Not Oakley, anyway.

'Who is it?' she calls out.

'It's me, Adam.'

Shit. Why is everyone wanting to come and socialize tonight?

Rose opens the door.

Adam is wearing a thick wool coat with a dark beanie hat and a turquoise scarf wrapped under his chin. It makes him look younger. He flashes her a smile, eyes betraying a slight nervousness at not being welcomed over the doorstep.

'Hi,' he says. 'I'm about to start the night shift but I realized that I forgot to fill this. Is it OK to get some tea in there?' He holds out a purple flask and gives it a little shake.

'Of course,' says Rose, blushing as she gestures for him to come inside.

'Bloody cold out there,' he says as he follows her down the hall into the kitchen.

'Have a seat for a minute,' she says and begins to busy herself with putting the kettle on.

His presence feels so alien in this house of fusty old belongings and female detritus. Almost as though he is taking up more physical space than he should. Or maybe it's that Rose always feels extra conscious of his body, his male presence. It's pathetic, she knows. He's got kids, for Christ's sake. He's a proper grown-up.

Brain buzzing with these thoughts, she almost misses what he says.

'So how are you doing with all this then?' he asks. 'I mean, the nights? Can't be much fun.'

Rose attempts a breezy laugh as she turns and holds up the box of PG Tips.

'I'm OK,' she says, 'but how do you do this? One teabag?'

Adam gets up.

'Oh dear me, no,' he says with mock severity. 'I like a proper cup of tea that you can stand your spoon up in. I think you'd better let me take over this delicate operation.'

As he takes the teabags from her, she finds she is very close to him and their hands briefly touch. Rose experiences a stab of desire that roughly goes in a line from her hand to her stomach to her groin in the time it takes for her to jump away.

Again she gives that fake laugh. *God. What's wrong with me?*

It's the stress getting to her, that's all. Sex would be a welcome break from living in a constant state of anxiety, that's why she is suddenly getting hot under the collar about a married colleague.

Adam appears to have picked up on the awkwardness as he pours water into the flask, eyes averted.

'So,' says Rose, trying to change the weird, charged atmosphere. 'Have the kids got used to you working at night?'

She takes milk from the fridge and hands it to him, both avoiding each other's eyes.

Adam pours some milk into the flask and gives it a stir.

'They live with their mum in Stevenage,' he says. 'So they don't get to see too much of my work life.'

'Oh, right,' says Rose, unsure what else to say.

'Anyway,' Adam holds the flask aloft and gives Rose a tentative smile. 'Thanks for this. Should keep me going for the night!'

At the door, he pauses and says, 'Take care, Rose, and remember I'm right outside.' His eyes are warm but serious.

45

Her two visitors occupy Rose's thoughts for much of the evening. Scarlett clearly picking up on *something* about this house should have been a comfort, but her feelings on the matter are too complex to process. And Adam . . . well, who knew what that was all about.

She has been delaying going to bed these past nights. The prospect of having one of the nightmares is bad enough, let alone the idea of waking up to see a man lowering a pillow to your face. Most nights, she has been getting by with a series of short naps before coming to with a blast of shock before she can work out she is perfectly safe. Alone.

It's starting to take its toll. Tonight she watches television until she is dozing on the sofa. Around midnight she slowly begins to get ready for bed. Her body feels pleasantly tired from the physical work she has carried out today and she tries to hold onto the sleepiness she felt on the sofa.

Before climbing into bed, she looks out of the window and can make out Adam in his blue Nissan across the road. His head is lowered, looking at something in his lap, but he happens to look up then, almost as though he knew he was being watched, and gives Rose a thumbs up and a quick grin, which Rose returns.

It does make her feel safer.

It's with this thought that Rose pulls back her duvet and gets into bed. She turns the radio on, a very old clock radio that is almost as old as she is, and tunes in to a talk station. Then she decides this will prevent her hearing anyone coming in and turns it off.

Turning the lamp off feels like a bridge too far. So she gets back out and puts on the landing light, which casts a reassuring wedge of soft yellow light on the faded pink carpet of the bedroom floor.

Finally, Rose allows herself to snuggle into the bedding, which she changed earlier today, and tries to slow her racing thoughts. The bed smells comforting and clean – although she avoids any washing powder with lavender in it – and she focuses on relaxing each limb, the way she'd been taught at a Pilates class she only attended once.

Going to sleep is like a very slow, faltering walk down into a dark place tonight and she jerks awake several times as she feels her thoughts become disordered.

There is so much activity in her mind and she needs to process it all one way or another. Everything that has happened since they got the call to that crime scene – from the strange nature of that murder and the subsequent attack, to discovering the Force she had invested her whole life in had a side to it she could never have anticipated – keeps churning around in her mind.

Eventually, despite all this, she drifts off into proper sleep.

Sometime in the night she dreams about desperately needing to find a toilet. She searches in all sorts of places that seem logical in the dream; under sinks and inside strangers' cars, but still she can't find the right spot. The urgency in her bladder pulls her properly awake at last and she sleepily curses herself for drinking so much tea earlier in the evening.

It's pitch black in the room. Darker than usual, surely?

It feels like someone has thrown ice-cold water over her, from crown to feet, as she sits up in bed.

The landing light isn't on any more.

Rose's heart thuds as she reaches down under the bed for where she keeps the taser she has been authorized to carry for the duration of this 'experiment'. Then she thinks, the bulb has blown, that's all. It's only the bulb in the hallway. She can't remember when she last changed it.

But why is it quite *so* dark? It's like being in the middle of rural Yorkshire again, instead of a suburb in the capital city. That's when she realizes. The streetlamp outside the window, which casts light through the thin curtains, isn't working. Quickly, she reaches for the lamp and flicks the switch, but nothing happens.

'Fuck,' she whispers, as though speaking loudly will conjure the bogeyman even faster. She tries to think logically, holding the taser straight in front of her body with trembling hands. There could have been a power cut to the whole area, so she must make herself go to the window and look. Or she can call Adam.

Phone. Where is the phone?

She fumbles for where it charges on the bedside table, but it isn't there. Panic is around her like the sharp, loud cracks of beating wings, so she can't concentrate. But someone has been in this room and she needs to act. Now.

Getting out of bed, she places one foot down and then another in the darkness, the taser held out straight in front of her. Breath coming in jerky puffs, she edges towards the window, slowly, slowly. All she can hear is the distant hum of traffic outside and the tick-tock of the old clock in the hallway downstairs. The house feels as though it squats around her, a malign darkness filled with hiding places.

As she reaches the window, she tears the curtain back to see that yes, the three nearest streetlights are out. A house across the road has a small light on and so it is clearly not a power cut. She knows it is relatively easy to disable streetlights on a sensor using any cheap laser if you have a mind to.

The blue car across the way is in darkness, but there is still enough background light here for Rose to be able to see Adam.

His head is still forward, but the angle looks wrong. Is he asleep?

That's when Rose notices that the window on her side is all the way down. That's not right. It's far too cold to have the window down, surely?

Breathing heavily, Rose swings open the biggest window and yells, 'Adam!' at the top of her lungs.

He doesn't move. And that's when Rose realizes Adam can't move. His head is slumped forward because he is unconscious. Or worse.

46

It feels incredible to him that she can't hear his thundering heart. He can picture hers, pumping even faster than his as she hovers in that doorway, trying to decide what move she can make.

'I know you're here, you bastard!' she shouts. She's more confident now the curtains are open. He can see the shape of her more clearly from behind, where he stands next to the large old wardrobe. There is room for his entire body to be in shadow there. Her phone is disabled and in his pocket. Gently lifting it from beside the bed was maybe the highest risk part of this whole thing. But he is used to creeping around on soft, socked feet in the dark.

The policeman in the car had been so easy. He'd been watching him for a couple of hours from his own car, parked a little further down the road, wondering how he could get him out of the car. But in the end, the guy had made it easy by lighting up a cigarette and winding the window right down. He has always been fast, and light. He couldn't do what he does without this. So it took him no time to hurry to the driver's window and appear next to him, a friendly smile on his face.

'Hi,' he'd said, 'did you know that your front tyre was flat?' The man wasn't taken in and was clearly about to move when he plunged the hypodermic needle straight into his upper arm, through his clothes. He is a large man, so he had gone for 10 ml of Midazolam, a powerful hypnotic/sedative drug, to be certain. It's one of the drugs used in the cocktail given in lethal injections in America, which made it all the more amusing to administer it to a cop.

Rose Gifford is much slighter and smaller. She is only going to need 5 ml.

He simply has to get close enough.

When she steps across the threshold of the bedroom, body coiled like a spring, she lets out a high-pitched scream of pain and that's his moment to act.

47

Rose is in a rolling, tipping world where light and dark are coming in stripes, first one, then another.

She can't move and her body feels like something that's out of her reach, apart from her feet, which she is aware in a dim way are *not right*. It's not pain, exactly, but like a shadow of pain, or a precursor of pain to come. It scares her but, like the pain, fear is prowling around the edges of this twilight place where the dark and the light come and go, come and go. She knows something terrible is hovering outside her consciousness, but she can't get there, not yet. There are sounds, but they are beyond the boundary of wherever she is, and she can't identify them as such. Then it comes to her. It's the sound of an engine, rumbling beneath her and she is lying in the back of a van. Where is she going? She's too sleepy to care, so she closes her eyes again.

It's impossible to judge how much time has passed, but it's the violent spasms in her stomach that bring her awake. She manages to turn to the side before hot, sour vomit spouts from her mouth and onto the ground next to her.

Groaning, she attempts to raise her hands to wipe her mouth, but they are joined together at the wrist like one arm and she is clumsy. Squinting through aching eyes, she sees her hands are secured in front of her with plastic ties around her wrists. Her feet, which throb as though something has been switched on underneath them, appear to be bandaged. It comes back to her . . .

Edging out of her bedroom door into the black void of the landing and, because of the anaesthetizing effect of terror pumping through her, only realizing once the second bare foot meets the old, worn carpet that she is standing on what feels like needles.

The shocking violence of that pain.

Screaming, and then hearing a voice that is somehow behind her, not in front, saying, 'Hush, Rose, hush.' A sharp scratch. Then nothing much at all until now.

It's too hard to sit up from this angle, so she lies on her side trying to keep her face out of the vomit and looks at her surroundings.

She is lying on a double bed covered in an old-fashioned shiny bedspread. It's a pale gold colour, splattered with the small pile of carroty vomit. It's a bedroom, oddly familiar in its old-person furnishings of faded patterned wallpaper and bulky brown furniture.

James Oakley is standing in the doorway, she sees with a jolt. He's staring at her, utterly still. He looks like a different man to the one she saw a few days ago in his surgery. His eyes are hooded and bloodshot and his hair is wild and tangled, sticking up on one side.

'What the fuck are you doing?' Only a small part of her fury makes it to her voice. Her throat is so dry and raw that she sounds scratchy and weak instead.

He gives a strange little laugh.

Then, even though the words are pointless, she reaches for them like a talisman and they spill out of her. They are all she has. All she has ever had.

'James Oakley,' she rasps out, barely audible, 'I am arresting you for the murders of Ronnie Betts, Mary Donovon and

Hannah Scott, the attempted murder of Kirsty Perryman, and the assault and false imprisonment of a police officer.' She has to take a breath because tears are coming, but she ploughs on: 'You do not have to say anything, but it may harm your defence if you do not mention when questioned something which you later rely on in court.'

This is met with silence, then, 'I need to get you cleaned up,' he says quietly, his tone flat. It's much more frightening than anger, like he has totally dissociated from himself. Rose has seen this before in people who are in shock, but it's usually victims of crime, not the perpetrators.

As he approaches, she kicks her legs in a bicycling movement and squirms, trying to get away from him. But her limbs are all weighted, so it's like moving in deep water.

Her feet are throbbing, and he must see her wince.

'It's OK, Rose,' he says, hands raised in supplication. 'I'm going to give you something to make the pain go away. All this is going to be over soon. You're going to sleep like a baby, more deeply than you ever have before.'

'What do you mean?' she croaks. 'What are you going to do?'

His shoulders sag and his face drops, as though some sadness in him has gravitational force. He looks even more tired than she feels right now.

'We're going to sleep,' he says, 'both of us. Together. I don't want to be alone any more. I'm so tired. And I know you are unhappy. I think you want this too, deep down.'

'What?' this comes out as a shriek. 'You know nothing about me whatsoever!'

Such a patronizing expression washes over his face that Rose longs to lift both her legs to kick him in the head, but they still feel heavy and cumbersome.

'I know that you live alone in a run-down house that probably belonged to a grandmother. Did she leave it to you? What a depressing little dump it is.'

'None of your business,' says Rose tightly, feeling an illogical pinch of shame at his words.

'It doesn't feel like a home, for some reason,' he says. 'And you have no boyfriend, or social life. You sleep so badly.' He manages a short laugh. 'Oh, don't think your performance at my surgery convinced anyone,' he says. 'I saw it on you the first time we met. You carry the weight of something around like a permanent rucksack on your back, and you're so tired, Rose, aren't you? Maybe even depressed.'

His words are like small jabs. It's a strange time to care, when she is trussed up and helpless in the face of a madman, but they still somehow hit. Is that how she presents to the world? A sad, worn-out woman with no real life, when she is still so young? Is that what they all think – Mack and Sam, and everyone else?

Despite his words, Rose feels an intense and protective nostalgia for the time before all this, when she could pretend the ghosts were only in her head, and she was free to do whatever she wanted. She makes a pledge to herself: if she can get out of here, she is going to sort her life out once and for all. She's going to live out of the shadows at last.

'Anyway,' he says, going to a heavy, oak dressing table that squats in the bay window veiled in ancient nets. 'I want you to have another short rest while I attend to your feet and get everything ready.'

'What's wrong with my feet?' Rose says, flinching away from him as far as she can without falling off the side of the bed.

'I had to put some broken glass down,' he says. 'A broken bottle I brought with me. I'm sorry. I didn't want to hurt you, but you're a policewoman and I'm not a large man, as you can see. I needed to slow you down so I could give you something to make you sleepy.'

'What did you do to Adam?' she says. 'My colleague in the car outside.'

'He'll be OK,' he says. 'He'll have slept for a few hours, that's all, like you did. I'm going to give you another dose of Midazolam. Just a small one.' He pauses. 'For now, anyway.'

'What do you mean *for now*?' cries Rose, panic stoppering

her throat. 'What is that? And what do you mean about getting things *ready?*'

He looks at her, almost benevolently. 'We're going to lie down together and rest soon,' he says, 'properly rest. I'm going to do it with you, so you won't be alone. Think of it as the ultimate journey between two places.'

'But why?' Rose cries. 'Why do you want to die? We can talk about this, we can—'

He cuts her off, his voice razor sharp.

'I've done everything I set out to do,' he says. 'I have achieved things beyond most people's imagining. I've travelled in a way no one else has done. And there is only one journey left to me. Plus, I'm . . .' he pauses and his voice cracks, betraying emotion for the first time. 'I'm tired. I want to be reunited with the only person who ever understood me.'

Then, faster than Rose was expecting, he grasps hold of her leg and she can feel the strength of him as he climbs onto the bed, squatting over her bucking body. Then she feels a sharp scratch and her screams become gasps and everything becomes so very, very heavy again.

48

Rose is in the twilight place and she isn't able to differentiate between the moments she is dreaming and when she is awake. People keep talking to her – random strangers she doesn't recognize – until, finally, a welcome face.

Mack is here, telling her a funny story about an arrest and she is laughing hard. The relief is so sweet, it's pure light inside her, but as she goes to the kitchen to make them both a tea, she understands that this is a dream, she still isn't safe. She's not at Silverton Street, making tea and joking with colleagues. She's lying, immobile on this bed, waiting for a psychopath to finish the terrible thing he has started.

The realization is the most intense sadness she has ever experienced. The pillow is wet against her cheek and she doesn't know if it is from drool, or tears. Maybe she has been sick again. But he somehow wants her to be clean, so he would have sorted this out.

And that thought, about wanting her sleeping in a bed and looking neat and tidy sends a bolt of fear through her that's almost painful and she jolts awake. She hopes he won't brush her hair. She wants to mess it up, cut it off, burn it, rather than let him do that.

The room is in semi-darkness, but it feels like late afternoon.

A movement in the corner makes her cry out and her heart crashes against her ribs. But it's not Oakley.

It's a girl, of about eleven or so, with long dark hair and a pale, oval face. Large dark eyes stare, unblinking, at Rose. She is wearing a pink nylon nightdress with a ruffled neck. She holds a finger to her lips and gives Rose a sad smile.

'Who are you?' Rose whispers, her voice harsh and raspy, and the girl inclines her head, watching her.

'Can you give my brother a message?' she says, but it's as though her lips are moving silently, and the voice is inside Rose's mind. Her voice is high and her accent Northern. She doesn't wait for a response before continuing. 'Tell him Helena says she is waiting for him.'

She disappears into shadow and Rose squints, trying to see her. She drags her gaze around the room, and it falls to the dressing table, where she can see two syringes, neatly laid out next to each other. What the hell is in them? Something awful. Something lethal.

The knowledge of this makes her start to weep but she is somehow carried away again. When she next comes close to consciousness, her eyes sticky and seemingly jammed shut, she understands that she must stay awake, whatever happens. But how?

Her back is stiff from lying in one position and her feet are sore, but in a muted way. She is desperate to pee, and her arm begins to itch, adding to her overall discomfort, but it gives her the glimmer of an idea. It's not a very good one, she'll be the first to admit, but it's all she can think of to stay awake, when waves of sleep keep trying to pull her down.

Shuffling onto her back, she cranes her head backwards to look at the top of the bed. There are bedposts at the corners with pointed tops and she begins to edge backwards, inch by inch, until she can loop her arms up and over the one on this side of the headboard. Then she starts to rub the tender part of her arm, the part that flares up all the time and never heals despite all the various creams she puts on it. She scrapes it against the wood until she feels pain there. Gritting her teeth, she forces herself to do it harder and then there is tell-tale wetness that stings.

The pain of this is horrible now, worse than all the other sensations. Is it enough? She is scared about making him angry, lying vulnerable like this, but it's all she can think of, so she releases her pelvic floor and allows the hot urine to seep out into her knickers and pyjamas, which she still wears.

She lies there like this, miserably cold and in pain, for another period of time she can't assess but every time sleep starts to pull at her, she pushes her arms back over her head and rubs at the bloody rash on her inner arm.

Finally the door opens, and he is there. He's holding some manner of white cotton garment over his arm and for a terrible moment, she thinks it is a child, before realizing it is a white puffy nightgown of the type rich women who think they live in some country idyll buy.

'You are such a sick bastard,' she says, but her words are a slur. He flinches, but it's more at the sight of her, lying there with blood all over her arm, and a dark, wet stain where she has peed.

'I'm going to have to get you cleaned up,' he says. 'This is annoying, Rose, and in all honesty, you're not doing yourself any favours. You are only delaying something that is going to make you feel so much better. Don't you want to rest?'

'No!' She wanted it to be a shout of anger, but it has come out as a smeary sob instead. 'I want to live.'

That look again, almost of sympathy, and he comes over and begins to tug at her to get her up from the bed. She complies, because being on her feet surely has to be better than lying here, and pretends to come meekly in a shuffle out of the bedroom, all the while trying to work out how she could overpower him. But she is so weakened from whatever he has been giving her, her legs can barely take her own weight. It's like being drunk, but the stage when the room spins, and you wish only for oblivion.

They shuffle-walk along a corridor, painted in pale yellow and framed with watercolours of flowers, and into a bathroom. It has the same kind of light green toilet, bath and sink that Rose knows from home, reinforcing the feeling of odd familiarity.

'Is this your house?' she says as he pushes her gently towards the bath. Taking off her clothes in front of him is an appalling thought and her brain burns with the need to think of something, anything she can do.

He starts to pour hot water into the sink, steam rising up, one hard hand gripping her arm.

'Don't understand why you're doing this,' she slurs, and he briefly meets her eye, before looking back at the slowly filling sink.

'I want to know,' he says. 'I only want to understand it once and for all, what it's like. But,' he hesitates, 'I don't want to do it on my own. I want to make the journey from sleep to death, warm and comfortable in a bed. With you.'

A strange laughing sob rips from Rose as he begins to tug off her pyjama bottoms, grimacing as he does so. Her own sour, hot smell rises up.

'I have a message for you,' she says, but the words are all mangled.

He is sponging her with a large pink bath sponge, delicately and efficiently like the doctor he is, and he only barely acknowledges her speaking.

He hands her a towel then and lets her dry herself as best she can with her wrists tied. The plastic ties bite deep, and her hands are starting to go numb.

'Shister,' Rose continues. The effect is as if he has been frozen in place.

He looks at her, eyes narrowed, breath noticeably faster from his lips.

'What are you talking about?'

'Saw your sister,' says Rose, 'Told me t'tell you.'

'What?' his face has paled.

'Says she's waiting for you.' It comes out as 'Shays shez'.

Oakley is gaping at her, his mouth slightly open, then he gathers himself.

'I'm going to give you these to put on,' he says, reaching into a laundry basket and bringing out a pair of soft trousers that smell sweetly musty. She is so grateful for being covered up again she lets him do this, but as soon as it is done she raises an elbow up hard, so it connects with his face. It shocks him, but he is still stronger, and she is still semi-drugged and bound, and he cracks her across the side of the head and half drags her back along the corridor.

Then there is a sound, a sound that makes hope burst inside Rose like a thousand fireworks at once.

Three sharp raps on the door, followed by shouting through the letter box.

'This is the police! Open this door!'

Rose somehow finds a voice from deep inside. 'I'm up here!' she cries 'Here!'

'Fuck, fuck,' says Oakley and pulls the squirming Rose, energized by new adrenaline, back into the bedroom where he throws her hard to the bed.

The door is battered in with a splintering crash. Rose tries to wriggle away as Oakley gets the first syringe and moves quickly towards her.

'It wasn't meant to be like this,' he says with a moan. 'It was going to be *beautiful*.'

There is a sharp stab to her leg and the Death Row drug enters Rose Gifford's bloodstream.

49

Sinking deeper and deeper into a soft place. It tugs at her limbs and her brain, and she doesn't resist. Shouting and too-bright lights, though, are coming and then receding. But she doesn't care all that much and letting go of all the fear and worry feels so good.

Wriggling free of the worrisome sensations around her, she begins to fall. But then the very last person she wants to see is leaning over her, shouting something into her face.

She says, 'What do you want, you annoying old bat?' to her mother but the words are only inside the squiggly lines of her own head. She tries to block her out, but Adele Gifford is yelling and yelling and punching her in the chest. Rose is so angry, because why won't she let her sleep? And it *hurts*.

What's more, she's angry about all the rubbish things Adele did when she was alive, like not caring for her enough, for being a crook, for humiliating Rose when all she wanted was a normal home and she decides she will tell her. She'll tell her how she fucking feels at last.

The fury brings a warrior cry from deep inside and Rose opens her mouth and her eyes at the same time.

Someone says, 'She's back! She's back!'

Another voice – one she recognizes -says, 'Oh fucking hell, thank God!'

SIX WEEKS LATER

50

'If you think dying for a couple of minutes is going to be your get out of jail card on the tea making then you're in for a shock, young lady.'

Rose pretends to look outraged as she turns, halfway to the kitchen. Where she was, indeed, going to sneakily brew up only for herself.

'I think you'll find it was actually three and a half minutes, not two,' she says, and Mack rolls his eyes theatrically.

'Will you ever stop milking it?' he says.

'Dying permanently is the only thing that is going to get you off the hook round here,' says Ewa with a grin.

Rose laughs and, accepting defeat, fills the kettle to the brim.

As she waits for it to boil, she looks down at her hands on the counter and clenches them into fists. They are shaking again. Joking about it all helps, momentarily. It seems to be the only way anyone knows how to deal with it, including herself.

It's six weeks since her heart stopped in that bedroom.

The house belonged to an old lady called Janice Fellowes, who had gone into hospital for a hip replacement a few days before.

It had been Adam who had the idea to look at vacant properties belonging to patients of Oakley. Oakley had offered to check on the place for her, because she was nervous about

305

leaving it unattended for so long. She'd been grateful at this extra level of care from her kindly GP and handed over keys without hesitation.

In the frantic hours in which they had been looking for Rose, it had also been fruitful to look at what medicines Oakley had checked out in the last few days.

So it was that the ambulance crew were able to quickly administer the drug – Naloxone – that reverses the effects of Midazolam once they accessed the room and found both Rose and Oakley lying on the bed, apparently dead.

Rose's heart had stopped. But, along with administering the drug, they'd had to resuscitate her using CPR. Her chest still aches where they thumped her quietened heart back into pulsing, beating life again.

Oakley was attended to second, but it was too late.

When she thinks about being in the space between death and life, her vision darkens, and she has to catch her breath because her chest goes all tight and funny.

It's all a bit much.

Her mother being there at the end is another thing she is struggling to process. Did she effectively save Rose's life? She isn't scared to admit that rankles. She would have dismissed it as her oxygen-starved brain hallucinating in the past. Now, she isn't so sure.

While she was recovering at home, in the aftermath of all this, Scarlett had come to visit.

Rose had surprised herself with the flood of emotion she had felt, seeing the bright red coat and the beacon of yellow hair through the glass of her front door.

The two women had hugged, wordlessly, and when they pulled apart, Rose had swiped at her cheeks, embarrassed at her show of weakness. But Scarlett had been unashamed at the tears rolling down her own face.

*

Rose had wondered if she would ever sleep again. But she did, in the deep and healing way her body needed. There had been no more visits from Adele.

But Scarlett had picked up on something that first time in the house, on that fateful night, and when she gently questioned Rose, Rose found it all spilling out.

Well, the part about seeing her around the place, anyway. She didn't want word getting out that she had grown up in such a crooked home, even if Moony knows.

Scarlett's opinion had been that Adele Gifford had been trying desperately to get Rose to understand something, in the only way she had available to her. Being a nuisance.

'But what, though?' Rose had wailed and Scarlett had puffed out her cheeks and said, 'I don't know. But there's obviously some kind of unfinished business and she isn't going to leave until you work it out.'

Yet another thing to think about. To worry about.

Oakley didn't make the papers. But it was all written up and stored, along with all the other cases the public doesn't hear about, in the database of UCIT. The official line is still that Russ Meehan was responsible for the murder of Hannah Scott and the attack on Kirsty Perryman. James Oakley's kidnap and attempted murder of Rose is a separate case. Rose isn't sure who knows the full story at Silverton Street. The silence from her colleagues is either professional discretion or some form of embarrassment.

Sam had hugged her a little too long when they were alone in the kitchen and she had felt herself melt into him, almost like she was falling. They'd had a brief conversation in which he told her he was so glad she was OK.

But then she had accidentally seen an email about his stag do on Mack's computer, while bending over his desk. So that was that.

At first, Rose was so grateful to be back at Silverton Street station that she attempted to put the whole episode – including UCIT and Moony – out of her mind.

But it isn't working. As she lifts down mugs and grumbles quietly at some of the badly washed ones that have been stored on the drainer above the sink, she thinks about the feeling she has had of not fitting in here any more, not after the things she has witnessed.

She has been wondering whether she has skills to offer that may not be appreciated by Rowland, however hard she works. The boss has been polite and clearly glad Rose survived. But she is never going to feel comfortable with her, that much is clear.

If one thing has come out of this, it's that Rose finally understands something about herself. She may mess-up occasionally. But she is no ordinary copper, however much she has tried to pretend she is.

Rose finds her hand straying to her pocket, where her mobile sits.

Her heart starts to beat a little faster as the thought that keeps swirling to the surface of her mind rises once again. *Ba-dum, ba-dum.* She'd never thought about her heart before. Now she thinks about it quite a lot.

It's a stupid idea, she tells herself. There probably isn't even a vacancy.

But as the kettle begins to boil, Rose finds herself flicking the switch off again.

She stares down at her phone for a minute and then swipes to a contact.

Rose dials and holds the phone to her ear.

It's picked up a couple of seconds later.

'DC Gifford,' says Moony. 'I thought you'd never call.'

Acknowledgements

This book started with a spark of inspiration as I was climbing into bed, late one night. My heart sped up and I thought, 'dare I do this?' I didn't get much sleep that night as the thought took shape in my mind.

Aware that it was a departure from my other crime books, I nervously shared the idea with my agent Mark Stanton (AKA Stan the man) who instantly gave me an enthusiastic thumbs-up. I am aware that I am extremely lucky to have an agent who is so supportive of all my ideas, even the mad, risky ones!

So now that the book is finally here, I need to thank the huge bunch of people who also helped make it happen.

I will forever be indebted to Detective Constable Nigel Horner of Hampshire Police, who held my hand through all the police procedure. He received so many emails from me, that I found myself often starting off with, 'sorry, sorry, but can I just . . .?'

He was never anything but gracious and helpful, however much I bombarded him.

I was also given incredibly useful advice on Met Police matters by Neil Lancaster and James Norman. Thanks, guys. Any police procedure errors are entirely my own fault.

For criminal justice information generally, my husband Pete Lownds was absolutely brilliant and continues to be a huge help as I navigate the early waters of book two. I'm incredibly lucky to have you on my side, Pete, and not just because of your clever barrister-brain.

I was given crucial advice on pharmaceuticals by Amit Dhand and my superstar sister-in-law Rachel Lownds. Tech Supremo Paul Dengel helped me navigate the business of secret Facebook profiles.

Thanks to Charlotte from a company called Fastkey for explaining how someone might get a key from a photograph (I'm still a bit shocked at how easy this is . . .)

Thank you to my brilliant editor Phoebe Morgan, to Julia Wisdom, and to the whole team at HarperCollins for helping to make this idea real.

I'm not sure I would ever finish a book if it weren't for the support, advice and laughs I get from my friends in the writing community. Thank you, as always, Emma Haughton, for reading early drafts of books and always making me feel that things are possible. There are too many other brilliant writers to name individually but I have to tip my hat at Colin Scott, because, well, he is a bit special.

I'm writing this in week eleven of the Coronavirus lockdown and finally want to thank my two sons, Joe and Harry Lownds, for always supporting my writing, being an absolute pair of belters during this period, and making me laugh ten times every day. (Love you, lads.)

Caroline (CS) Green, London, June 2020